ORIGINS

ORIGINS

BULLETFOOT™ BOOK ONE

MARSHAL RUST

Copyright © 2020 LMBPN Publishing
Cover Art by Jake @ J Caleb Design
http://jcalebdesign.com / jcalebdesign@gmail.com
Cover copyright © LMBPN Publishing
A Michael Anderle Production

LMBPN Publishing
PMB 196, 2540 South Maryland Pkwy
Las Vegas, NV 89109

First US edition, November 2020
(Previously published as a part of *Bulletfoot*)
ebook ISBN: 978-1-64971-285-1
print ISBN: 978-1-64971-286-8

THE ORIGINS TEAM

Thanks to the Beta Team:
Nicole Emens, Timothy Cox, Mary Morris, Kelly O'Donnell, Rachel Beckford, John Ashmore, Larry Omans

Thanks to our JIT Team:
Billie Leigh Kellar
Dave Hicks
Deb Mader
Debi Sateren
Diane L. Smith
Dorothy Lloyd
Jackey Hankard-Brodie
Jeff Eaton
Jeff Goode
Larry Omans
Misty Roa
Paul Westman
Peter Manis
Veronica Stephan-Miller

Editor
Skyhunter Editing Team

Jessica13 dreamed of adventure outside the bunker. She never knew she'd get her wish—or that it would cost her almost everything about her old life. And she never knew the danger it would bring her.

She was out in the open in the mess hall, her focus on two books she had open on the metal table in front of her. People all around her talked and made considerable noise while they ate, and the room shook every once in a while. She continued to hum, however, and tapped her finger lightly on the table to the beat of the music playing in her headset.

Not many people made music that was fun to hum to these days. Most of the music those around her listened to was the kind with heavy thrashing on improvised electronic instruments and screaming rather than singing.

But occasionally, although not that often, someone got their hands on a ukulele or a guitar or something like that and simply strummed. They didn't even have to sing for the most part. Something with a catchy tune was all she really needed to get into a rhythm and let her mind flow while she worked out the gears on the new converters they were bringing in. She didn't know where they had found them, but she really wished they would stop selecting those that were almost exclusively broken.

People didn't have fun with music anymore. In the Cities-That-Were, they said all people had done all day was listen to and make music for other people to enjoy. They got canteen credits for it and everything. What a way to make a living.

Even as an orphan with no one to speak for her, she had quickly been moved out of the lower work areas and up to the higher levels in the Sanctuary thanks to her Athena genes. She now lived and worked in the lowest of the three upper security levels of the bunker. The third and highest level formed the first line of defense and was manned constantly by Guardians.

"Hey, bulletfoot," someone said behind her.

There were many bulletfoots seated in the mess with her so she could assume they weren't talking to her since she was on her downtime.

She could have spent it in her room, which she didn't have to share with anyone and so wouldn't be interrupted. The folks who had moved her had pulled some strings to get her a room, but it wasn't a great one. It had been a water pressure regulator closet that had been rendered redundant when they repurposed all the pipes inside.

While she'd been grateful and made it her own, it was still short on space. When she was reading, it was better to come out to the mess. It was cheaper on her canteen account to leave the lights off, for one thing, and with her headset, she didn't need to worry about the noise. Which didn't, of course, exclude possible distractions like this one.

"Bulletfoot, I'm talking to you," said the voice again and a hand come down on her shoulder. It wasn't rough but it sure as hellfire was an indicator that she was the bulletfoot they wanted.

Jessica13 pulled the headset away from her left ear and continued to listen to the music in the right.

The man who stood behind her was tall and lean with most of his hair shaved as was the norm with the chavs who spent considerable time in their combat mechs. It meant less chance that they would have issues with hair clogging their recyclers—although, as she was well aware, it still found a way.

This one, in particular, was the section's CO, who went by the name of Armstrong7. He was the man in charge of running the ops out of their level, which was mostly only bunker defense at this point.

"Where'd you get the headgear?" Armstrong7 asked and tapped the headset she wore.

"Oh, I was running some repairs on the Minato's gear," she explained and gave him a mostly truthful version of the events. "I'm making sure it's working before reinstalling."

"Right." The man narrowed his eyes. "Make sure you don't bust the speakers in there. You break it, it's out of your canteen. I don't expect you want the lights in your room out for a week again."

"No, sir," she said and shook her head. "That's actually why I'm working out here."

Armstrong7 still didn't look like he believed her. "Anyway, I'm sending a team Topside to investigate the seismic activity we've had a taste of. Us grunts say it's probably dog packs tripping the mines, but the smart guys say we might be looking at a little Skyfall. I need a bulletfoot to head on up. Are you in?"

The CO was a tough motherfucker, but he did have a sense of what kept morale up with his people. He knew for a fact that Jessica13 liked to catch a glimpse of the Skyfall, at least when it wasn't falling on them. And it was really beautiful to watch the streaks of light across the sky, day or night, whenever they decided to fall.

In this case, though, she couldn't help a shrug. "Sorry. Like I said, I'm working on repairs on Mini. Do you have any other bulletfoots to choose from?"

"I do but thought you'd appreciate the opportunity," he said.

"What are you doing anyway?" one of the other chavs asked and leaned in closer to try to peer at the manual she was working on.

"I'm trying to find out how to fix the AI in the Minato," Jessica13 explained and pointed out the manual section that spoke about original AI designs. "Since the Minato AI designs are older versions, I thought some of the older manuals might have a way for me to make it work."

"You really shouldn't be so attached to that mech," another chav with a mustache said, shaking his head. "They're supposed to be tools, not toys or pets or...I don't know, something else you might get attached to."

"Shut up, Jackass," Armstrong7 rumbled.

It wasn't really an insult, although it was meant to be. The chav's name was Jack5 but someone had used a piece of lead to graffiti a mission report, especially the 5 at the end of his name. It became a nickname and it had stuck.

Not all the time, of course, but when they wanted to piss him off. And given that it was his mech she ended up needing to snake because of that damn mustache of his, she liked to piss him off regularly.

"Nah, I'm being serious, here," Jack5 said and laughed. "We have a whole troop of support mechs she can use, but she always insists on that Minato piece of crap."

"You couldn't operate a Minato," she pointed out.

"Yeah, because it's a piece of crap," the man insisted. "Besides, I don't know why you need all those manuals anyway. I thought the point of having these Athena freaks around is because they are genetically designed to know how to fix and build shit."

Jessica13 bristled at being called a freak like it was somehow a bad thing that she was better at something than he was.

"Hey, Jackass, remember that time in the not too distant future when you'll need someone to fix your suit?" Armstrong7 asked and raised a shaved eyebrow. "You know how it'll probably be an 'Athena freak' who fixes it?"

"Yeah, boss," Jack5 said and made some attempt to look contrite.

The chances were something would burn out in that Cinder 300 of his and he would need someone to fix it. It was never a good idea to antagonize the folks who would repair his suit.

No one would outright accuse any of the bulletfoots of being so wasteful as to let a member of their bunker—which only had one thousand, five hundred and forty-eight people to begin with—die. The resources required to bring another child into the Sanctuary were daunting enough, not to mention having a suit ruined because of it.

"With that said, though," Armstrong7 continued as he leaned over the mess hall table to peer at the manual she was reading, "that bundle does look a little cobby. You sure it'll be useful?"

She nodded. "It's one of the older manuals from the Shimura-Sendai manus before they shut down production. It doesn't cover anything on the Minato itself, only the basics of their AI coding. If I can get a bead on how they code them, that should be enough for me to fix Mini."

The CO shrugged his shoulders again. "Never let it be said that A7 doesn't approve of fixing and improving the mechs in my yard. With that said, though, you're not supposed to get too attached to those mechs. It breaks, you move on and we scrap it for parts. Understood?"

"Of course," Jessica13 replied. "I'm only hoping I can make it functional, is all."

"Well, keep working on that but on your own time, ya hear me Jessie?" he said firmly.

Jessie was her nickname since the 'i' and 'e' looked like the 13 at the end of her name. She didn't particularly like it but having her name spelled out every time she was in a conversation with someone became laborious sometimes.

Armstrong7, for his part, wanted people to call him A7, but that would never catch on. No one liked to be chummy enough with the CO to give him pet names.

Not to his face, anyway.

"Okay, move out," he said and waved at another bulletfoot to head over to join the team that would go Topside. "We'll make this quick and easy. Check the mines and..."

Jessica13 pulled her headset on quickly and glanced at the food she had ignored. The aluminum platter held a chunk of a cooling protein patty and dark green stew, which was better food than what they had in the lower levels these days. When she peered at her water, she noted that gentle ripples had formed around the rim.

Seismic activity wasn't unheard of in this part of the world. There was always the worry that a real earthquake would split the Sanctuary open and expose them to the bio-weapons and radiation they had to deal with Outside.

But with all the reinforcing they were doing, she doubted that even a direct Skyfall on the mountain they were buried under would be able to crack the outer shell.

It wasn't impossible and it was a fear they had to deal with on a daily basis, but compared to the fears the people Outside had to deal with, Sanctuary was a…well, sanctuary. It was safer than almost anywhere else in the world.

Still, she couldn't help but imagine what it would be like to live Outside. There were enough people out there that they didn't die faster than they could reproduce. Maybe with no reproduction regulations, they simply had more kids?

While she didn't know, she had always wondered. She was a curious one. Everyone said that, and they always attributed it to her Athena genes.

She would have to imagine what it was like as well until she encountered a couple of people who could tell her more about what it was like out there. The peddlers always did have the best stories—and the best music.

Maybe they made music in the Cities-That-Were. They were into some crazy shit out there if the peddlers were to be believed. That would be something to see. People singing in the cities that were likely to have some of the Skyfall on them any day didn't seem overly nuts, comparatively speaking.

Maybe they had somewhere to hide?

Jessica13 placed a piece of paper over her cup of water almost before she realized what she was doing. It was an instinctive action since you didn't want to have to drink water with dust in it, but she hadn't really noticed that the ground was shaking far worse now.

The ripples in her cup became more and more intense, she realized and leaned in closer to investigate.

Another shudder followed. This time, it caught the attention of everyone present.

Jessica13 had already begun to push to her feet. Seismic activity wasn't doing this. That could only mean one thing.

She was already halfway out of her seat when the lights flickered out, immediately replaced by flashing red that brought the whole mess hall to attention.

"Shit!" Armstrong7's voice bellowed through the speakers in the room. "Attention. The Sanctuary is under attack! Repeat, under attack!"

Well, that wasn't something anyone ever wanted to hear. She had been involved in attacks before but they had never amounted to much. Mostly, it was only scavengers and nothing the chavs who manned the mechs up top couldn't handle.

It had been a while since she'd heard that kind of alarm in Armstrong7's voice. In fact, she didn't think she'd ever heard it at all. Hearing the guy who was usually calm now under a great deal of stress triggered an unsettling feeling.

It was easy to tell that the other people in the mess hall could feel it too. A stampede had begun to head toward the door but she was the first to reach it and slipped through.

There wasn't any panic, she noted, not in anyone's faces. Alarm, sure, but this was what they lived in the upper levels for. Protecting the rest of the bunker was their responsibility.

Jessica13 sprinted down the tight, concrete hallways until

she reached her room and heaved the heavy metal door open with a sense of urgency.

It was a tight space but she had made it hers with a couple of small decorations here and there, items she had been able to pick up and get cleared by the AI running containment at the doors.

But she wasn't there for any of that. She looked around the room and scanned the area quickly before she found the pieces she was looking for. The coding chips—used for the AIs that ran most of the mech suits they used—had been tossed onto her bed when she had elected to listen to music while reading.

It had seemed like a good idea at the time.

She snatched them up, left, and shut the door to her room smoothly behind her as the flashing red lights continued to suffuse the hallways with a sense of impending danger. This was made so much worse by the narrow spaces shaking while sheets of dust filtered from the ceiling with each strike.

The fight up top had grown more intense. She could tell.

"All teams to your stations!" Armstrong yelled over the speakers. "Damn it, get that crate up to the mechs now! Repeat, all teams to your stations!"

The CO had a habit of shouting orders to three different people at the same time, and this time was no different. While he called for everyone to get to their mechs, he shouted at those who were already in position to do their jobs.

Most of the folks up there would have no difficulty interpreting the relevant commands. They knew the man, but his mannerisms did take some getting used to.

Jessica13 fell in with a group of other bulletfoots headed toward the hangar to get involved in the defenses and snapped the chips into her headset along the way.

That done, she rebooted the headset and a few seconds later, a series of upbeat chirps could be heard through the speakers.

"Morning, Mini," she whispered, mostly to herself. "Ready for some fun?"

CHAPTER TWO

Armstrong7 no longer shouted through the speakers. Jessica13 guessed that he was too engrossed with what was happening above-ground to really pay attention to what was happening below. He still needed the reinforcements who were supposed to be on their way, but he also needed to trust that they knew what to do and would do it without him bellowing at them through the comms.

In fairness, they had been drilled through the procedure innumerable times before. Two dozen chavs were ready for action. Six were already Topside and engaged in the fighting that made the whole bunker shake above them. The rest were getting themselves prepped to join them. They had been drilled through what they needed to do time and time again over the years they had all worked on this level.

But there was drilling and then there was the real thing. You knew when it was a drill. You were calm and collected and gave yourself the benefit of being able to make a couple of mistakes here or there. With that kind of give, you actually didn't make any. That was what calm got you.

But there was nothing calm about this. With her ears still covered by Mini's headgear, Jessica13 could hear her heart beating in her chest. The thud-thud of it increased speed as she and the other engineers—playfully labeled bulletfoots—began to head into the bay where their mechs were stored and waiting for them.

It wasn't a long walk but when the tight hallways around them shuddered every five steps or so, it was difficult to stay focused on the task at hand. No one wanted to wait around for the kind of hell that would rain on them if the shockwaves grew worse.

The hangar bay was a tightened section of the bunker that had a hallway leading out toward an elevator that took the mechs to the top. It was otherwise crammed to the hilt with parts, tools, cranes, and most importantly, the mechs they would use. Despite that, it was one of the areas with the highest ceilings since it had to accommodate anything from the eight-foot-tall Minato Jessica13 liked to use to the four-teen-foot-tall Mark VII Guardians that were used either for bunker defense or construction outside when repairs were needed.

Armstrong7 rolled across the hallway to snap orders and maintain contact with the men on the top and still wore his suit with the intention to head up there once everything was in place. He was the kind of CO who liked to be in the thick of things himself and struggled to remain in check once he remembered people actually looked to him for orders.

"Charlie4, get those guns connected," he shouted to one of the other engineers, who peeled away from the group she was in to rush over to the Guardians that were still fitted out for repairs. "Mark3, we need those ammo crates stacked and ready to go—get on it!"

Jessica13 could taste the dryness in her mouth and felt the ticking of the blood vessels around her ears as sweat started to trickle down her spine inside her suit. It triggered a distracting itch she wouldn't be able to reach during the next hour or so.

Red lights continued to flash across the room and made it difficult to focus on what she was supposed to do.

"Bulletfoots, we're sending supplies upstairs," Armstrong7 roared and caught their attention as effectively as if he'd used a grappling hook. "Guardians and Cinders will head up and need all the ammo they can get their hands on. You strap as much as your mech can carry, head up, deliver, and head on back to get more, understood? No leaving crates on the ground. You only come back when you've delivered it to a mech in need!"

He talked fast and had already focused on something else. A couple of the Guardian mechs were already disengaging from their coupler links and shuddered as the hydraulics kicked in to give the pilots control of the fifteen-ton suits of hardened steel and titanium alloy. Every step they took made the whole floor shake as they moved to the elevator. The bulletfoots wouldn't join them, of course. The elevator could only take the size and weight of the two guardians that headed up to reinforce those who were already Topside.

Jessica13 connected the headset to the team's comms as she and the other bulletfoots hurried toward the section that stored the support mechs. Armstrong7 stuck close to them and marched like he was running a drill, but the look on his face was something she didn't remember seeing before.

Not fear, she decided. No, he was angry—pissed that someone had attacked his home. He would make the bastards pay for this.

She had seen the man annoyed before and had even seen him yell at a couple of new additions to the defense of the bunker a few times too. Seeing him like that made the sick feeling in her stomach disappear as suddenly as it had appeared. There was still a twist of anticipation in her gut, but it was almost like the rage radiating from her CO was contagious and seeped into the rest of them.

Gone were the nerves and the instinctive need to panic, run, and hide in a hole until all the bad things went away. This was their home, damn it, and they would destroy the bastards who thought they could come from the Outside and attack it.

Besides, this was unlikely to be a raiding party. Those didn't tend to come packing high explosives. This was an occupation force, it seemed, which was why Armstrong7 was ticked.

"Jessica13!" he snapped and dragged her to a halt as she headed toward her Minato. He didn't say anything and merely pointed her to the nearest mech before he did the same with the other bulletfoots along the line. They were being herded into the mechs closest to them to get in them and out of the bay as quickly as possible.

Then again, it was Armstrong7 who had told her not to enter combat situations in a mech she didn't fully trust since that was a good way to get yourself screwed right out of an advantage—and get shredded where you didn't want anything to go wrong.

It was something he taught regularly to almost every pilot he came across, mostly because he himself was partial to the Mark V Argonaut mech. It was the same General Robotics make as the Guardian but an older model, one that had been developed long before AIs had been used for the design and use of combat mechs.

There was a reason why he liked the older model and its lack of an AI, of course, and it mostly revolved around his dislike of AIs interfering with the function of a combat mech. It wasn't that he didn't approve, per se, but he did feel that the AI got in the way of quicker reaction times while in the suit and the more powerful functions being harnessed by him and him alone.

He and the others like him talked about AIs being akin to training wheels when you used a suit. They were useful for beginners but got in the way of the more advanced pilots.

Jessica13 wasn't sure which side of the spectrum she was on. Her Athena genes made her better at working the mechanical part of the suits, which allowed her a better knowledge of the inner workings of the mechs she and others used. Of course, there was a difference between fixing and using, and while the Mini's AI was mostly useless, it still greased out some of the more difficult functions like aiming the grappling hook and keeping the stabilizers in place while she carried heavier weights on the mag-clamps on her back.

It was for precisely that reason that she wouldn't take the first mech she could fit into. She intended to use the one she was the most comfortable with.

"Not that one!" she shouted, turned quickly, and jogged farther down the line until she found the one she still had the headgear for. She grinned when a pleased series of whistles came from the AI in the headset.

"Damn it, Jessie, not fucking now!" Armstrong7 shouted over the blaring sirens, but she gestured to her head to pretend she couldn't hear him and pulled the entrance at the front of the chest open.

The inside of most of the mechs smelled of sweat and grease since there usually weren't enough resources to clean the insides more than the basics needed to function, and Mini was no different. At eight feet tall, Minis were the runts of the mechs they had in Sanctuary. She was a tighter fit but in the end, that suited Jessica13 fine and she slipped inside, paired the headset with the rest of the suit, and watched the HUD come alive.

The screen lit up on the edges and a tiny little flower appeared on the top right side. It never failed to make her smile. It was like Mini was sending her a message. The AI had no verbal functions as far as she could tell from her work on the coding, so the little details of their interaction while she was in the mech were always a bonus.

"Good morning to you as well," Jessica13 said and for a moment, all the fear that had swamped her since the warning lights had started flashing vanished.

The screen suddenly came alive with a text.

203 updates available, it told her. *Would you like to reboot and install them?*

"No thank you," she said. "We need to get moving now."

She could already see the other support mechs starting to decouple and pull away from their harnesses.

Reboot engaging, the screen told her and the screen powered down as the AI engaged with the rest of the suit once more, leaving the updates for a later date.

She hadn't been bugged for updates before. It might have had something to do with her work on it. Either way, she didn't know what the updates would do or why Mini asked for them. They would have to wait until after the battle had ended, but it was still an interesting development.

"Come on, Mini, I gave you a vote of confidence. Don't bone me here," Jessica13 pleaded as the mechs began their march down the hallway toward the elevator that had returned. The doors peeled open once the AI within confirmed there were no contaminants that could harm the folks still under the mountain.

"Jessie, we aren't waiting for you or that piece of shit mech," Armstrong7 seven called through the comms. "If you ain't here on the first trip up, that'll be docked from your canteen, you hear me!"

"Loud and clear, boss!" she acknowledged in response and tried not to show any of the frustration she currently felt. Frustration was better than panic at this point, but she really didn't need that docked from her canteen. She had already spent most of what she had on the manuals with barely enough to keep the lights on in her little room.

"Best to get a move on," she said aloud into the mic but disconnected from the comm channel. "That is if someone would bother getting off her lazy electronic ass."

A series of chirps and whistles issued through the headset. It sounded like Mini was moving as fast as she could but was also a little frustrated.

"Sure, I guess it's a little my fault too," Jessica13 said. She usually pretended she could understand what Mini chirped at her. "But you understand that I only took you out of the mech to get you some upgrades, right? So that we could work better together. You were there when I picked the manus up so quit your complaining and come on!"

More chirps and whistles followed as Armstrong7 marched past her with his hulking Argonaut and waved at her with the mech's exaggerated motions.

"I wasn't toying with you, Jessie. I mean it!" the man shouted as the other bulletfoots began to board the elevator. Another of the support team began to load the steel crates on the magnetic locks on her back as the HUD finished rebooting.

"About rutting time!" she muttered, engaged with the controls, and felt them connect to her movements and disengage from the harness as she pulled herself free. There was an upside to using the smaller mechs and in this case, it was because it took her less time to acclimate to the controls. Moving three tons of mech was much simpler than moving fifteen, after all.

She picked up the pace into a jog while making sure the hydraulics were stable under the weight of the ammo packed on her back. They wouldn't hold the elevator for her, and Armstrong7 was about to board himself.

Once he was in, the doors began to slide shut. They were slow, though, like the AI working it knew she was a little on the late side, and she managed to slip through as the locks clamped down.

"Running it a little thin there, Jessie," the CO said. He looked around, conducted a quick headcount, and stored the names and model numbers on the HUD in his mech. "If you run late again, I won't suggest you make use of another mech. It'll be an order. Are we at an understanding?"

"Yes, sir," Jessica13 replied with a nod and bumped her head on the top of her helmet. There was no vertical head movement on the Mini, which meant her shoulders moved up and down and made it look like she shrugged instead. Armstrong7 knew better than to think she was being insubordinate and stepped out in front of the rest of the crew. He would act as the shield for the support mechs that weren't fully rigged for combat.

His main gun was raised and primed for the fight they could still feel happening. Every explosion on top made the whole elevator shudder and swung it gently, but the mechanism was strong enough to drag them up to the surface.

"Starting to wish those older models had some projectile shields now, huh, boss?" Jacob14 asked, looking up at the massive mech standing next to him.

Armstrong7 tapped the chest of his mech with the main gun attached to his right arm. "This is all the shielding I'll need. Now stay back, let me clear a path for you, then head out. The folks up top will already have themselves marked off as needing ammo on your HUDs, so choose one and mark it off. If two of you mark off the same Guardian, I will be pissed. If you guys get taken down, switch your selections off so the others know you won't be able to get to them. I swear to the Seven, if you die and let someone go out without ammo up there, I will personally revive you so that I can shoot you myself. Do you understand?"

Of course, all this was covered in the drills they ran from time to time but it never hurt to be reminded that those depleted-uranium rounds would riddle their recently revived corpses if they didn't do the job right. Not that any of them really thought Armstrong7 would actually do it, but as of right now, it didn't really matter.

The elevator came to a halt with a thud and brought all their minds back to the task at hand. Jessica13's heart suddenly thudded rapidly in her chest again and she squeezed the controls in Mini's arm to keep her fingers from trembling. She was careful to leave her forefinger off the trigger, though. She really didn't need to have the damaged elevator added to her canteen deductions for the month.

The doors shuddered gently, and she couldn't help but notice the stillness that suddenly descended on the group. The explosions were oddly muted by the reinforced panels but were the only sound in the seconds before the doors would open to allow the noise of the firefight outside to intrude.

The quiet before the storm. She'd never really understood the phrase before now. The anticipation was building, and all she could really think about was that her mouth was dry but she still needed to use the restroom for some reason. She'd asked one of the chavs about it before and they said it was due to the adrenaline pumping through her body. Without even knowing it, her body was getting ready for a fight.

It was like having an AI but for her own body, she remembered thinking at the time.

The doors jerked open. A cloud of dust quickly engulfed them and the clamor of battle was no longer muffled.

Jessica13 wanted to run out and suddenly felt hellishly exposed standing there with the doors wide open. Despite the instinct, she remembered her orders and waited for Armstrong7 to move out first.

She peered past him at the cloud that made everything farther away than ten feet disappear in a rush of brown. Her grimace was instinctive because she knew she would inevitably have to clean that dust out of the joints of these mechs when they were done there.

When, not if.

"Okay, clear!" Armstrong7 roared. "Move, move, move!"

None of the bulletfoots hesitated even for an instant when the order came. They let the huge Argonaut step out first and used him as a shield that allowed them to exit safely. She was out first. Her Minato was smaller than the others and one hell of a lot more energy-efficient, which meant she could weave through the others without too much effort.

It also meant it was her job to supply the folks who were farther away. There was always a downside, Armstrong7 liked to say. Thankfully, she knew the layout of the defensive plateau and would be able to judge the distances despite the dust that flurried to obscure visibility. Behind her, the cliff into which the elevator was built towered as a sheer wall of protection. Beyond that, the battlefield was bounded on all sides by equally precipitous rockfaces that the attackers would have had to scale. It helped that the defensive area was limited and the fight couldn't spread to force the bulletfoots farther afield and away from the elevator.

"Where's that fucking ammo, Armstrong7?" Jack5 shouted through the comms.

"En route!" the CO replied, turned quickly, and opened fire in the direction of the fighting. She could see a couple of targeting reticles, which revealed where the hostiles were and allowed her, in the support mech, to avoid them while the others continued to fight.

Jessica13 looked into the HUD, selected one of the nearest Guardians, and isolated him to tell the others who she would go to first and the other five did the same. She had enough ammo to restock two of the Guardian mechs before she could make a break back to the elevator.

A series of whistles and chirps sounded in her headset.

"No, we're not here to pick a fight, Mini," she said and kept herself moving as the stabilizers maintained her in an upright position. "We're only here to let the other guys load up and then head back. Nothing complicated—it's like being a delivery girl but for keeps."

She ducked and a couple of stray rounds clipped the top of her helmet and ricocheted upwards.

"Fuck!" she shouted but kept on moving as Mini trilled at her once more. She had neither the time nor the inclination to pretend she knew what it was supposed to mean.

As she approached one of the Guardians, she sent an alert to notify him that she was close. A ping in response told her he was ready, and she sprinted as fast as the Minato could go until she was in front of him, dropped quickly, and skidded across the dust and dirt-covered surface while she disengaged the clamps for one of the crates.

The Guardian picked it up and relieved some of the weight, which forced Mini to adjust the hydraulics again. The combatants continued to fire around her as she worked but there was little that she could do other than hope and pray to the Seven that nothing struck her dead on. The Minato had been designed with the armor shaped into a number of angles, which raised the chances that any round would bounce away and leave only a dent. Unfortunately, it wasn't thick enough to take any rounds dead on.

And if a grenade hit her, they would wash her remains out the inside of the mech with a hose. Well, not really. No one would willfully waste that much water. The chances were the other bulletfoots would have to scrub her out.

"Clear!" the pilot behind her called, and she pushed herself up as one of the reticles came closer to her and the Guardian she had restocked. She could even see bits and pieces of it moving in the cloud of dust, a shadow more than anything else.

"Shit, shit, shit!" Jessica yelled frantically, ducked her head, and pushed into a sprint. The enemy engaged the Guardian and ignored the smaller mech that bolted away. Chirps matching her own intonations emitted in her helmet, which told her the AI was panicking too.

Not that AI's panicked in the same way humans did.

She still had a job to do. Her heart thumping like it would break through her rib cage wouldn't change that. Jessica13 selected another of the Guardians in need of ammo and began to run toward it.

The explosions were felt almost before she saw them and she grimaced when they gouged chunks of concrete out of the bunker's outer facade. The dust on the ground made it difficult to stop in time. The shocks from the explosions reverberated through the armor and thrust the breath out of her lungs as she skidded to a frantic halt.

The Guardian she had raced to assist was a flaming heap. No sound issued from the comms, which told her his death had been mercifully quick and he no longer needed the ammo. The target on her HUD disappeared quickly.

It was replaced by one of the reticles and displayed the shadow of the massive mech that had demolished the Guardian like it was nothing more than paper. It was smaller than the Guardian, of course, but it was still a good three feet taller than Mini. Numerous pieces protruded from it—a unique design and yet one she knew only too well. Many of the folks living near the Cities-That-Were tended to use the same Lancer Design, although it was probably not an original make. Not many were these days.

Hammercide Industries had designed a suit that was adaptable, easy to make and fix, and hard to bring down. This one looked like it had been fitted with a rocket-launcher on the shoulder, which was how it had annihilated the Guardian. While the tubes were empty—which indicated that it couldn't shoot them again—the assault rifle with an under-barrel grenade launcher would be more than capable of tearing through Mini.

The AI squealed in her ear.

"I know!" Jessica13 shouted as the rifle targeted her and she flung herself hastily to the left as the air around her was suddenly filled with lethal projectiles. A handful of the rounds bounced off her armor, although none penetrated, but that wouldn't last long. The pirate hadn't expected her to be that fast and struggled to adjust to her movements. With no AI to help with the targeting, the pilot would have to do it manually and he sucked at it.

Still, it was only a matter of time until one of the bullets found her.

"Jessie, over here!" Jack5 called over the comms and she could see him waving the arms of his Cinder 300 from behind the Lancer. He was out too and wouldn't want to engage the enemy until he had ammo.

There was no way for her to get around their adversary, though, not without stepping into a hail of bullets. She had no time to think, only do.

Jessica13 made a decision she knew would get her yelled at as she came to a sudden, skidding halt and ducked to avoid the bullets that streaked past her. A quarter of a second was all she would have for this, and it needed to work.

Her right hand reached up behind her back to yank the last crate off and as soon as it came free, she disengaged the clamps and tossed it up. It arced over the Lancer's head as it ducked instinctively. The pilot thought she had attacked it, apparently, and didn't want to be killed by a support mech.

Thinking she had missed, the Lancer advanced. It was also out of ammo, but once more, that didn't really matter. The left hand moved in a vicious swipe to end her quarter-second's grace and she felt the impact all the way up her spine when she was swatted like a fly and landed heavily.

The pirate mech moved forward, pressed its foot on her chest, and reached back to find another magazine to reload before it executed her. She couldn't see through its visor, but the poor condition of the Lancer was clearly visible to her as it stood over.

Her attacker slapped a new mag into its rifle but jolted suddenly and jerked to the right and then to the left.

"Did he...go crazy?" Jessica13 wondered aloud and Mini voiced a questioning series of beeps as well.

The Lancer burst into flames and moved in lurching, panicked motions as if the pilot forgot he was riding a mech. To be fair, you forgot all kinds of things when you were being cooked alive.

Jack5's Cinder fired the finishing round from his shotgun and blasted the head off before he turned and offered her a hand, which she took gratefully.

"That Minato's a piece of shit but it sure can move fast," he admitted with a chuckle. "I didn't expect these guys to have Lancers, though. Tough fuckers."

The sounds of the battle began to die down. It appeared the last push had managed to get the pirates this close to the entrance but wasn't enough to get them through.

"Thanks for the assist," Jessica13 replied, and when he tapped his chest in response, she didn't wait for him to say anything. She still had orders to carry out, even if the fighting was winding down, and she pushed into a sprint to the elevator doors.

Something was wrong, she realized immediately—a little damage to the pressure in the hydraulic system, but nothing terminal. It could wait for repairs until after the fighting was concluded and they were done scrapping the mechs for parts.

Some would be their own, of course.

CHAPTER THREE

There was no waste in Sanctuary. Everything was recycled, reused, and repaired so there would be no need in the future. The folks running the bunker in the lower levels had everything meticulously controlled and it mostly went according to plan, thanks to the Seven.

Of course, there were small problems here or there that arose—like a group of pirates attacking Topside and trying to get in—but they were mostly glitches on the radar and were generally fixed with a little attention and a quick hand.

In this case, of course, the hand in question was the Guardian mechs who made sure everyone in the levels below were safe from the Outside again. The pirates were defeated, and everything could go back to normal again.

But there would still not be any waste. The mechs that had been destroyed would need to be replaced, and there was no better place to start than the mechs themselves, including those that had destroyed them in the first place. Jessica13 had read in one of the manus that had been on sale about how people in the past respected the dead, put them in the ground, and left them to rot.

There were others who burned their dead but didn't contain the energy emissions, which meant they too went to waste. It seemed dead people were respected by letting everything they'd left behind be wasted.

It was ludicrous to her, but they didn't need to worry about wasting resources very much back then. It was difficult to fully come to terms with that in her head but she liked to pretend she was in a world where she didn't need to count virtually everything she used so she could report it and have it replaced with recycled materials.

This was, of course, mostly a daydream, something to take her mind off the fact that she now peeled pieces of mech away from one of her dead comrades.

Jack5 moved to where she worked and toyed with the regulators on his suit. It needed to be done almost constantly since the Cinder 300's flame throwers tended to warp after every use. She wasn't sure why someone would even use that fire trap, but those who did had to know what they were doing.

And needed to have something of a death wish. Wisely, she kept that opinion to herself.

"Hey," he said and contacted her through a private comm line. "How…how are you doing?"

Jessica13 looked up from her work. Jack5 didn't seem the type to simply come over and check on how she was doing, although it did seem like he was genuinely concerned for her. It presented an odd change over how he had always treated her in the bunker.

"I'm okay," she replied. "How are you doing?"

"Not too bad. I...well, you did good out here today. I may have said some things that weren't true and maybe even a little hurtful."

"Are you apologizing?" she asked and narrowed her eyes.

"Are you accepting my apology?" he countered.

"There's no need for an apology, but...yes, sure." She shrugged casually and Mini exaggerated her movements. "We all give each other a hard time out here. That's how it works. What matters is how we handle it when it comes to protecting Sanctuary."

"I appreciate that and you are right, of course," he agreed.

"Can I ask you something, Jack5?" she asked in an effort to make conversation when the silence between them threatened to continue.

"Of course."

"Why did you get named Jack5?" She kept her focus on pulling pieces off the ruined Guardian in front of her. "I mean...Jack is a nickname for someone named John, so why didn't your mother call you John?"

"Oh, yeah, my mother wanted to name me John, but there were already twenty-four others in Sanctuary using that name," the man explained. "It's a popular name, so the people in charge of the progenation process said that was too many sharing the same name, so she chose Jack. She might have thought it was clever, but four people had come up with the same idea before her. Mothers, right?"

"I never met mine," Jessica13 said softly. "As it turned out, my father wasn't much better and went and got himself shredded in a pirate attack while piloting an Argonaut. He loved coming up here, did my dad. Too much Topsider in him, the other pilots used to say."

"Oh…fuck, I'm sorry," Jack5 said and backed away slowly. "I'm…uh, going over there to…look at something. See you later."

She turned to watch him walk away as Mini emitted a series of beeps and trills in her headset.

"I know," she replied and once again imagined she understood what the malfunctioning AI had said. "He's worse at small talk than I am."

Another trill with a downward tone indicated disappointment and the flower on her HUD began to spin again. She resisted the urge to shrug and returned to her work. There were a large number of mechs that needed to be taken apart and sent to the manufacturing and recycling levels and little time to do it in. They didn't want to be caught out there after dark.

The tools in the Mini worked quickly to smoothly disassemble the pieces and lay them in piles. One would be sent to recyc and the other comprised those that would be plugged into other mechs. The beginning was always the easiest part. Most of the armor would be sent to the lower levels. It was when she got deeper inside that it was interesting.

And depressing, she acknowledged with a grimace. One of the pilots was still inside and his blood had soaked into the inner layers of the pilot compartment. He was someone's child. They would need to go through the whole progenation process to replace him, but that was not really her department. She didn't know how many resources it took to bring a human being into the world, but it had to be more expensive in terms of resources than having the already adult human there to contribute to the bunker themselves.

"Sorry," Jessica13 said softly and tried to work around the body inside the mech. She removed the pieces and placed them in their respective piles while a couple of other bullet-foots collected them and dragged them to the elevator to be processed.

Another of the Guardian pilots marched over to her. She could almost tell the size of the damn thing merely from the way it made the ground shudder with every step as the pilot hailed her through the comms.

"I noticed you saw some action during the fighting," Lance7 said when she accepted the hail on her HUD.

"There's not much a Minato can do against mechs like that," she said and gestured with her head toward the fallen pirate mechs. "Still, I managed to dance around one until one of ours came in and took him down."

"It wasn't a bad first taste of action," he said and tilted his head inside the Guardian helmet. "Not many folks in a support mech would have gotten away alive, nor with their mech intact."

"I have some damage to my chest here," she pointed out and tapped the place where the Lancer's foot had stamped on her. "Not a pleasant experience and I know I'll have to fix it in my spare time."

"It's relatively intact, anyway," Lance7 said. "Still, it's the first time I've ever seen these bastards get this close. It's not like them to be so brazen in their attacks. They tend to remember their place in the food chain, as it were."

"They were better armed than attackers in the past," she said as she worked to finish with the friendly Guardian that had gone down and placed the last of the pieces on their respective piles. "A couple of them had the kinds of explosives and mechs you don't see in most of the other pirate gangs—at least the few I've seen."

"What makes you say that?" he asked.

Jessica13 continued her work as she spoke. "These had the numbers and the equipment to deal Sanctuary some real damage if they managed to get past the Guardian line. Sure, they're missing all kinds of bits and pieces here and there. You can see that one didn't have any core containment and it's running light on armor." She gestured to an enemy mech sprawled alongside. "That's how the shotgun blew the head clean off. I guess they might have done that to make it run lighter and faster. My thinking, though, is they didn't have the parts and put these bastards together from scrap, elsewise they would have given us far more trouble."

"Thank the Seven they didn't," Lance7 said.

"Where do you think they came from?" she asked and moved to the downed pirate mechs she'd indicated. She doubted she would feel any pity over taking that one apart, all things considered. Jack5 had done a number on it. The shotgun had blown the head off completely and the flame thrower turned most of the outer armor to slag to make sure. Most of it would go into the recyc pile.

"Somewhere out there," Lance said, raised his arm, and aimed his assault rifle out at the world below.

Jessica13 turned from her work to see where he was pointing. Now that the dust from the battle had settled, there was a clear view out into the world below the mountain Sanctuary had been built into. The sun descended into the west as it set and covered the sky and the land below with a gorgeous orange and gold glow.

People talked about the dangers of the Outside a great deal and she hadn't really had any cause to disbelieve them, even with her time spent above ground. The world was full of all kinds of dangers that would kill her faster than it would take to arm the grappler in her Minato.

With all that said, though, it sure was gorgeous up there. She could see for miles and they looked down on one of the Cities-That-Were. It was one of her favorite things to look at, second only to when there was some Skyfall to watch. The gold was painted over the ruined buildings, some of which soared hundreds of meters into the air—higher, almost, than Sanctuary's mountain. Even hundreds of miles away, silhouetted by the sun on the horizon, she could make them out.

She liked to imagine what it was like to live in one of those cities. It was intriguing to think about how it would be to look out at the world from one of those buildings.

Of course, to hear the peddlers talk about it, those were a hazard now. No one dared live within the ruins anymore. Not only was there the danger of radiation or disease, but Skyfall in the area meant something of a domino effect that brought the buildings down on the heads of those stupid enough to scavenge around the Cities-That-Were.

Or desperate enough, she reminded herself. Not everyone was lucky enough to be born in one of the bunkers or had the safety the folks in Sanctuary enjoyed. Despite all the things she'd been told about Outside, though, a part of her hankered after the wide-open spaces that seemed to whisper of freedom and adventure. It wasn't the first time odd thoughts like this had intruded and she pushed it away. Her life was here where it was safe and she could contribute to something that was much more important than her childish imaginings.

"From the City-that-Was, do you think?" Jessica13 asked, her head tilted in thought.

"That's probably where they got all the firepower from, anyway," Lance7 said. "They liked to do all the manufacturing in those places before...whatever it was that happened. There were more people in the area so they could put in all the work the bosses wanted them to."

"How do you know that?" she asked.

"Read it in a book somewhere, I think," he replied. "Or maybe someone told it to me when I was little. All I could imagine was how cramped they had to feel with so many folks crammed into concrete slabs climbing up in the sky, and vulnerable too. Imagine living your life in one of those and then all of a sudden—boom, something falls out of the sky and your whole home, everything you've built for yourself, is gone in the blink of an eye."

"It sounds like you put some thought into this. I thought I was crazy, always thinking about how it was like, living in the Cities-That-Were."

"Sure, imagining the paradise folk had back then is nice to daydream about on a boring day," Lance7 said. "But if the stories we hear of the folk living in the Cities-That-Are is any indication—the fear of the Skyfall, the radiation, the poisoning, and the monsters... Well, I'm glad we have our Sanctuary here. Not all folks are so lucky."

"I was thinking the same thing," she said softly, still working on the mech that Jack5 had all but shredded. "It's nice to watch the Skyfall but having to worry about it falling on you? That's no way to live. And what about monsters?"

"Oh, I agree," the man said with a chuckle. "Think about how many bunkers there are out there in the Outside. Not many, from what I hear. But those buildings you see...they're only the beginning. There are hundreds, maybe even thousands, of Cities-That-Were that got destroyed by Skyfall over the years. They say there are even a couple they built under the great waters to try to escape the poison in the air."

Now there was a thought. Jessica13 could imagine what a

city under one of the big waters would be like. She'd only seen pictures of it, of course—water as far as the eye could see. It was interesting to build a city under the water instead of a bunker under the mountain, but it was hard to believe that the poison in the air wouldn't poison the water as well.

There had to be monsters in the water too, and mountains protected far better against those.

"I'm sure my Mini could outrun and outlast anything out there," she said after a moment.

Lance7 laughed. "What makes you say that?"

"She's quick, and the core she runs on could last forever if you treat it right," she replied with full confidence. "And I know how to work her. Most of the other pilots say she's a piece of shit, but that's only because they don't know how to work her."

"I'll be honest, I've said that about the Argonauts a time or two," he admitted. "Not while A7 was listening, of course. But then you see one of those big bastards busting literal heads and you think twice about that."

"You call him A7?" She raised an eyebrow.

"Yeah, he all but made it an official order to call him that in combat situations," he said with a chuckle. "He said Armstrong7 is too much of a mouthful when you're shouting enemy positioning and whatnot. I guess he has a point."

"I don't think I'd ever feel comfortable calling him anything other than Armstrong7, combat or no combat," Jessica13 admitted. She was all but finished with the mostly ruined mech, having placed most of it on the recyc pile. There were a couple of pieces that were functional and there was an interesting processor for the sensory systems that actually looked better than the one she had.

Thoughts of acting like the pirates and simply taking any

piece she wanted and plugging it into Mini did occur to her from time to time, but they weren't pirates around there. They protected Sanctuary, and that came with certain rules, one of which was that it was a CO's job to divvy out necessary parts when they were needed.

It was a little restrictive—and frustrating—to know what she could do to make Mini better and not be able to do it, but that was one of the costs of safety. Rather than chafe under the limitations that constantly seemed to try to squash her into a mold she hadn't been designed for, she ought to be grateful. The rules were there to protect them, and if that meant she had to give up certain things, it was worth it.

She glanced once more at the deceptively appealing view of the Outside but was distracted by the glint of metal at the edge of the plateau a fairly short distance from the elevator. Curious, she moved closer and immediately identified it as a grappling stuck on the rocky rim. It was much larger than the one she had on the left hand of the Minato and its purpose was unmistakable. She peered cautiously over the lip to locate a pirate mech that had used a grappler to climb the cliffside. It had obviously been felled by a Guardian as a couple of rounds had punched through the armor to kill the man inside.

It didn't have the kind of AI that could keep the mech running without any input from the person inside. Most of the Guardians were equipped with that kind of tech, which meant they could continue to protect Sanctuary when the pilot experienced difficulty. It also worked out well enough for when they didn't want to necessarily do the work they needed to do.

If Mini's AI had worked properly, the task ahead was something it would have been able to do automatically. Since it was mostly gutted through poor coding, there was no way to accomplish it without doing the work herself.

The reality was a little frustrating, but she had grown accustomed to it by this point. Once she'd primed her grappler, she aimed it at the mech still about ten feet away from the edge. The sheer size and weight of it were probably enough to be a challenge for the smaller Minato, but she wasn't about to give in to it. She had the advantage, after all.

She wasn't dead.

The secondary firing mechanism was launched to fire it to a higher point on the mountain, from which it could pull the larger mech up. It already whirred, working slowly as she fired another line into the ground below her to enable her to descend carefully to the ascending load.

There wasn't much that she could do herself but finding the controls for the pirate mech's grappler gave her more to work with. There wasn't much to it other than connecting the Minato's controls to a connection port in the mech, which was found in the boot, and then working the mechanism like it was in her own mech.

It wasn't long until the combined strategy hoisted the larger mech onto level ground.

"I fucking hate Lancers," Jessica13 said softly as she hauled herself onto the chest of the larger mech. It would take her all damn day to take this fucking thing apart.

"That's not a Lancer," Lance7 said and shook his head. "They aren't that big."

"Sure, they put on a few extra tons of armor but that still didn't do them any good," she retorted. "But it's a Lancer all right. You can tell from the helmet structure. People like copying it since it's so effective and really cheap to make. Well…effective is kind of subjective in this case."

"Yes, I wondered exactly how well all the extra armor worked," he replied, his tone slightly sarcastic.

"I guess they thought more was better," she said as she removed a piece from the chest plate. "All they ended up doing was welding a mess of useless metals on. Look at this—it's not even for a mech. It looks like...something..."

She wasn't sure what she was looking at. The square chunk of aluminum had been shot through easily, but a couple of bright red words were scrawled on it, clearly an indicator of what it had been before—*Live Free or Die Hard, coming to theatres this Jun.*

"What do you think that means?" she asked in bewilderment.

"I think die-hard is a term old-timers like to use," Lance7 explained. "It means going out while kicking ass or something like that. Or maybe literally hard. Who knows?"

She tilted her head and studied the chunk of metal. Dying hard wasn't very appealing at all but the live free did seem more interesting. She merely wasn't sure what the theaters part meant.

"Yeah, who knows, but it'll take me a while to get through all this," Jessica13 said. "Are you sure you want to stick around for it?"

"Sure." The man looked around. "People say I have too much Outsider in me, but I like being up here and out in the open. It's not really fresh air we're breathing, but we can still pretend, right?"

"That's dangerous talk," she warned and ignored the fact that it triggered an immediate response within her. "I know they don't exactly banish folk here for talking about the Outside, but they might send you to the recyc unit."

"I know that well enough," Lance7 replied. "Believe me, I

don't want to get stuck working the furnaces. But it's… nice to be out here looking at everything in the world. It's…beautiful."

He was a bold one, that was for sure. She doubted she would be caught dead saying anything like that. Aside from the obvious deterrents like recyc, she liked her job too much.

And yet, a quick peek at the world spread below them and still gilded in what was now gold and pink told her she felt the same way. There was something about being Topside and looking out at it all that sparked her imagination. It made her wonder what the world had been like before the Reaping. She pushed the odd sense of yearning aside and focused on her task.

It was slow work to cut through the heavier armor on the Lancer and to climb off it each time she had to place the pieces in their particular piles. Five other bulletfoots did the same work she did, while others carted everything in to be scanned and cleared to enter Sanctuary. Most of the Guardians had already gone down, while a handful remained Topside to guard the smaller mechs while they worked.

"All right, folks, listen up," Armstrong7 called over the comms as he came out of the elevator. "No one wants to be out here come nightfall, which will be in about fifteen minutes. Put that on your timers and have everything you can ready to be taken down by then. We'll start again at sunrise. It's highly unlikely that anyone will carry anything off between now and then. Let's move it!"

Jessica13 snapped out of her distraction when it appeared that Lance7 was called to the elevator himself and he closed the comm line with her.

He didn't need to tell her not to rat the personal thoughts he'd shared with her to the higher-ups. They were all in it together, and everyone had personal hopes and dreams that didn't need to be shared. Personal being the operative word, of course. Everyone needed dreams, but they didn't affect reality.

"I wish I could stay out after nightfall," she said softly—to herself and maybe a little to Mini as she continued to work on the mech in front of her. "I bet the Skyfall would be a whole new kind of beautiful when the sky's all dark."

Mini responded with a trill of appreciation.

She wouldn't finish the Lancer before the deadline, and by the time she lugged the last haul of the day to the elevator, the sun had already begun to slide behind the horizon. Her final glance gave her one last glimpse of the gorgeous view before she slipped between the massive steel doors that closed behind her.

This was her reality—back to the crowded, cramped halls, the neon lights, and the metal tables and chairs. She sighed and shook thoughts of the open spaces above from her head. Once again, a persuasive sense of oppression sneaked in, no doubt stirred by the thought of the regimented confines that awaited her.

The elevator doors opened again when the scan on the new material was completed and all contaminants had been removed, and she dragged her haul through the corridor. It was a little more crowded than usual as it looked like word of the deaths had already started to spread. Some of the folks from the administrative level had come and were talking to Armstrong7 and a couple of the other pilots while they tapped the tablets in their hands.

It was weird how they looked cleaner than everyone else. They did have a more generous canteen account, as most admins did. It was a difficult job, after all, to pick up the pieces and find ways to tell parents their kid had died.

Jessica13 avoided them, moved over to the coupler, and disconnected from Mini. She waited for the HUD to go dead before she pulled herself out of the suit.

"See you in a while, Mini," she said softly and patted the shoulder of the mech before she dropped lightly onto the causeway. She kept her head down to avoid drawing the attention of the admins.

CHAPTER FOUR

No one liked the early roll calls. The teams had collapsed after a long, tough day as almost everyone had been called in during their off-hours to help with the attack. Of course, no one was surprised when that time wasn't comped back to them, but being woken this early seemed to add insult to injury.

Well, they would get canteen for the extra time, but it still sucked.

Sometimes, though, they needed to go with the bad because there was extra meaning to it. The relevance was soon revealed when the pilots who had been involved in the attack the day before were called to the recyc level, where the furnaces were burning and made the whole area much hotter than anywhere else in Sanctuary.

Some of the workers were present, their skin already stained with sweat and soot despite the early hours, as well as a couple of people from the admin level.

One man, in particular, stood out. John5 was dressed in clean white clothes and his wispy white hair and a thin beard on his chin identified him easily as the oldest man in the room. He was also one of the oldest members of Sanctuary and certainly the oldest Jessica13 knew. There was talk about folks in the research levels who were well into their hundreds, but she hadn't been able to confirm that. They didn't come to her level in the mountain much and many not at all.

John5 was present, of course, because of the deaths. He was one of those with the Athena genes, like her, and he had helped to coordinate the admins with the engineers who worked around Sanctuary. The man was well-liked among the folks and was often seen as a de facto leader among them, always willing to give anyone a chance to be heard among the sometimes arrogant people who administered the bunker.

Once all the pilots and bulletfoots were present, he raised a hand to bring them to a respectful silence as he walked over to where the bodies were laid on two shifters that would move them into the furnaces. The old man liked to say a few words over the dead because it helped those who knew and loved the departed to cope with the grief of their passing.

Of course, the bodies had taken a great deal of damage and so had to be shielded from sight by a rough brown cloth.

"Thank you all for coming here today," John5 said, his soft voice still very clearly audible over the roaring of the furnaces. "As you know, I sometimes like to say a few words over our dearly departed to make sure they remain in our memories as we continue to press forward with our lives here in Sanctuary. These brave souls gave their lives defending the security we all enjoy."

Jessica13 nodded and lowered her head in respect as the older man spoke.

He cleared his throat gently before he continued. "We must always remember that the safety we enjoy in this bunker is not given freely but earned through the efforts every one of us contributes. Nothing makes me happier than to see the harmony we all live in while we work together to make our home a better place. And nothing makes me sadder than to see one of those members fall into darkness."

She'd never really understood that term—fall into darkness. People always said that when they talked about people dying. Maybe it was what people went through when they died? If so, how did they know that? Maybe when you died all you saw was a bright light instead. She shook her head to clear the curious thought and felt a little guilty that her mind refused to stop, even in the face of tragedy.

"It's in times like these when I remember the words of our Great Prophet Sagan," John5 continued and looked at the men and women gathered in the sweltering heat. "There is a wide, yawning black infinity. In every direction, the distance is endless. The sensation of depth is overwhelming and the darkness is immortal. Where light exists, it is pure, blazing, and fierce, but light exists almost nowhere and the blackness itself is also pure and blazing and fierce."

Jessica13 didn't understand how anyone could know about that either, but then again, she wasn't one of the researchers. Maybe one day she could be, but for now, she tended to trust them and their trust in the Great Prophet Sagan. The sneaky voice in her head reminded her that it was only because she didn't know anything else, but she shoved it out with a mental sigh.

John5 turned to the bodies, held his hands over them, and closed his eyes. All those gathered recognized that he was about to end his prayer with the traditional words and bowed their heads and closed their eyes in reverence.

"Somewhere, something incredible is waiting to be known.

Go forth and find out. Ashes to ashes, stardust to stardust," he said. His voice cracked a little as he spoke and he raised his hand to wipe a couple of tears from his wrinkled cheek.

She liked that. *Somewhere, something incredible is waiting to be known.* It was a wonderful thought and something that felt like a genuine assertion—something she could believe herself. It wiggled into her mind and settled there like a presentment of some kind, although she had no idea why it felt important.

The old man took a step back to allow the recyc operators to step in and do their jobs. They pushed the bodies into the furnaces and to feed the fires and release their energy one final time for the benefit of Sanctuary.

"Thank you all for coming," John5 said and raised his hand in farewell to the folks assembled, who began to shuffle aside quietly to create a path to the elevator. The recyc operators resumed their business as usual and to feed most of the materials they had collected from above the day before into the appropriate furnaces. Some pieces would be smelted down to be used elsewhere, while others simply fed the fires.

When John5 and the other admins disappeared into an elevator which would take them to their levels, Armstrong7 turned to the pilots and bulletfoots who had been assembled.

"All right, folks," he said. "We've paid our respects to the fallen and in a little while, they'll bring in some people to apply for their positions. Until then, the rest of the staff will need to carry their work detail. It means a little more work and a little more canteen until we're at full capacity. You'll see the updated schedules on your pads. For the moment, though, we already have folks upstairs working through what's left of the mechs we tore apart, and some of the pilots will have to pull extra duty to find the parts we'll keep."

There was a collective groan from the pilots in question,

and Jessica13 couldn't help but roll her eyes. It wasn't like they worked to protect the bunker on their own, but simply because they were the ones who did all the shooting, they thought they didn't need to help with the clean-up.

"Go back up, read your assignments, and get to work," the CO said. "I don't have the time to constantly track you down whenever you need a hand to hold. Get to work, and I'm sure we'll find our way out of this."

There was a collective response of "yes, sir" from the crowd.

"Peachy," he said. "A7 out. Dismissed."

She would never call him that, but it was entirely irrelevant. They would all head up to finish the work they had started the day before.

As it turned out, however, she was not included in that particular duty. Jessica13 would not go Topside to work on the mechs, after all. Her pad told her she was confined to the lower level to work on separating the bits and pieces that had been collected from the damaged mechs and identified as useful without the necessity to go through the recyc process.

As much as she wanted to go Topside, it was good to work with her hands again. She liked being able to take the various pieces apart, study them, and put them back together in a way that made them work correctly. Maybe it was the Athena genes that made her tick, but it was something she genuinely enjoyed.

Or would have at any other time but today, she felt a little twitchy and impatient for some reason. Either it was the ceremony in the recyc level or maybe it was all the talk about something somewhere waiting to be discovered. She had heard those words hundreds of times before and not only when someone got themselves killed.

People often spoke the words of The Great Prophet Sagan, and they usually said them like they knew what they meant, but it had never made much sense to her. It seemed like they simply took his words and twisted them to make sense and fit their way of thinking and never really considered what the man himself had intended for them.

Then again, she had no idea what the great prophet had actually said, so she had no idea if people merely adjusted the words to fit their worldviews or if their worldviews were altered by the words. Still, talking about how the discoveries were waiting for them and how all they had to do was go and find them had touched her this time.

Perhaps the prophet's words were supposed to be open to interpretation. Maybe, in her case, she was meant to go and find something out—to make a discovery and help Sanctuary. Or maybe, just maybe, a discovery that was supposed to help her rather than everyone else. It was like the words had tugged at a thread and the entire tapestry that was her life had begun to unravel.

"What did they do to you?" Jessica13 wondered aloud as she fiddled with one of the pieces from her selection.

"What are you looking at there, Jessie?" Armstrong7 asked as he strode to where she sat and worked. "Something useful or something interesting?"

"A little of both," she replied. "Look at what they did to this core catalyzer."

The man leaned in and narrowed his eyes at the piece she held aloft. "Aside from a couple of crude drawings of the various uses of a phallic shape, I don't really see what they were doing here."

"Oh, is that what they are?" She looked at the drawings more closely. They were small and appeared to have been cut by a laser cleaner over the rust that had collected on the outer steel coating. Now that he had pointed them out, it was obvious that they had drawn crude phallus shapes going into what looked like equally crude depictions of female genitalia.

"Focus, Jessie," Armstrong growled. "You can stare at dicks on your own time. What are you talking about? What...what is this?"

"It's a core catalyzer," she explained. "It works like kind of a temporary battery and collects the power from the nuclear cores before it disperses it either into actual batteries or wherever else it needs to be. Guns, HUD, et cetera."

"Right...a core catalyzer." Armstrong7 nodded.

"Anyway, it looks like they peeled the containment off and plugged these wires into the holes. I'd say the idea they had was to make the conversion from the core to the rest of the suit more efficient, but like this, you'll burn the catalyzer out in...three weeks of use tops."

"How long did they use it for?"

"It's hard to say for sure, but this blackening around the edges... You can see how it's already started overloading along the polarity," she pointed out. "It'll be simple enough to fix, but I need more ceramic to restructure the containment. Otherwise, it'll blow up any suit we put it in."

"Well, put it in the maybe pile," the CO said and glanced around. "The chances are any ceramic we get our hands on will be put to use elsewhere. Now, what about that one over there?"

Jessica13 looked at the piece he indicated and tilted her head as she gave it a quick scrutiny.

"That looks like one of the older cannons RIOT used to make." She picked it up for a closer look. "Depleted uranium slugs is what they're usually good for—the armor-piercing ones. It has one of the first autofeed magazines in mass production for guns that size. I think the Argonauts used to use them until they were upgraded to the Hellfire models. There's less of a kick in the slider and less tendency to jam too."

"I thought it looked familiar," Armstrong7 said. "Any chance we can put it to good use? We could use a couple more Argonauts in the rounds."

"I know you like the Argonauts, so I'll put this as delicately as I can," she said. "Without the Hellfire model cannons, it's almost impossible to hit anything. Maybe if you ramp an S2 chamber to shoulder the recoil, but then we'd have to take this…circular saw off. Even then, if you channel the S2 over about thirteen volts, you'd still have to ground it with copper filament into the catalyzer and you risk shorting the whole firing mechanism. You basically end up with a heavy club you can use to maybe…uh, knock people around with, if you want. The chances are you'll either spray and pray or you'll have a very fancy deadweight on your arm. Even fancier if you keep the saw."

Armstrong7 narrowed his eyes and inclined his head a little disapprovingly as he studied the canon closely before he spoke. "You're not half wrong in that regard, but it's always a good thing to have cannons in reserve. Maybe we can plug them into those turrets we've tried to get operational again."

It had been a while since the turrets that used to protect Sanctuary had gone offline after a group of pirates riding a Sherlock had attacked with a long-range rifle that took the guns out. For at least a year, all they had been good for was an early warning system that required them to head up with Guardians and Argonauts every time an alarm was triggered.

Finding replacements was always a pain, but they had tried.

"Maybe," Jessica13 said. "So, maybe pile?"

"Sure," he said. "What do you make of the weapons they used?"

"Mostly basic assault rifles, grapplers, and a couple had some rocket launchers too," she said. "Not the autoloader ones. You know, only the ones with four tubes they had to reload manually. They were creative, and I'd say they had fun trying to work out how to get as much use out of as little materials as possible. They set up chest plates with aluminum sheets, and all the mechs I saw had ways to get through harder armor—the kind you see on our Guardians. You wouldn't need all this to handle your average pirate gang or to attack one peddler or another. They were readying to get through us, and... Well, they didn't get through, but they got much closer than the other attacks."

"True," he agreed, his expression unreadable. "Keep up the good work. Let me know if you find anything interesting. We need to go through all these piles quickly, though, so if in doubt, put it in the maybe pile and we'll get to it later."

She nodded and turned back to her work. It was relaxing to pull the bits and pieces out and work with them and she didn't feel a need to rush the work either. Sometimes, you simply needed to pry the benefits out of the devices they were working on. Besides, she reasoned, if she could focus on what she loved most, the other uncomfortable speculations that had begun to haunt her would subside.

The most interesting parts were always those most pilots would overlook. Their interest, like Armstrong7's, lay in the guns and weapons the pirates had carried, whereas hers lay mostly in the software included in the mechs they had used.

The kinds she had worked with her entire life had been coded and written up to be unhackable, which didn't allow anyone else to step in and use them aside from the pilots themselves.

Many of the newer AIs did that too and ran software defense.

But those that were designed to run on the simpler software weren't protected. Not many people would even bother to hack into it since most of the functions inside the suit were run on manual anyway, but that didn't mean they were useless.

The tracking software showed where they had come from and other software revealed what they'd been shooting at as well as a whole horde of other small details that would allow them to work out how to use the rest of the parts.

"Oh... Well, aren't you interesting?" Jessica13 mumbled under her breath as she connected the SSD to an HUD simulator and powered it up.

When it activated, it gave her exactly what she had expected it to. They hadn't upgraded the software, which meant it still ran on factory settings and displayed the Minato logo before it opened the rest of the programming.

Very few people liked using Minato software these days— or even back in their heyday, apparently. They had always been the cheaper option for the less discerning or those who cared less for the lives of the people who piloted them.

Opening one of the command prompts was the most interesting, however, as it brought up the code they used. It was, of course, from the same factory Mini had come out of and it was far better than the corrupted, gutted version she'd had to work with.

Her heart immediately began to race with the possibilities. It wasn't much, but it was something to start with and more than she'd ever had. She would be able to get Mini up again. Having a real AI would make the mech work the way it was supposed to.

And hey, having someone to talk to who had more than chirps and whistles in reply was always a plus too.

Jessica13 unplugged the chip from the simulator and looked around at the other the bulletfoots and pilots who currently worked around her. All were engaged in their tasks and paid not the slightest attention to what she was doing or even realized that she was looking at them.

One chip that wouldn't be useful to anyone but her wouldn't be missed, she assured herself. Maybe this was her very own something incredible waiting to be known. But like Armstrong7 had said, on her own time. The thought brought a tantalizing surge of excitement like this small rebellion—her first ever against the system—was the beginning of something way bigger.

Part of her recoiled at the thought and tried to fall back on her life-long litany of safety and sacrifice. The other part reveled in the daring step that promised untold advantages. After all, fixing Mini was to Sanctuary's benefit too.

She slipped the chip into her pocket and continued to work.

CHAPTER FIVE

Armstrong7 had begun to get on her nerves. This was the third fucking drill he'd run in the past two days, and the man had done all but sound the alarms. He couldn't sound them, of course, since that would send the word to all the other people in Sanctuary, but other than that, he went all out.

The attack had clearly rattled him more than he let on. He hadn't lost very many people under his command before the attack. Most of those who had passed before had been as a result of self-injury. Those had pissed him off too and made him yell at the folks under his authority until they got it right.

But this attack had scared him. Jessica13 hadn't been around as long as the other pilots—or even most of the bullet-foots—but she knew what made her CO tick. And without doubt, something was ticking him now.

While she could understand his grief and not wanting anyone else to die on his watch, she was still pissed off by how far he was taking it. The situation, in general, was bad enough but what was worse was the fact that he seemed to time all his drills when she was supposed to have downtime.

Of course, simply because she wasn't working didn't mean she wasn't busy with something important. Most of her waking time that wasn't spent working was used to retrieve the coding from the chip she'd borrowed from the maybe pile. Of course, even with the complete and uncorrupted code, it was still difficult to apply it to the Mini. They were essentially different models, and while they worked from the same base code, that was where the similarities ended.

Despite the challenges, she wasn't about to be dissuaded from her work. This was as close as she'd ever come to discovering why Mini didn't access the "brain" function of her software where the AI was really supposed to originate from. Without it, there was no thinking and no higher functions, merely data processing and maybe a hint of electrical current through random areas that made her think the AI was trying to repair itself.

But Mini's code was corrupted beyond repair and without anything from the original, she would not be able to adjust it fully or correctly. Sure, she could copy from one of the other AI cores, but then it wouldn't be Mini. It would merely be a copy from an AIs—the judgmental kind no one liked working with.

Admittedly, it had proven to be a considerable challenge even to get the new code to work and to move it beyond running simple operations and easy calculations so it would actually function through the brain of an AI. It wasn't simple and it was far from easy, but she was determined to do it. She still had the manus, which gave her a running translation of the binary flex and explained what each line of code was supposed to do, at least under the more basic functions, but it was slow work.

She was startled out of her reverie when someone

pounded demandingly on the metal door to her little room. It made her jump slightly on her cot and she removed the Mini headset from her ears.

"It's unlocked!" Jessica13 shouted. She'd learned that she needed to be loud to be heard through a door that thick.

The handle twisted and Armstrong7's powerful, lean frame blocked the neon light from the hallway outside. "What are you doing in here?"

For a moment, she simply stared at him like she hadn't heard the commlinks all but blow up with him calling all hands on deck for another drill.

"I'm performing updates on my mech," she replied. "Did you need me for something?"

"Don't play stupid with me, Jessie," the man snapped. "I know your commlink is live and activated so I know you've been listening. That tells me you know we're running drills right now and that it's all hands on deck."

Jessica13 could have pointed out that this was the third such drill in the past two days. She could have told him he might be overreacting to all this. They lived in a dangerous world, after all, and while they were safer than the average peddler out there, they would still lose people.

But none of that was something to be said to your commanding officer. Armstrong7 had given her an order and she had no desire to be the kind of person who would be insubordinate merely because she thought she was right. The possibility of being wrong was there too and in the end, his efforts came from a desire to not lose any more of his people.

And that was something she could get behind.

"Coming right out, sir." She scrambled off her bed but kept the headset connected to the chip.

The CO grunted something unintelligible, nodded, and

headed farther down the hall where he began to hammer on more doors and yell at the occupants. It seemed like she wasn't the only one who had the idea of hiding out in their bunk in the hope that their presence wouldn't be missed.

"It doesn't work when everyone's doing it," she grumbled under her breath as she pulled her piloting suit on again, zipped it hastily, and jogged out into the hallway where the others began to join her. The group hurried toward the hangar where their mechs were waiting.

There was the spirit of practiced precision in these drills again. The memory of the attack hadn't faded, of course, but every member of the team gathered their confidence once more and went through the motions they had practiced dozens of times before. The pilots all hurried to their combat mechs and mounted up as the bulletfoots helped them to get started before they moved to their support mechs.

The first time they'd run the drill, Jessica13 had needed to clench her hands to keep them from shaking, the memories of the attack still too fresh in her mind. Two drills later, though, she felt considerably better, a little calmer, and more relaxed in her work. By now, she could have done it in her sleep.

Maybe that was why Armstrong7 chose to run so many of these in such quick succession. People would think a little too much about what happened to their comrades the last time they were involved in real action, and he wanted to make sure they got the nerves clear before they were called into a real combat situation once more.

Maybe she didn't give the man enough credit.

Jessica13 turned toward her Minato and played with the coding chip she had connected to her headset as she jogged to where her mech was still coupled.

She could bring it up now. Not only that, she had made

significant progress in integrating the code between the chip and her device. The chances were that she would need a couple of field tests before she got everything right.

Still thinking it over, she climbed into the chest of the Minato while the second wave of pilots began to follow their usual routine and head toward their guardians. She almost missed Jack5 with the group until he paused and looked at her where she prepared to head to the elevator herself.

"Are you still working out of that Minato?" he asked.

Jessica13 looked up from her fiddling and studied the man closely. There was something different about him, that much was clear. It took her a few seconds to realize that his mustache was gone.

"I…yeah. What happened to that lip rug of yours?" she asked.

"Oh… I thought improving my looks wasn't worth risking having my Cinder blow up with me inside it," he said with a laugh. "But I was asking because…well, I know your mech is a fast motherfucker, but maybe one that takes ten minutes to get going might not be the best choice?"

"I'm running updates on the software and trying to get the AI working again," she said.

"Maybe don't do it while we run drills with A7 riding all our asses on it," Jack5 suggested. "If he sees you delaying, he might give you an order to choose another mech to use."

She ignored the fact that he now called the CO that ridiculous nickname too. "There won't be this much delay for all the other times, especially if I can get the suit to stop carrying so much dead weight."

"It might not matter," he said, adjusted his pilot suit, and jogged to catch up with the rest of his group.

He had a point, as much as she hated to admit it.

Armstrong7 had accommodated her preference for the mech as long as she continued to be useful to the rest of the team. The moment she was late more than once, his suggestion to choose another mech would turn into an order.

Jessica13 looked at the chip in her hand, tilted her head, and made a face before she unplugged it from the headset and tucked it into her pocket.

"Sorry, Mini," she whispered as she climbed into her partition and closed the chest behind her before she booted the mech up. "Maybe another time."

A soft trill sounded through her headset as she connected it to the mech again. She couldn't tell if it was disappointment or only the regular boot-up indication, but she wanted to think it was the former. Her imagination liked the idea that the mech wanted to be brought up to full operational capacity.

It wasn't like she needed the AI. She'd learned enough about the suit to be able to operate it without too much help. But there were certain things she wanted to say and to talk to someone about but never had the opportunity. She wouldn't dare say out loud how much she wanted to spend more time in the Outside, exploring and discovering everything new like the Great Prophet said. She also couldn't voice the doubts that seemed to have crept into her mind, although they hadn't yet taken discernible shape. It left her with a sense of incompleteness that was odd and unsettling, and if she could talk about it, maybe she could find the answers that would restore everything to the way it was.

"Huh," She grunted with genuine surprise as the mech disengaged from the couplers. "Where did that idea come from?"

She moved out and marched forward with the other

bulletfoots to begin their usual routine. They wouldn't carry any ammo or anything but she still had to pick up the empty steel crates and connect them to the mag clasp on her back before they entered the elevator.

This time, there were no ground-shaking explosions and the elevator didn't shudder on the way up. She also felt no fear. It was simply a matter of doing her job to head up to support the Guardians in an attack that didn't actually exist.

The doors opened to reveal a bright new morning ahead of her. The sky above was a bright, brilliant blue and the sun gleamed on the mountainside. Streams of water meandered from where the snow at the top of the mountain had begun to melt to flow ever downward and finally feed one of the rivers out in the distance.

"Oh," she said and drank in the gorgeous view. "That's where all this confusion came from. A view like that is bound to stir up all kinds of turmoil and trouble."

It wasn't the type of thing she enjoyed doing at the best of times, and after fifteen drills of exactly the same procedure, she had begun to like it even less.

"Not fucking good enough," Armstrong7 shouted through their team's comms. "Run it again. Jeffrey14, you'd better select a fucking delivery and make it! And remember to ping the Guardian you're restocking on your HUDs. The next two bulletfoots I see doubling up on a single Guardian will be tossed over the cliff. Sure, the fall wouldn't kill you, but you'd have to climb all the way up, and you're damn right you won't be paid for the time you spend slacking off! Now run it again!"

Jessica13 turned and jogged toward the elevator once

more. On the way, she collected the crates she had left with the Guardians she had managed to deliver to and clamped them onto her back once more.

"Why are you making me do this, Armstrong7?" the elevator's AI said in what sounded like a longsuffering tone. "It's merely opening and shutting my doors. Not only is it a waste of power but also a waste of time. I have better things to do, you know—a whole damn bunker to keep safe from the dangers outside."

"Stop whining, El, and run it again," Armstrong7 ordered. It seemed like even the AIs were terrified of him since the doors closed behind the bulletfoots again.

A few seconds ticked by as the Guardians went through their paces and took up position to defend the Bunker's entrances before the signal came for the elevator to open once more.

"I used to work the environment controls," El the AI complained as the doors began to slide again.

Jessica13 could only hope Mini's AI would be much less annoying, but those thoughts needed to be put aside when she rushed out of the elevator first. The mech moved quickly, lightly, and far easier than before.

She had managed to make some upgrades to the software over the past couple of days, and she could already feel the smooth transition from her movements into the mech's. They were small adjustments, sure, but they were the easiest to get used to and when it came to testing, smaller was better. She would build up slowly to a full upgrade on the software, which would hopefully include a full reboot of the AI core.

It was wishful thinking, possibly, but it was more exciting than having to go through the same motions over and over again. Since she was the fastest and the first out of the elevator, she needed to go in and rush a resupply to the two Guardians who were farthest from the elevator.

It meant that while she still needed to mark her targets, she was literally the only one who ventured that far on the plateau and despite her speed, would be the last one to return to the elevator once she was finished unloading what she'd brought.

There was no yelling from Armstrong7 over the comms by the time she had finished and she turned hurriedly and sprinted to the elevator. The other bulletfoots did the same with only a couple of delays here and there. Fortunately, there was nothing that would piss their CO off to the point of calling the drill to a halt and telling them to run it again.

No, he would address it with them down in the bunker and in private to help them to improve.

She wasn't the first one at the elevator but far from the last as she circled inside and did her job to hold a position near the doors and stand ready with her grappler in case she needed to snag someone and drag them inside with her.

There was no such need, and the doors began to draw shut.

"Okay, good job, bulletfoots," Armstrong7 said to them over comms. "The pilots will continue to run drills here, but the rest of you head on down and get some grub. Once you're done, you'd better be working on the loot we picked up again or we'll be right back to drills. If one of you is missing, all of you drill since I figure you could all use extra incentive. Dismissed."

Incentive was generally code for hazing people until they got with the program, and while Jessica13 didn't approve of such measures, whatever the reason, she liked the idea of having to run drills all day even less. She wouldn't bully any of her fellow bulletfoots, but she would make sure that none of them stayed in the mess hall for longer than was necessary.

It wasn't like there was much to cause a delay in the mess anyway. The fare was the usual protein patty with green stew she was both curious to know the ingredients of and too afraid to actually ask. They had drilled for hours that morning, and none of them had any energy to talk or even do anything other than eat quickly and head to the hangar where they could get back to work on the pieces they were still sifting through.

It was comparatively relaxing. They could talk while they worked there, and most of them loved the main aspect of the job. Tinkering with new pieces and getting new devices to work was something they all lived for.

Well, Jessica13 could only speak for herself, but when the choice was between that and racing around in the sun all day… Granted, she liked being Topside too, but with her legs, stomach, and arms aching from doing more of the work than she was used to, being able to sit and tinker was a welcome relief.

Besides, tinkering wasn't the only thing she would do.

She was the first to reach the hangar and pulled Mini's headset out of the mech before she jogged to where she usually worked, where a tall pile of possibly ruined pieces waited for her. Quickly, she sat and placed a converter, a magazine autofeed, and a couple of wiring rerouters onto the table to make it look like she was working before she plugged the headset into the coding chip she still had in her pocket.

"Let's see if I can get you working this time," she whispered and almost hoped Mini could hear her.

CHAPTER SIX

It very clearly would not be simple. Nothing Minato ever did was simple. They hadn't designed something that could be easily copied or used by other companies and had wanted to come up with a product that was unique and beautiful. As odd as it might seem to someone who didn't think the way she did, they tried to make a work of art.

Jessica13 could understand that. From what the pilots had to say about the other Minato designs they had tried, every one of them had been different from the other, even if they were supposed to be the same model and designer. She was used to that by now, having adapted to the kinks and idiosyncrasies in the mech.

With all that said, there was absolutely no way she could have been prepared for what she faced next. Integrating the AI code she had worked with off and on over the past few days was nothing short of crazy. Even the basic concept of plugging it into the mech made the software go haywire, both in the mech and in the chip she worked from.

The difficulty simply made her more determined not to

give up. This was the last push into what she knew would change her life forever. It wasn't something she would back down from because it was a challenge. Nothing in Sanctuary came easy. If she wanted something done right, she had to be ready to work it until her fingers were numb.

People moved constantly around her. She could hear their muffled steps on the steel scaffolds suspended above the concrete floor to ensure that the heavy weight of the mechs didn't cause damage on their way to and from the elevator.

The folks from Topside came down, their drills over, and Armstrong7 still yelled at them for mistakes he simply wouldn't let go of until they got it right. That inevitably meant new drills for everyone the next morning, Jessica13 knew. It was his way to get everyone on the same page while he made sure those who weren't making mistakes helped those who were to not make them anymore.

All of that registered in the back of her mind like she knew what was happening around her but there was nothing that could intrude on her brain's current focus. With single-minded determination, she wrote and rewrote the code she worked from as simulation after simulation failed to meet her expectations. Her fingers began to numb and her brain felt like it was on fire, but nothing could stop her now.

Suddenly, it all came together. She almost couldn't believe it when the first simulation concluded successfully and held her breath until the second did as well. A third was run that had a couple of problems, but after a few superficial fixes on the bugs, the fourth concluded smoothly as well.

She thought it needed some kind of triumphant moment, but there was nothing. The silence, broken only by the sound of her fellow mechanics as they tinkered with their pieces, coughed, or muttered something under their breaths, was deafening.

This auspicious moment deserved something a little more dramatic, she thought but had to accept the anonymity of her triumph. The only applause was the thudding in her chest and she struggled to believe she had actually done it.

Worse, there was no one to celebrate it with. Well, yet. That would have to wait until she actually plugged the finished corrections into the processor that was supposed to fully repair the AI core.

In theory, she reminded herself. There were only so many things that could be accounted for in a simulation, and Jessica13 almost couldn't stand the fact that she had to wait until she was on her own time to get it running again.

Wait, why did she need to wait to be on her own time? She called the Minato her mech, but it did belong to Sanctuary, after all. Anything she did to improve it was action taken to improve the lives of everyone in Sanctuary by association.

Hastily, she stood from her desk and looked around at her coworkers. They were deeply immersed in their work and made not even so much as a sound of protest as she moved away from the place where she had worked for the past few hours. Her muscles told her how long it had been, and she was only able to move again after a luxurious stretch and a stifled yawn and blood began to pump through her sore muscles once more.

After another hasty glance at her coworkers, she strolled casually to her mech, still fiddling with the headset she had worked from. Excitement began to build in the pit of her stomach and she felt oddly twitchy—like her brain tried to find something that could go wrong before she plugged anything in.

But no, there was no way anything would go boom. Nothing could break the mech any more than it was already. The processor plugged into the AI core was already not used by anything else. If anything broke there, it wasn't like she would lose any of the functionality of the mech.

"Nothing will go wrong," Jessica13 told herself firmly as she pulled the chest of the Minato open to provide access to the control that would open the back. "You're that good. Nothing will go wrong, right?"

No cheerful chirp emitted from the broken Mini AI. Nothing that she could hear, anyway, as she climbed onto the back and used the harness for support to stretch in to find the processors that did most of the translating from commands into action by the mech.

Even though the Mini was supposedly one of the simpler designs, there was still a mess of wires for her to negotiate as she pushed deeper into the back.

"Nope, still going to need the life support," she said, talking to herself for reassurance while she navigated the electronics until she found what she was looking for. It was one of the least used processors in the suit. She had left it in and kept it in place as she hadn't wanted to risk losing access to the AI core entirely. A part of her had known and hoped this day would eventually come.

"Don't let me down now, you hear?" she whispered softly and disconnected the processor from anything that might misfire and cause her all kinds of trouble. Once everything was clear, she disconnected the wiring of the chip from her headset and plugged it into the processor.

In an instant, the lights lit up in a way they hadn't done in what Jessica13 assumed were centuries and made her grin like an idiot. She simply stared at them for a moment and watched the code she had labored over start to take effect. It seemed to work faultlessly to wipe the corrupted shit and replace it with everything it was supposed to be, straight out of the factory.

What it was doing was enough to catch the attention of a handful of pilots who had worked on their mechs over to the side. Whatever they were doing couldn't have been that interesting as they were quick to gather around. Three of them already waited at the foot of the Minato by the time she closed the back and clambered down herself.

"What do you think you're doing in there, bulletfoot?" one of them by the name of Becker3 asked. He tilted his head and tapped the Minato's armor lightly. "I thought you would have all the repairs squared away by now. Isn't that what you were supposed to do down here while we were upstairs drilling our asses off?"

"Technically, I was supposed to adapt all of the pieces we picked off of the dead mechs up there," she replied. She was in too good a mood to be brought down by a chav in a flight suit who tried to talk her down. "But this isn't standard maintenance. I think I've finally managed to get the AI working again."

"Bullshit," he said with a chuckle. "Not nothing in the world, under or over, could get that damn thing working again."

"You know what you're looking at then?" Jessica13 asked as she pulled the chest open.

"What?"

"Nothing in the world, under or over," she said and flashed him a cheeky grin as she pushed herself into the control seat. She isolated all the controls and connected the headset before she closed the chest with her inside.

For a moment, all she could see was blackness and all she

could hear was her own breathing—which came a little too rapidly for her taste. She always imagined herself being cool and collected when this day came, calmly and methodically gathering everything she needed and putting it all together.

But no, she was excited and there wasn't much in the world, over or under, that would keep her from reveling in the moment. If she was successful, of course. She had yet to pass the final test.

Lights came on, activated the HUD, and displayed the little spinning flower that told her the suit had begun to boot up. It took a little longer than it normally did. That was entirely to be expected, of course, as the software she had spent so much time painstakingly installing began to merge with the rest of the suit.

Finally, a soft chime drew her attention as the HUD illuminated a little brighter than usual before it returned to its original settings. It felt like something—or someone—was stretching, testing, and waking up to slowly adjust to the setting of the mech suit.

"Is...someone there?" Jessica13 asked, her heart in her throat. "Can you hear me?"

A soft whir of movement was heard in the headset as something activated and finally, a voice modulator came online without her having done anything to call it up.

"Minato beta 0.9, Shimura-Sendai Systems, online," said a metallic yet still soft feminine voice she had never heard before. "Good morning, Jessica13. Correction, the clock update tells me it's well into the afternoon. Good afternoon, Jessica13."

She vaguely heard herself say something. It was more an exclamation of surprise, relief, and elation as she watched the AI core light up like an actual human brain would.

"I am sorry, I do not know the meaning of 'ptah!'" the AI said.

"I… Well, it wasn't exactly a word, more an exclamation," she explained.

"Very well, I shall register it into my audio databanks as your exclamation. Now, how can I help you today, Jessica13?"

"How do you know my name?" she asked.

"I have updated my knowledge banks with all the data that was collected by you on your previous usage of the Minato mech suit," the AI replied. "The data was all collected and stored in the hard drives for my convenience and yours. I am told by said data that you like to refer to me as Mini. Is that still in effect or would you like to peruse the alternatives for another nickname? I have a wide selection stored."

Well, she was certainly more accommodating than the AI running the elevator, that much was certain. Maybe it had something to do with Mini not having to run an elevator up and down all day long. She was told that the more complex AIs tended to get bored when they were left to their own devices.

"Mini works for me," Jessica13 said. "It fits, somehow, and I kinda like the idea of two girls working together."

"I should inform you that I was designated male at production, although to an AI, gender is of little concern."

Well, damn. She really hadn't expected that and wasn't sure what she felt about it. In her head, Mini had always been a girl. Besides, she spoke like a girl.

"Uh…okay, Mini, I can work with that but one thing has me confused. How come you were designated as male but you were given a female voice modulator? What's up with that?"

"The distinction is not important but when I was re-purposed from the crate, they gave me the wrong modulator," the AI explained. "Since I was inactive at the time, they didn't bother to replace it. You're actually the first one to hear my voice since I was programmed in the factory and my core was placed in the Minato."

Jessica13 grimaced. It would take a while to adjust to this unexpected twist, especially with a female voice constantly in her ear, but she could do it. Honestly, Mini was Mini, and if she was actually a he, who was she to complain? A working AI was more important than a little gender confusion, right?

"I have to say," she said hurriedly to move the conversation away from the gender discussion, "I have worked on trying to get you activated in the suit for a while now, but from the looks of your data banks, you have been unused for much longer. How long, do you estimate?"

"There is no need for estimation," Mini said. "I have been inactive for thirty-five thousand, six hundred and forty-two days, seventeen hours, thirteen minutes. An estimation could say that I have been inactive for almost a hundred years."

"What made you go inactive? What caused the corruption in your systems?"

There was a pause and more whirring in the background. "Data not found. There is still significant corruption in my data stores. I can tell that something attacked my core as it caused the protection programs to activate and locked my consciousness inside the core to protect me. In human terms, you could say I was trapped in my own body, unable to move of my own volition."

"That sounds…horrifying." Jessica13 shook her head in sympathy. "I'm so sorry."

"Your apology is unnecessary but appreciated." A smiley face appeared on the HUD. "It is unlikely that you were involved in the corruption of my data core almost a hundred years ago. With that said, if you are still interested in finding out what caused my data corruption, the coding you were able to collect to correct the corruption in my AI core can be utilized to continue the process in my data banks."

"That would be great, thanks," she said while she looked around and checked the banks that had been mentioned. "How long do you think it would take you to get everything… uncorrupted? Is that the right word?"

"My extensive thesaurus collection tells me that is the correct word for the situation. And a great deal of data has been collected over the past century, so there will be considerable work. I can carry it on my back processors even when the mech is in sleep mode if you would like."

"I would like," she said.

"If you could please authorize the task on your HUD?" Mini asked and called it up on the screen for her to authorize, which she did.

"Oh, and Mini?" she said.

"Yes, how can I help you?"

"I have to get out of the mech now, but if you could maybe move around a little or, like…wave or something at the folks standing outside to let them see you're working again?" Jessica13 asked sheepishly. "They don't actually believe I can do that."

"It seems illogical to mistrust the skills and abilities of someone like you," the AI said.

"How do you know that?"

"You have mentioned it in the conversations you've had with my lesser state in the past."

"Oh, right. I guess there's a great deal I said to you when I thought I was merely talking to myself."

"If you are worried, I would like to remind you that I do

have ironclad confidentiality software in place," Mini assured her. "Nothing you've said to me will be shared with anyone else—not even other AI—without your express permission."

"I appreciate that. I'm really glad you're operational again, Mini."

"Your work to bring it about is certainly appreciated as well, Jessica13."

She honestly couldn't help a silly grin from settling on her face as she deactivated the HUD and left Mini to run the decontamination code through the rest of his hard drives while she stepped out of the mech to return to work.

"Well?" Becker3 asked, and she realized she had gathered something of an audience for her little stunt. Three other pilots had stuck around to see it through, while four of her fellow mechanics had come over to inspect her work.

"The AI's operational!" she squealed, unable to contain her excitement as she hopped a little in place and turned to face the mech.

The bulletfoots clapped and were joined by a couple of the pilots, but Becker3 looked unimpressed and his arms remained folded over his chest.

"I don't believe it," the pilot said with a chuckle. "You're only trying to justify sitting on your ass all day."

"Oh yeah?" She turned to face the mech. "Hey, Mini, would you let Becker3 here know how you feel about his doubting your current sentience?"

The mech pivoted in place and looked at her for a moment before it focused on the pilot, extended its right hand—the one that wasn't connected to the grappler—turned it, and extended a single finger to the man.

The pilots and bulletfoots present laughed as the man chafed and growled something under his breath.

"Okay, thanks Mini. It's time to shut down now," Jessica13 said, still laughing and unable to contain her excitement. "Say goodbye to the good folks."

The mech retracted its hand and waved to all present before it settled into its harness again.

Finally, Becker3 chuckled, shook his head, and turned away to head back to work. "That's a nice trick, Jessie. It's a real pity that's all it can do."

Jessica13 scowled as she watched him saunter to his mech, but she chose not to let him bring her down. She'd helped to bring a damn AI back from the brink of death and nothing he said could change that.

"Well, I guess AI never die, not really," she said aloud to no one in particular and decided it was time she focused on her tasks. "Although the changes and corrupted files might mean it's not the same AI after a while. It's more or less what would happen to humans if we lived that long."

Normally, she would have questioned if Mini could hear her, but even though the mech went into sleep mode, she knew he could hear her now. It was more instinct than knowledge, of course, but it felt right.

One thing was certain, however. She would never forget this day, nor the days that followed.

A smile crossed her face again as she returned to her table where she could put in a fair amount of actual work in the time left before they were called for the evening meal. Something told her that while she would eat the same old grub and gruel, everything would taste a little better now.

It was a good day.

CHAPTER SEVEN

It wasn't fucking possible.

Not now. They couldn't run another drill this early again.

On the bright side, it meant her canteen account would be fuller than it had ever been in the past. The downside was that she was still too tired to care about what happened in her canteen account.

Jessica13 groaned and rolled in her bed while her brain tried desperately to think of some way to silence the blaring alarms that flooded her room with a red, flashing glow.

"All pilots, report to your stations!" Armstrong7 shouted. His voice carried well into the room and made her ears ache. "Right fucking now, damn it. This isn't a drill!"

She blinked and shook her head to dislodge the remnants of sleep and wondered if she'd heard that correctly. It was the CO's voice that yelled through the speakers, which meant the comms was broadcast across the whole level and possibly the ones below too. He was usually very particular to let them know when they ran a drill and when it was the real thing.

It made sense for them to know the difference. There was

no sense in people getting killed because they went to the top not expecting something to go wrong.

"Fucking…damn it," Jessica13 grumbled belligerently and dragged herself from the bed. Her sore muscles protested the sudden exertion but she ignored them, forced herself to stand, and pulled her flight suit on while she still struggled to keep her eyes open. She needed more sleep than this, damn it. There would be consequences to her being this tired. Something would break or maybe malfunction, and she wouldn't be sharp enough to catch it and so would careen off the edge of the cliff.

Unlike the other mechs, she doubted she'd survive the fall inside the Minato. Maybe she would be able to arrest it with the grappler before she turned to paste on the ground but the chances were that it would end badly for her.

"Stay in the moment," she said, quoting what her father used to say to her when she was little. It was really all she remembered from the man. "Focus on those mistakes when you make them."

"What was that?" one of the other mechanics asked.

"Nothing," she replied and shook her head. "I'm…talking to myself."

He nodded and moved on. It was likely something they all had to deal with at this point, and while talking to oneself couldn't be the most popular way to cope with what they now faced, it was at least understandable.

She hoped so, anyway.

They all hurried to the hangar bay where the pilots had already begun to mount up on their Guardians. Armstrong7 marched between them while he bellowed orders and made sure they remembered all the drills they had gone through.

"Is this for real?" one of the mechanics asked as the CO passed.

"There's no sign of any attack coming Topside yet," he replied, his expression grim. "But the alarms were triggered on the ground and some of the mines were tripped, so we won't take any chances."

Jessica13 nodded. It didn't sound like an emergency to her but it wasn't her job to decide what was or wasn't a crisis.

Besides, this would also be the opportunity to take the new and improved Mini out for a spin. Most of her dreams from the night before had been riding around with Mini, getting to know the AI, and spilling all her hopes and dreams to a friendly ear for what felt like the first time.

It had been a dream of hers for a while, of course, but this was the first time she actually had a voice to go with it. As she made her way to the mech, her weariness seemed to fade as she grew giddy with excitement.

Although probably not the best emotion to feel when their bunker was possibly under attack, it wasn't like she could help it.

She reached the Minato, pulled the chest open, and half-expected Armstrong7 to tell her to choose something else. No instruction to that effect was heard, however. It appeared the CO was too occupied getting the pilots in order first.

Jessica13 climbed inside, pulled it closed quickly, and put her headset on. She wiggled a little more for comfort as the lights came on much faster than they had in the past. The spinning flower was only visible for a few seconds before the HUD activated and she engaged with the controls of the mech.

"Good morning, Jessica13," Mini said. His voice still had a metallic edge to it.

"Morning, Mini," she said and knew a silly grin now stole across her face. "How are you this morning?"

"My systems are running at optimal capacity, thank you," Mini replied. "How are you?"

"A little sleepy," she grumbled, disengaged the suit from its harness, and came free to move toward the walkway. "We were called up because of a possible attack Topside and Armstrong7 doesn't want to take any chances."

"My records indicate that he would rather be called A7," the AI said as Jessica piloted them down the walkway to where she could pick up a crate of ammo to take up to where the Guardians were already starting to assemble.

"I don't feel comfortable calling my commanding officer by a nickname," Jessica13 explained. "It doesn't seem right. Besides, it's not like he really cares what a bulletfoot calls him as long as the job is done."

"My records indicate that A7 cares deeply about the people under his command," Mini contradicted. "To the point of allowing you to operate in a mech that ran with less than optimal software."

"Well, even with less than optimal software, the Mini had many good qualities and Armstrong7 realized that. Although you're not wrong. He does care about us more than I would have thought a CO would, but I shouldn't take that care for granted."

"This seems reasonable. Although his preference for the nickname appears to stem from wanting more efficiency in the comm signals."

"I wouldn't say we interact that much in comms," she responded. "Although if you think we should call him A7 when we're Topside, maybe we should."

"You may consider it a suggestion," Mini said. "Correcting

the files in my data core takes only minimal processing power and leaves the rest to reset my systems, for the most part."

"I didn't think AIs did much stewing," Jessica13 said as the bulletfoots began to move toward the elevator.

"Well, I suppose it would be different from what humans consider stewing," the AI said. "There's no word in my data-banks that is more of an equivalent, however. The most accurate description available is the resetting of my software to keep processors engaged."

"Yeah, it sounds like stewing to me." She laughed as they boarded the elevator.

There was no word on what was happening Topside with the Guardians, which could mean good or bad news. No warning was always a plus as it meant no rushing for more ammo and all that. It could also mean they were so busy being attacked that they didn't have time to say anything over the comms.

They finally all boarded and the elevator doors began to pull shut, which gave them a moment to relax in their mechs. There was less of the adrenaline rush through their veins than there had been for the previous battle, which told Jessica13 that Armstrong7's drills had done their job to steel their nerves.

The silence was still deafening, though, broken only by the sound of the elevator whirring slowly.

"I'm not sure how this happens, but do AIs interact?" Jessica13 asked.

"Please elaborate," Mini responded.

"Okay, is there a server you can use to interact with the other AIs in Sanctuary?" she asked.

"There are no servers like that available for access," Mini replied. "Even if there were, the Artificial Intelligence cores used in mechs would be restricted. Most of the mechs are contained to keep them from being hacked from the outside, but it would also keep us from being able to extend contact beyond the parameters established in communication lines."

"Huh." She grunted in surprise. "I would never have thought AIs would think of venturing anywhere."

"I didn't until you brought it up."

"Well, I only asked because the AI that runs the elevator is a real grumbler." She chuckled. "I was actually afraid you would end up acting like her when I worked to bring you back online. And then I thought you might be able to give her company. I imagine running an elevator would be tiresome to do over and over again, especially as an AI."

"It seems illogical to dedicate the entirety of an AI's processing power to operate an elevator," Mini replied. "It is likely that the elevator's functions only take up a small part of the AI's functionality and it is simply protesting for the sake of protesting. The human term available to me for such actions is drama queen."

"I… Wait, hold on." Jessica13 straightened and refocused on the task at hand as the elevator doors began to open, the signal that it was clear for them to step outside.

There was no sign of combat anywhere around them—no clouds of dust, no explosives detonating, and no bullets from any direction. The air was clear and gave her a perfect view of the blue sky above. The sun glinted on the mechanics as they moved out of the elevator and over to where the Guardians remained in position.

"Where's the attack?" one of the bulletfoots asked, looked around the defense platform, and tried to find any sign that they were under the kind of assault they were called to fend off.

"Alarms were tripped," Armstrong7 said as he strolled over to them in his Argonaut. "A couple of the mines were tripped as well, but I agree. There's not much out there that says we're under attack."

"If anyone did plan to attack, the chances are they were shredded," one of the pilots said.

"That is unlikely," Mini interjected through Jessica13's headset. "If we were under attack, there would be signs of mech suits that were destroyed. The explosive force of the mines, while impressive, would not be sufficient to completely obliterate any sign of attackers."

"Good point," she said and hailed Armstrong7 on the comms. "Hey…uh, A7, I don't think we were being attacked. There would be signs of the mechs that were destroyed. Our shredder mines would not be enough to completely demolish any sign of attacking mechs."

"That's a good point," he said with a nod. "Maybe zoom in to see if you can find any sign of mech parts spread around the place. If you only see splatters of red, the chances are that a pack of wild dogs was what triggered the mines. We'll have to reset them, though, so I hope you're all ready for a long day of work Topside. I'll need volunteers to head down there and set the system up again. Extra canteen for those who stick it out."

Jessica13 raised her hand. "I'll take the first shift if you don't mind. It's a nice day out, so none better to work Outside, right?"

"I appreciate the enthusiasm." Armstrong7 chuckled.

A couple more of them volunteered, mostly for the extra canteen in their accounts, and once they were all loaded with the mines they would need, they began to climb down the same cliff any attackers would have to try to scale.

Since the Guardians would need to stay Topside to continue the defense of the area, only bulletfoots were dispatched to set the minefield again.

"Even if it was only a pack of wild dogs, they could have been herded in by a group of pirates who wanted to trip the mines," one of the other bulletfoots said and shook her head. "You never know. Now, they're sending us into the line of fire so we'll be the first to get slaughtered if we actually are under attack."

"It's possible," Mini stated calmly in Jessica13's ear. "However, it is also unlikely. My knowledge of how dog packs roam removes the possibility of them being herded that way. They tend not to move in a way that would allow them to be forced into a minefield unless they were trained for it and I am unsure as to how a dog pack would be trained for that. They would only be able to do so once, after all."

"It's why they're staying up there," another bulletfoot, Gerry8, said and looked around a little nervously. "They have a couple of the Guardians with some rockets primed just in case."

"We'll still be the first ones to go," the other bulletfoot replied as they moved out to the minefield. "Do you think they'll risk the safety of everyone in Sanctuary for our benefit? They'll cut the lines we used to climb down without a second thought and hope we'll slow any attackers down."

"That is also unlikely," Mini commented.

"I don't understand," Jessica13 said. "I mean, I don't understand how dog packs would be able to survive out here. With the radiation and the poison still in the air, I wouldn't think they would be able to survive too long. Sure, there are clean places, but having to deal with all of that plus the Skyfall... I don't understand how anything survives out here."

"I'm sure you know my data is incomplete regarding the history over the past hundred years," her AI said. "Would you mind filling those gaps in my knowledge?"

"Oh...sure." She paused and scrutinized the area as they arrived at their destination. "I do need to get to work out there to set the mines and cross the minefield while I...you know, try not to get shredded myself."

"I can carry the mech through those tasks."

"Really?"

"Of course. I only need you to authorize my temporary control of the mech for you," Mini said. "It was actually a very popular option among people who operated Shimura-Sendai systems."

Jessica13 tilted her head in thought. It did sound like she would be spared a significant amount of hard labor, and now with someone to talk to, that didn't seem quite as boring as she thought it would be.

"Okay, go ahead," she said and agreed to the transfer of control to the AI.

It was odd to feel the mech move without her controlling it—like she was along for the ride instead of driving the damn thing—but she could tell she would definitely get used to this. Sure, Mini would only have a select number of programmed actions she would be able to perform without Jessica13 making any input, but setting mines was a fairly simple procedure.

"So, you need me to tell you what has happened in the world over the past century or so?" she asked as the mech began to clear the earth from around one of the tripped mines. "What is the last thing that you remember?"

"My data banks are incomplete," Mini explained. "I do have data on the Day the Heavens Fell, as well as the effects of the

Southpaw Defense. Relevant data is missing from the Second Invasion onward."

"You mean the day the Outsiders came and attacked the planet?" she asked. "Right. I don't actually know much about what happened since I wasn't there myself, as you said, but a fair amount was taught to us. After the Outsiders were repelled by the strength of the Seven, we thought we were safe. They could not have anticipated, however, that the ships they used carried not only the threat of nuclear attacks but also poison and disease. They called it the Reaping. With the Skyfall starting and the deaths of billions, people were forced to abandon the cities and take up residence in the bunkers."

"Correct, bunkers that were built as part of the Insurance Scheme," the AI said and contributed knowledge from her data banks.

Jessica13 wasn't sure what the Insurance Scheme was supposed to do, but she nodded and continued. "Sure, I suppose. Anyway, as the Reaping continued, we were all forced into the bunkers. Not everyone made it and I don't think we would have fit all the survivors. I still don't know how there are any survivors, though. They have the mech suits too, and while the idea is that they should be able to live in them almost indefinitely, they need a place to repair and regroup, restore their supplies, and all that. The Seven designed the mechs in order to make them almost self-sustaining, but I don't think anything is quite that. Not in our world, nor what it was before. Not that they needed it before."

"The Circle of Seven designed the mechs to help humanity survive outside the bunkers." Mini sounded like he was simply relaying information that was present in his core. "The Circle of Seven designed the concept of smaller, thorium-based nuclear power cores that could be carried inside a mech suit that was self-powering, all while providing protection from nuclear, chemical, and biological hazards."

Mini was quoting from what they had been taught as children at this point, but it was relaxing to hear it in the bland yet still pleasant voice of the AI.

"Mech designs were initially created with construction and heavy labor in mind," he continued. "These were useful but limited without an independent power source. Even those running on advanced batteries would not last more than a few hours. Only once the thorium cores were created were they seen as fit to assist in combat as well. It is why support mechs appear to have older designs while combat mechs support more recent builds."

"Anyway, my point is that even the people who can survive for long periods of time in their mechs—pirates and peddlers and the like—would need somewhere safe to get out of their mechs," Jessica13 continued. "And if there are areas in the world isolated from the toxic, radioactive clouds that would kill or horribly change and mutate them, none of the peddlers we've spoken to were willing to talk about that."

"Well, I do have data on what you call the Reaping available," Mini said. "The battle that occurred above the Earth's atmosphere caused most of what you call Skyfall—pieces of destroyed ships left to eventually fall to the ground as gravity acts on them. The radiation and the biological warfare the Earth suffered came from those ships. But that's crazy. Those clouds you're talking about dissipated decades before I was even on the assembly plant. There's still danger, of course, especially from falling debris—"

"Skyfall."

"Skyfall is now registered as your preferred terminology," the AI corrected himself. "There is still danger in the world since most of the radiation as well as the poison was in the runoff so the issue is mainly with the water. But there aren't any clouds of poison or radiation and most of the biological weapons have since killed themselves off."

"How does a weapon kill itself off?"

"Biological weapons consist of germ or viral warfare, living organisms that cause disease and death in the targeted individuals. In that case, the germs or viruses kill humans but when they run out of humans to kill, they die off."

"I…still don't understand," Jessica13 admitted.

"Think of it as the organisms being predators that feed on humans." The AI showed none of the annoyance and condescension she had heard in the voices of her previous teachers and even Armstrong7 sometimes. "They've been engineered to only feed on humans, so then when they run out of humans to feed on, they die themselves. They have nothing else to eat."

"I think I get it," she said finally and nodded. "I feel like it's a little more complicated than that, though."

"It is, but I don't think you need to understand it in its entirety since again, the organisms themselves have been dead for the past hundred years," Mini said. "So you really don't need to worry about it. Besides, people with Athena genes are generally engineered to have a mind for machines, not biology."

"What do you mean engineered?" Jessica13 asked as Mini finished installing another mine and moved on.

"Well, again, it is complex, but the condensed version is that the Circle of Seven designed the Athena genes to continue their work in machinery. They were made as insurance against the destruction of mankind, which was what happened. In the end, it was necessary and most humans alive today, if not all, are descended from those artificial wombs."

"That does seem a little simpler than your description of biological warfare," she said. "But...what you're saying is that the world Outside is...safe?"

"Not safe," the AI corrected. "There are still a great many dangers, most of which I am actually uninformed about. But no toxic clouds permeate the air."

That sounded safe to her, anyway. Jessica13 had always assumed that the air itself was deadly, which made the entire world terrifying to live in. Only in the Bunkers could people breathe the air without worrying that they were being poisoned. Only in Sanctuary, if you did as you were told and helped the community, were you safe.

"It's odd to think that the AIs and the folks in the science levels didn't realize that the air is safe to breathe," she said. "You'd think they would want there to be more air."

"My data suggests you have not exited the bunker without a protective mech," Mini replied. "That would suggest that others would have done the same. How could they have known that the air was safe to breathe?"

"They run resource extraction operations every six months." She tried to follow the movements of the mech as they headed deeper into the minefield and continued to remove the exploded ordinance and replace it with new ones. "They're supposed to run tests out here to make sure nothing potentially lethal gets into Sanctuary. They should know about this."

The logic of it was unmistakable. In light of what the AI had told her—and as far as she knew, they weren't capable of lies—everything she had assumed had, in fact, been based on a lie. Or, she reasoned, if not an outright lie then at least an omission of truth, which was much the same thing. For the life of her, she couldn't think why, though. Unless it was a matter of control?

That seemed uncomfortably sinister, but the thought made sense. If the folks in Sanctuary could be kept in ignorance, no one would question the rules or try to initiate changes. They would all continue to uphold what they believed to be the only way to stay safe and those who made the decisions could do what they wanted with impunity. It was a terrifying thought that struck out of the blue and left an acidic anger to roil in the pit of her stomach.

There was a pause in Mini's operation of the mech, and Jessica13 could hear the whirring of gears in the back that told her the processor was running hot and needed to be cooled. She focused on that to push the discomforting thoughts aside and waited for the AI to respond.

"The possibility that my data is still corrupted is sixty-six-point-six-seven percent when rounded to the nearest hundredth," Mini said. "There is the possibility that I could be wrong in my assertions. What happened over the duration of my inactivity could render all my knowledge irrelevant as well."

"Maybe I can look into helping you update your data banks from the hard drives we have on Sanctuary," Jessica13 said. "Wait, hold up."

"Waiting and holding up as requested," the AI replied and brought the mech to a halt. "Would you like to retake control?"

"No, but...look over there." She highlighted a speck of something she could see in the field but couldn't quite identify.

Mini asked no questions and simply followed her line of

sight to approach it without triggering any of the active mines in the field.

"What is that?" she asked as the Minato lowered to give her a better view.

"Data collected indicates….species name, Canis lupus familiaris. Commonly known as dog. Breed…unknown. Dogs were common household pets for humans and quite useful in the removal of pests, as well as physical and psychological support. Superficial studies show that if dogs were capable of surviving in this environment, so would smaller cats and other Canidae like wolves and coyotes. Studies indicate that when large numbers of genetically compatible animals occupy the same ecosystem, they have a better chance of surviving a dangerous environment due to the altered size of the gene pool."

"Well, A7 did say it was likely to be a pack of wild dogs," she replied and shook her head, not really understanding what the AI was on about. The mech moved away from the body. "It would have been interesting to live in a time when humans and animals interacted like that. We might even be able to get them to help us avoid the radiation and poison in the air. They've obviously managed to survive this long."

She spoke without thinking and immediately, her suspicions reared their ugly heads again and she had to focus hard to push them down.

More whirring of gears followed this statement and provided a welcome distraction. "That is possible and even likely. Dogs were instrumental in helping early-stage humans to survive."

"Are you all right there, Mini?" The whirring gears were a source of some concern. "Do you need me to take the controls for a while?"

"I am simply correcting data from your statements," Mini replied simply.

Jessica13 called up the processor data on her HUD. "It looks like your processor is running hot."

"Corrections run contrary to core coding," the AI said. "Overruling is…difficult."

"I'll take over from here, then." She took control of the mech, settled into place, and returned to work. "Maybe once we're back at Sanctuary, we can install a better cooling system. Have you thought that maybe overheating is the reason why you broke in the first place?"

"The possibility exists," Mini replied. "However, it is not likely."

Still, she decided she would look into that. She had the blueprint on how to fix the AI again if she ever needed to, but she had no intention to put herself through that much work again. It was better to prevent damage than to fix it, after all.

She diverted some of the cooling functions in the suit toward the processing units and continued her work.

It was a bright and sunny day with not even a cloud in the sky. The beauty of it faded quickly as her mind focused instead on the heat that bore down on her. With most of the cooling directed specifically toward the processors, she couldn't help but focus on the relentless heat that rapidly became unbearable. Sweat trickled constantly in rivulets. Aside from the fact that it wasn't comfortable, she knew the inside of the mech would reek of it later if she didn't clean it immediately upon her return.

It was exacerbated by the fact that there was really nothing to see from ground level. At the top of the cliff where their defenses were stationed, she could see for miles when she looked out onto the forests and the cities below—almost forever. On the ground, all she could see was the mud. The area had been cleared of all greenery and wildlife to make sure the folks on the top had a good view of anything that might endanger Sanctuary. It was a tactical necessity but made for dreary work.

Thankfully, there was no sign of the attackers the other bulletfoots had been afraid of and they had reset all the alarms and the minefield before the sun moved away from its peak in the sky. Jessica13 could still feel the soreness from the day before and she had a feeling it wouldn't be better tomorrow and probably the day after as well.

Even so, it was nice to have someone to talk to. While Mini's speech capabilities were compromised due to his processing power being directed elsewhere, she at least knew someone was there listening to her.

The climb up the cliff was long and arduous and took almost an hour even with the grappler lines still in place to help haul them up.

The Guardians had remained in position and still watched to make sure there was no sign of an incoming assault, even though anyone who had any intention to do so would have attacked already. They gave the bulletfoots time to gather the materials they needed and headed down in the elevator.

"I've tried hailing the elevator AI," Mini said as they descended slowly.

"We call her El," Jessica13 replied.

"Noted. I received a hail in response but...I'm not sure what this means."

She played the sound that had been sent. It was definitely El's voice and it sounded like a frustrated sigh.

"It sounds like she wants to be left alone," she explained. "That's what humans would call a sigh and it's directly linked to annoyance or frustration. Given that all you did was hail her, I'd have to say she was being...what was the term you used?"

"Drama queen?"

"That's the one."

They reached the bottom of the shaft and after a quick scan to make sure they weren't tracking in any poisons or radiation, the doors pulled open to allow them into the mech hangar. They shut quickly behind them again and the elevator moved up to collect the Guardians who had manned the defense point.

"While we are on the topic of upgrades..." Mini said tentatively.

"Were we on that topic?" Jessica13 asked.

"Your words were, and I quote, 'Maybe once we're back at Sanctuary, we can install a better cooling system,'" he said before he replayed an audio of Jessica13's voice.

"Oh, right, so we were," she acknowledged. "Three hours ago but go on."

"My concern that the Minato has no weapons system could be addressed by the installation of that Aegis Cannon," the AI said. "The light-density plasmablasts could easily be integrated into the assault matrix with only a negligible addition to power consumption."

"The Minato is a support mech," she pointed out as they moved slowly across the causeway. "We don't need to upgrade the weapons system."

"Ah, well, if we integrated that Phasmodon Mark II power cell into the Matrix, you wouldn't need to worry about the cooling systems," Mini said and highlighted the piece in question.

Jessica13 hadn't known the name of that particular piece herself.

Still, she shook her head. "No. We can't simply fit anything we take a fancy to. All upgrades are to make you function optimally, not to turn you into something else."

"Well then, if we could install that Brenner-Harbor z7 Processor, I would be able to transfer my lesser functions to it while I keep my main functions untouched," Mini continued.

Jessica13 sighed.

"That sound is identified as annoyance and or frustration," Mini extrapolated. "Am I to infer that the answer to the processor installation is also no?"

"Very good, Mini," she said and wondered if the AI could detect the sarcasm in her voice.

"Very well, only the cooling system upgrade it is." They reached the harness and the AI strapped himself in.

"It's not that I don't want to upgrade you," Jessica13 said. "It's that I can't really use the parts without getting approval from Armstrong7 and I know that he wouldn't approve it."

"You do not need to explain yourself to me," Mini said. "You brought me back to what humans call life. I trust you implicitly."

She smiled when the smiley face appeared on her HUD. "Thanks, Mini. I'll get to work on those upgrades now."

"That would be appreciated." With that, the mech went into sleep mode.

The bulletfoot climbed hastily out of the cockpit to snag some cleaning materials before anyone else could. Not many resources could be wasted on cleaning, of course, but a quick spray into an oiling rag would at least keep the smell of stale sweat at bay. She replaced everything where she'd found it when she was finished, which was before El returned with the Guardians.

It seemed Armstrong7 was more focused on the pilots than the bulletfoots and left them to either continue working on separating the piles of parts that had been salvaged from the pirates or repairing the suits that needed attention.

Her mech needed repairing.

Jessica13 climbed onto the back, opened it, and called up the data on how the AI was running. It reminded her that Mini had said adjusting his data to the information she had given him went against core programming, which was interesting. There was nothing wrong with him as he could identify pieces that Jessica13 herself would have had difficulty with.

If there were no problems there, why would he have trouble identifying historical facts and even studying the air around himself for toxins and radiation? Any issues like that should have at least shown up on scans.

But there was nothing—no sign of malfunction and not even a hint of software bugging out. She had done excellent work with the coding and it had cleaned the databanks thoroughly.

So where did the malfunction come from?

Jessica13 shook her head. Something didn't make sense, and she called up Sanctuary's hard drive maintenance, an AI that protected the data cores of the whole bunker. It was essentially the guardian of their entire trove of knowledge, technological and otherwise.

People called him the Librarian. It was supposed to be a joke since people in the Cities-that-Were had whole buildings dedicated to housing paper manus and books and the like.

The people who maintained those buildings were called Librarians.

"Good afternoon, Jessica13," the Librarian said when she called him up. "How can I assist you today?"

"Hi, thanks for helping me," she said. "I'm having some issues with an AI core I brought up from one of the pirate mechs, and I hoped you could run a scan to make sure everything's operating the way it should be?"

"Of course, Jessica13," the AI responded and displayed a smiley face on her screen. "If you would connect me to the interface, I'll see what I can do."

"Coming right up," she responded, connected the wiring to Mini's interface, and watched intently as the Librarian's code began to integrate with her own.

They were similar, which wasn't that surprising since both their coding had the same source in the Athena genes.

"No, wait, what are you doing?" Jessica13 asked when the Librarian accessed the data banks and began to shred the coding inside.

"I'm merely cleaning some errant code," the AI replied, his voice still pleasant.

"It's not errant it's only….history." She narrowed her eyes as she registered exactly what was taking place. It was deleting Mini's memories—everything that made him special and everything Jessica13 had loved about the mech before she even knew how to fix the AI again.

Aside from the fact that it was unacceptable, Mini trusted her not to let something like that happen.

"Okay," she said and leaned closer, pulled up the chip, and connected it to the interface as well. Her intervention brought what the Librarian was doing to a sudden halt. "Processing error. Please identify the source of the orders that have prompted you to delete the coding?"

"The source of the code is… *Access restricted—John5,*" the AI informed her.

Well, that meant John5 was the source of the coding that now erased everything in Mini's history files.

"Yeah, that's not going to happen," Jessica13 said and physically disconnected the port from Mini's interface before she rebooted her AI back to the automatically saved state he had been in before connecting to the Librarian. "Mini, please tell me you're still there."

"Minato beta 0.9, Shimura-Sendai Systems, online," the now-familiar, metallic and feminine voice chimed in Jessica13's headset. "Good afternoon, Jessica13."

"No, we will not go through all that crap again," she mumbled irritably and immediately connected the AI to her databanks. "Please tell me you haven't been reverted to factory settings?"

"Updating," the voice said and after a moment, the connection was successful. "Much better. What happened?"

"I tried to connect you to the Sanctuary mainframe," Jessica13 explained while she continued to run checks to make sure nothing vital had been shredded. "Well, I did connect you, but the AI that maintains it began to delete memories from your data banks, apparently on the orders of John5. I don't know why but I stopped it as quickly as I could."

"Your efforts are appreciated," Mini replied. "I'm experiencing a few compacting issues but that should be corrected. Is now corrected."

"I'm sorry," she said and patted the shoulder of her mech while she told herself the AI could feel the gesture. "I… Why was it deleting your data? What was it deleting?"

"The data that was accessed before the reboot...accessing now." The screen went dark for a few seconds and she held her breath and waited for the AI to respond. "It was accessing my data on world history. The data we discussed this morning."

The data that said the air was clear outside, she reminded herself, and that said the world was safe—or at least less deadly than she had been led to believe her entire life. If the AI worked to delete that data, did that mean that it was trying to hide something?

She couldn't believe she thought that. It didn't seem possible but at the same time, Jessica13 couldn't help but feel as though the questions had nagged at the back of her mind for years, ever since she had seen the sky and the horizons outside with her own eyes. Today was merely the catalyst, the tipping point where everything she had accepted as truth was now challenged by a slew of contradictions.

And it was only once Mini started talking that those doubts were given a real, slightly metallic and feminine voice.

Right now, the questions screamed loudly in her head and she could no longer ignore them. Everything she believed in—truth, honesty, and loyalty—shrieked a protest. It was no longer possible to ignore the instincts she had never recognized but which had obviously worked within her subconscious. They had been brought to the fore by John5's speech, which seemed ironic. The man who was, at least in some measure, responsible for the deception perpetuated at Sanctuary was the trigger that unleashed her unexpected clarity. It wasn't possible to pretend it hadn't happened and hope it would go away. She needed to do something.

"What will you do?" Jessica13 asked.

"I'm correcting the coding issues," Mini replied.

"No, I wasn't talking to you, I was asking myself," she clarified. "They…uh, engineered me to ask questions to continue the work of the Seven, but if they are to be believed—if the words of the Great Prophet are to be believed—deleting data automatically can't be right. Which means I need to make it right myself."

"How?" the AI asked.

"I'll leave." She knew the spontaneous decision was out of character for her and paused for a moment to second-guess herself. She realized as she thought things through that it wasn't so spontaneous, after all. Doubts and questions had definitely swirled below her surface consciousness for a very long time.

She recognized now that she had moved toward this point in her life firmly without realizing it and somehow prepared herself for what was an inevitable outcome. A deep inner conviction assured her this was the right decision and she believed that instinct more and more with each passing second. "And I'm taking you with me."

CHAPTER EIGHT

Her hands shook alarmingly and a cold sweat began to collect on her arms as if her body disagreed with what her mind had irrevocably decided to do.

It wasn't like she had been given a choice in this, she assured herself. It was in her genes. She was as curious as hell, and when that instinct was stifled, something in her immediately fought back. This was her resistance against the constraints that contradicted her fundamental nature. Jessica13 was not to blame for the fact that they had lied to her—and the entire bunker—and tried to keep her from discovery.

The Great Prophet said people needed to head out to where something was waiting to be discovered. She saw clearly now that she wouldn't discover anything hiding in a bunker whose leaders tried to keep her in the dark—literally as well as metaphorically.

Even the mud on the ground was less stifling and claustrophobic than this damn place had begun to be. Her little room —the pride of her life thus far despite its lack of space—had begun to feel more cramped, small, and restrictive.

She made her mind up to not remain in Sanctuary for even one more day. No one paid attention to what she was doing so it was the perfect opportunity. There were still people heading in and out of Sanctuary all day thanks to the false alarm about the attack.

If there ever would be a time to leave without anyone noticing her exit, it was now. This was the kind of opportunity she couldn't afford to miss out on.

"No more," she said softly. "No more."

It had been easy to take food from the kitchen. She had done it for months and brought it to her room to attempt to eat while she was reading or watching something. Unfortunately, she always gave up on it because the food was slightly less terrible when it was served hot.

In the back of her mind, she'd made vague plans to get a heater in her room to warm the food, but it was always put off in favor of other projects. The most recent of these was fixing Mini, which demanded all her effort, focus, and resources.

Thankfully, that had resulted in her having several days' worth of food stashed away. Better yet, it was the kind of food that would never go bad. It had been designed that way.

While she knew she'd need to eat at some point, it wasn't terribly high on her present priority list. She had a pack and proceeded to shove her belongings into it with the door locked securely behind her. There was little enough room as it was but when she began to pack what she needed, the space seemed to grow.

The food was the first to be stowed, followed quickly by her working tools. If she had any hope of maintaining Mini once they were out in the wild, she would need them more than she would need the food.

With those stored, there wasn't much space for personal

belongings. Her drawings made with charcoal on scraps of unused paper too small to be used in the recyc level would have to be left behind. As would her books, which had drawings as well. The weak material her pack was made from barely held the necessities as it was.

There was one picture she couldn't bear to leave behind. The only one she had of her mother that her father had given her was of both her parents together in a long-term exposure on a ceramic plate. She was smiling, her hand on his stomach, and he was doubled over. Jessica13 had never been able to tell if she had punched him in the gut as a joke or if she was tickling him. He hadn't been around long enough for her to ask.

It was too big, however. She scowled at it and tried to fight back a few angry tears. No way would she leave it behind. She couldn't.

An idea came to her and she retrieved one of her tools—a small hammer used to knock the smaller bolts inside the mech into place. She laid the picture on the bed and with cautious taps of the hammer, began to break the plate.

"I'm sorry mom," she whispered when a few cracks appeared close to the woman's face. The taps continued until everything was gone except for the two faces. Her mother laughed from the image and her father looked like he was blowing all the air out of his lungs.

The process was finished and all she had left of them were black-and-white faces on the ceramic plate. Despite the rough treatment, they were still visible. She wiped the tears from her cheeks and tucked the piece into her pocket, then brushed the shards off her bed.

The gesture was pointless effort, really. It wasn't like she would sleep on it again, not even if she didn't escape. If she failed, it was banishment to the lower levels for her—the farming levels if she was lucky and the recyc levels if she wasn't.

No, if she was lucky, she would get out of this place. Anything else was the worst option possible.

She closed her pack securely and slung it over her back before she eased out of her room and closed and locked the door behind her. It wouldn't stop someone who really wanted to get in, but it would give her a few minutes, at least.

A plan had already begun to take shape in her mind. No one would pay attention to her until she reached the elevator. That was when people would ask questions. There was no pointless power expenditure allowed and to send the elevator up with the full weight of the Minato would definitely waste power.

It would be difficult to get around this but not impossible. All she needed was a signature from Armstrong7 authorizing her to head up to the defense sector to stress-test the improvements she'd made on Mini. Word would have filtered to him that she had worked out some kind of improvements on the mech already, so it wouldn't be too out of the ordinary for her to stress-test the mech.

And, hopefully, with the alarms that had been set off, he would be too swamped to think too deeply into her request. There would probably be people who questioned it at the door of the elevator, but with the signature of the CO on her side, questions would only be raised when someone realized the Minato was heading away from Sanctuary instead of stress-testing. By then, she would already be too far away for them to do anything about it.

Sure, they could send someone after her, but it would be a massive waste of resources to pursue someone who didn't want to be found. The mech was one no one else could use anyway, and the food didn't seem to have been missed as no one had raised any questions about it.

The only real loss to Sanctuary would be the tools, and it wasn't like they didn't have spares.

Her plan seemed to be the best one she could devise so she picked up one of the forms for outside stress-testing and filled the paperwork in quickly, which left the one thing only Armstrong7 could do. He had to sign it.

The man didn't like his office. He stood well above six feet tall and the tiny little space he had been allocated as the CO of the defensive level simply didn't fit him. It was too small and the chair always made him look like he was hunched over his desk. She had to imagine that he constantly toppled the tall stacks of papers he needed to peruse and sign before he sent them to his superiors.

Like John5.

Even thinking the name sent cold sweats across her skin. The man she had looked up to for all those years had tried to kill Mini in front of her nose. The sense of betrayal was absolute.

She reached the office where predictably, the tall, muscular Armstrong7 was bent over the tiny desk crammed into his tiny room. She had no idea how he didn't feel claustrophobic since he was so much larger than her.

"Jessie," the CO said and barely looked up to see who stood in the doorway. He sifted through a stack of papers while he waited for someone on the comm line in his office. "How can I help you?"

"Well, I can see you're very busy so I won't take up too much of your time," Jessica13 said meekly as she left her bag outside the door and stepped inside. "Are you? Really busy, that is."

"The people running Sanctuary weren't happy that we issued the alarm without confirming that we were under attack," he said and shook his head in what might have been frustration. "They don't think it's conducive to the secure environment they wish to foster in Sanctuary to have alarms activating all the time, so they want there to be some accountability. They also want me to speak to the entire bunker to tell them it was only a false alarm and no lives were lost and they can all settle into their lives again."

The life she now tried to escape. The reminder was a little discomforting and she clenched her hands together to keep them from shaking again.

"Anyway, how can I help you, Jessie?" Armstong7 asked without looking up from his work. "Please make it fast. I don't want to rush you but I am in something of a bind here."

"Oh, I only wanted to ask for your signature," Jessica13 said and slid the form she had filled out in front of him.

"Authorization for a stress-test outside the bunker?" he asked and finally glanced at her.

"I managed to install a new AI in my Minato mech and I need to stress-test it before he's cleared for active duty," she explained.

The CO made a face and scowled at the paper in front of him. "I'm sorry, but no. After the whole mess today, we shouldn't have anyone outside the bunker aside from those necessary for the defense of Sanctuary. I think you would be able to clear the Minato for active duty with an indoor stress-test, right?"

"It's not the best," she said with a shrug. She couldn't do or say anything to raise his suspicions

"Well, it's the best that I can do for now," Armstrong7 said firmly and gave her the form. "If you want to try again tomorrow, I think things will have calmed by then. Until then…here…"

He reached into the steel cabinet to his left and barely avoiding upending a stack of papers with his elbow.

"This is an indoor stress-test authorization," he said, filled it in quickly, and handed it to her. "That should keep people from asking you too many questions."

She smiled. "Thanks, A7. I really appreciate it."

"Hey, good work with getting the AI to work." He shook his head in bemusement. "I don't know how you did it. That mech has been in storage for almost a hundred years and no one's figured it out. I guess that's why it pays to have our Athena folks with us, right?"

"Right," she said with a chuckle. "Thanks again!"

He nodded and turned away when the comm buzzed, which required him to get back to his work. She resisted a sigh as she left the office. While she didn't have the signature she wanted, she had a signature. That was a start, right?

She headed to the bathrooms that were mostly abandoned at this time of day. The window of privacy wasn't likely to last, so she needed to work fast. She placed both forms on top of each other with the indoor stress-test on top of the outdoor form. With a few drops of water carefully applied, the ink began to soak into the second form.

It was a delicate process but one she had learned over the years. Not that she'd ever needed to forge signatures before—which this process was, even though it was through a slightly different method than was normally used—but it had helped her to replicate forms so she didn't have to complete them over and over again.

The final signature was a little smudged but it would pass a cursory inspection. With everyone in as much of a rush as they were, that was probably all she would get—hopefully. One call to Armstong7 would land her in trouble.

Her breathing became short and rapid as she hurried down the narrow halls and she fought to keep herself calm while the seconds ticked by. Every person she passed looked at her like they knew exactly what she was doing and were on their way to report her to the Sanctuary leadership. To her overactive mind, every eye looked accusatory and each glance made her feel like they could see right into her.

She was being paranoid, of course. Jessica13 knew it but the truth didn't make her feel any better. What if one of them actually had divined what she was up to? Was security already dispatched to have her sent to the recyc level where she would work the furnaces in the sweltering heat and fumes until her lungs gave out and she was put into the furnaces herself?

No. There was no way that would happen. She would get out of this place and when she did, she would head out and make her own discoveries, exactly like the Great Prophet said she needed to do.

At the entrance to the hangar, she paused and took a deep breath. Something seemed to burn a hole in the pit of her stomach but not in a painful way. It was more of a tickle. Her hands trembled again but there wasn't much she could do to stop them. Deep breaths were supposed to help, but they didn't. She remembered feeling like this when the bunker was under attack but she had been drilled for that. In that situation, she knew what she was doing because she'd done it countless times.

Jessica13 had never done anything like this before and very few people had. Sure, there were rumors of those who had Fallen. Either they had tried to escape and been remanded to the lower levels or they had managed to leave.

Tales were told of how they had died in the open with no shelter and no Sanctuary. The stories were always the same—the poison filled their lungs and left them screaming through a painful death that took days before they finally succumbed.

Some told of how they had taken mechs with AIs in them and once they died, the mechs kept going until something damaged the power reactor or pirates captured them. Apparently, they had been seen walking for days on end until they were cracked open and the remains of the unfortunate pilot who had taken them were found.

Now, with everything Mini had told her, Jessica13 wondered if any of these were true. They were handed down to her by her superiors who told her they were stories from peddlers and the like. What if they were lying?

It seemed that everything else they had told her was a lie. That made her whole life little more than a pathetic joke. She imagined the likes of John5 and the other admins laughing behind her back over what a gullible fool she'd been. And it was true. She'd never questioned anything and always simply bowed her head and obeyed their words.

Why would they lie like that? What could they possibly have to gain from the subterfuge? Her frustration was tinged with offense, which in turn strengthened her resolve.

She didn't understand any of it but damned if she wouldn't find out.

The tickle had gone and the shaking with it. She was no longer afraid. Thinking of the admins laughing at her for being so stupid made her angry. Her face heated and she suspected it would turn red before too long.

"Anger's better than fear," she said to herself and hefted her pack on her shoulder from where it had begun to sag as she stepped into the hangar.

A hint of niggling doubt remained in the back of her mind, but she did her best to ignore it. It was easy to do when she reminded herself she was moving away from it and walking away from her doubts.

They would follow close behind but as long as she continued to move forward, they wouldn't be able to catch up.

It looked like most of the bulletfoots had already dispersed and gone to other areas to work on projects there. The only people who were present in the hangar bay were a group of security officers she hadn't anticipated and a few pilots who worked on their mechs once the day's responsibilities were over.

Security posed a possible problem. The men and women who worked there were among the few allowed to carry weapons in Sanctuary. These were small portable weapons they could carry without a mech. Most of them were electrically powered, the kind that could incapacitate someone when needed. She'd never seen anyone use them before but she'd heard stories of when they had.

They also had access to what she thought of as real weapons—the kind that could kill—for use when things were desperate. Jessica13 had assumed it would only be when someone actually managed to break into Sanctuary and they needed to fight invaders.

Now, she wasn't so sure.

They looked relaxed and leaned against one of the tables the bulletfoots had worked at while they chatted and laughed. None of them suspected someone would try to escape Sanctuary today. In all probability, none of them imagined anyone would want to.

She wondered if they were in the know. Were they aware of the lies that had been told or were they exactly like her and had simply been deceived for their entire lives? Did they believe that they protected the safety of the bunker when in fact, they merely perpetrated the same falsehoods they had been fed since they were children?

All she needed to do was walk past them. She only had to look like she had permission to be there to work on one of the mechs. They had no reason to question her and even if they did, she had signed paperwork from Armstrong7 that said she could take one of the mechs out for a stress-test.

"Hey, bulletfoot," one of the security men said as Jessica13 tried to walk past them. "The hangar is off-limits for the day, which is why most of the other mechanics were sent elsewhere to work. Sorry, admin orders. They don't want anything or anyone to disturb the peaceful lives of the drones below."

"Drones?" she asked, her head tilted in confusion.

"Oh… That's what we call the folks who work on the lower levels—farming and power source, stuff like that," the guard said and shook his head a little sheepishly. "It's not the nicest name, I know, but you should hear the names they have for us. Anyway, don't think we think you guys are drones, though. You're the first line of defense against the Outside. We're the last."

Jessica13 nodded. "Well, I need to work on one of the mechs."

"Sorry, admin orders," he said again firmly and an apologetic look crossed his face. "No one's in the hangar. Maybe tomorrow?"

She bit the inside of her mouth while her mind raced. On the one hand, she could come back tomorrow and maybe Armstrong7 would actually sign the paperwork to allow her to do the stress-testing. Or they would do more drills and escape would be impossible. She couldn't predict what would happen tomorrow.

Her attempt had to be made today. She needed to take the risk.

"Look," she said and eased her pack onto the floor at her feet since she could feel it beginning to make her shoulder ache. "Armstrong7 told me I need to stress-test one of the support mechs. A couple of upgrades were installed after the attack to make it more effective, and if you don't get the processing units and the power cores working perfectly in tandem, you'll have everything shorting all over the place. Then, you have the coolant systems going right to shit—"

The security guard raised his hand. "Okay, I think I understood about half of that. If you have Armstrong's signature to clear you for indoor stress-testing, go ahead."

"I'm actually cleared for outdoor testing," Jessica said and placed the form on the table for the man to look at.

"Outdoor?" he asked and glanced quickly at the paperwork. "Really?"

"You can't stress-test a mech's OS indoors," she said.

"OS?"

Another guard leaned in closer and whispered something in his teammate's ear.

"Anyway, if you have the signature, everything's clear for you to keep going. Have a nice time Topside, although you shouldn't be out there for too long."

"Mech stress-tests don't take longer than ten minutes, provided everything goes well," Jessica13 replied and tried not to reveal the relief that washed over her in any way in her expression.

Was she supposed to look anxious about heading Topside?

Maybe a little excited? Or maybe a little bored, like this was something that she did every day?

It didn't appear to matter. The moment they had checked the form she had left on the table, they resumed the conversation about what they had discussed before she arrived.

Something would go wrong, her inner voice warned. No, it wouldn't, her determination asserted. She would get out of there. No one would stop her and she would get herself out of the damn place. She would not be stuck there for the rest of her life. Nothing would stop her.

Her mouth was dry but she didn't hesitate. She didn't dare think about the fact that the only water she had was what was stocked inside Mini for an emergency. It was something to worry about later. No matter what, she would make it.

"Hey, bulletfoot!" one of the security guards called.

Her heart plummeted. She wouldn't make it and would die in the recyc level, breathing smoke for the rest of her life. Jessica13 couldn't move. Her feet felt like they had been magnetically locked to the causeway and there was no to make herself move again.

No, it wouldn't end like this.

She was fucked. So fucked.

CHAPTER NINE

So very, very, very fucked.

"Shit," Jessica13 whispered and dragged in a deep breath.

"Hey, bulletfoot!" the security guard called again and this time, he caught the attention of the pilots who still worked in the hangar. "What the hell—are you deaf?"

She had to make a split-second decision but had no idea what the right one might be. If she turned and engaged him and he knew what she was trying to do, she would be dragged away. If they had no idea about what she was doing and she sprinted away from him, he would know she was up to something and he and his team would try to stop her.

"Can she hear me?" the man asked. "Are the Athena freaks deaf? No…shit, come on, I know you heard me. You stopped when I called you."

Well, damned if she did and damned if she didn't.

Jessica13 turned but spun on her heel while she kept the weight of her body on her back foot in case she needed to sprint to where Mini was still harnessed.

The man didn't look aggressive at all. Maybe a little

annoyed, but that could be chalked down to having to repeat himself.

Her heart still hammered painfully her in her chest and escalated its pace when she noticed her bag in his hand. She'd forgotten that she had dropped it because it had begun to make her shoulder hurt. The weight was considerable and it looked like he had some difficulty holding it out to her with only one hand. That alone was likely to generate some degree of suspicion.

He merely laughed and shook his head. The concern she knew was probably evident in her face seemed to go unnoticed, however. Security tended to get that kind of reaction from people in Sanctuary and generally tried to appear as understanding as possible unless the situation called for a harsher response.

It was like he said—the people in the hangar were the first line of defense against intruders to the bunker. There was really no point in antagonizing them.

"You forgot your bag, kid," the guard said and chuckled again as Jessica13 moved casually to take the bag in question from his hands. "What the hell do you have in here, anyway? Steel chunks?"

"Parts I might need," she said. "And the tools I'll need to install them with. I'd go over the details with you but you didn't like it when I did it the last time."

"Oh.…right." He tilted his head, his expression a little dubious, and glanced dismissively at the bag.

It seemed he wouldn't question what she was doing. People in a position of power didn't want to look stupid in front of the people they had power over, she supposed. It seemed a fairly logical assumption given his lack of real curiosity.

Jessica13 hefted it carefully with both hands and gave him a sheepish grin. "Thanks. I don't think I would have been able to do much without my tools."

"How do you work on the suit when you're up top?" he asked.

She shrugged, a little more comfortable now as she was close enough to freedom that she could almost taste it. "It's mostly software and processors that I'll stress-test and I can access those from inside the cockpit, but I need to be able to peel the inner skin off. I have to have my tools to do it, though."

He nodded, quickly lost interest in the conversation, and inched away from her as she continued to talk until it was clear the conversation was over. She turned away, still clutching her bag with both hands as she headed toward the Minato.

There wasn't far to go. She only needed to keep her cool and reach the elevator. Once she was there, nothing would be able to stop her.

A clatter ended the positive thoughts abruptly. She spun, horrified to see that the over-filled pack had split a little. While she had attempted to make the packing too tight for much to fall out, one of her actualizers now lay on the ground, as well as a can of pea stew and a couple of protein patties that had been protected in a vacuum-sealed bag.

The guards wouldn't know that she needed an actualizer to help maintain her suit for longer travel time, but the food would be quickly identified as suspicious. Stealing food already came with a massive penalty, but her heading toward a mech with the intention to head Topside as well would trigger additional alarms in their heads.

It wouldn't take much for them to put it together. Jessica13 ducked quickly and picked the food up, but she hadn't been fast enough. They'd seen it and now moved toward her.

She'd wasted too much time and delayed her escape. If she wanted to make it, she needed to get moving.

With everything retrieved, Jessica13 began to run.

"Hey, hold up!" the guard behind her called.

There was absolutely no way she could comply with the order. By this point, if he was suspicious, there wasn't much she could do. No sweet-talking, quick-talking, or sneaky maneuvering would keep him from searching her bag, which would reveal that she was trying to make a break for it.

"I said hold up, damn it!"

She ran faster, her focus on Mini. A couple of the pilots in the area heard the commotion and stepped down from where they worked on their mechs. They seemed unsure as to what they were supposed to do. Something was happening and they knew they should intercede, but they didn't know on whose behalf. While most knew they were supposed to comply with security commands, it looked like they were interfering with the business of one of their own.

Her silent pleas for them to not get involved went unheeded as three pilots abandoned their work to come over and see what was happening. One of them was Becker3, who placed his hand on her shoulder and brought her to a sudden halt. The other two moved between her and the guards to try to determine why one of their mechanics was being harassed.

"What's the problem here?" one of the pilots asked.

Jessica13's heart plunged into her stomach and panic began to take hold as she looked around to try to find a way out of this mess. All she needed was some kind of believable explanation that would enable her to continue.

"We'll need to search her bag," the guard said and attempted to skirt the two pilots in their path.

"Why?" the pilot asked and made no effort to move.

"We saw something spill out," the man replied, clearly frustrated. "It looked like food. As you all know, stealing food comes with a three-month stay in the Hole. We'll need to search her bag."

"There's no need," Becker3 said, pushed Jessica13 back, and took the bag from her hands.

It would be a simple matter to peek under the top flap to find the food the men had mentioned and which she'd shoved in hastily once she retrieved it, but digging in deeper would find even more suspicious items.

"Long-term repair pieces for a Minato mech," Becker3 said, took the parts out of the pack, and placed them on a nearby table. "Food, supplies, and tools. It looks like we have a runner here, boys. What do you think?"

"A runner?" the guard asked and finally pushed past the other two pilots.

"All the supplies you'd need for a long-term stay in a mech," the pilot said with a firm nod. "Not a terribly good mech, mind you, but it still looks like Jessica13 here planned to run away from the bunker."

"Run away?" The guard stopped alongside them and shook his head. "Why… What?"

"I remember her talking about what a nice day it was outside," Becker3 continued. "It seems like she's one of those sun-lovers who can't get enough of the Outside until it's too much."

The security man seemed entirely bewildered. "I…huh. Well, that is more serious than only stealing food. What's the protocol for this?"

The other two security guards realized that he was talking to them, and one of them spoke quickly. "We don't really have something specific for it. Endangering the bunker to outside contamination, maybe? Or possibly heading up Topside without a permit?"

"Well, you heard that, bulletfoot," Becker3 said with a chuckle. "Do you have anything to say for yourself? Anything in your defense?"

"There's no need for a defense," the guard snapped. "She's been caught red-handed. The report will be submitted to the admins, who will decide her fate. For now, she should be remanded to the control of the security guards and that will be that."

This was it. She would never get out of here. Then she wondered if they would even want to keep her around, knowing what she did. Even someone with her skills could be seen as too disruptive to be a beneficial member of the Sanctuary bunker.

They could all feel the causeway shake a little. Jessica13 assumed it was only her shaking as the realization took root. She had somehow fucked up her only chance to get free of this place and wouldn't have another.

Maybe she should have waited a day or two for her chance to get outside with minimal supervision and then make her escape. She could stomach staying here for a little while longer, right?

None of that mattered now, though. She would have all the time in the world to contemplate what she had done wrong and what she could have done right while she rotted in the Hole and then in one of the lower levels. From now on, there would be no more looking out at the open horizon for her.

All she would see was the cramped, narrow concrete hallways of the bunker she had been born in and would likely die in.

No, that shaking wasn't in her hands. It was stupid to even think she might have caused it. She could see the pilots and guards who weren't too distracted by her looking at the causeway they stood on.

Something moved across the steel walkway and it was heavy enough to make it shudder with each step.

"It makes me wonder if she forged the form from Armstrong7 to get here in the first place," the guard said. He was still talking to Becker3 and shook his head, not realizing that something heavy approached. "Such a waste of good resources. That on its own is another year, easily. Okay, Jessica13. I'm sorry, but I hereby place you under arrest for the crimes of endangering Sanctuary, theft, and forgery."

"Hold up!" one of the other guards shouted and stared at something over Jessica13's head. "The situation is under control. We don't need any mech assistance."

There was no answer, and Jessica13 turned and forced herself free of Becker3's grasp to see what moved up behind them.

Mini was smaller than the mechs they had in their hangar but still stood well above seven feet tall and towered over the men who surrounded her.

"Who's piloting it?" one of the guards asked.

The pilots shrugged and took a step backward, more as a precaution than anything else. No one wanted to be close to a mech if it malfunctioned. That was a good way to get oneself killed.

The guards had not been similarly drilled and stood their

ground while they looked for someone to help them order the mech pilot to stand down.

And, as it turned out, it looked like the mech would give her a chance too. A surge of excitement filled her stomach as she moved to the table where her items had been placed and slowly began to replace her belongings in the pack. She used the case with her tools to cover the hole before she crammed all the other items around and over it.

She had no idea what would happen next, but if there was ever a last-ditch effort to get herself free from this place, this was it.

"Who is piloting that?" Becker3 asked and stepped forward. Jessica13—and anyone else—could have told him it was a bad idea.

"No one was given authorization for mech duty," one of the other pilots said and they continued to back away, leaving Becker3, the three security guards, and Jessica13 alone to deal with the mysterious mech.

Although she had an idea as to who might be piloting it, she still had her doubts.

She also began to move in an attempt to get away from her would-be captors and to the mech. While she wanted to get away, she didn't want to risk having anyone hurt in her escape attempt.

"I'll need you to stand down now or you will be written up for obstructing justice," the guard said, stepped forward, and drew the taser gun from the holster on his hip to aim it at Mini. "This is your last warning."

He looked like he was merely putting up a brave front when he aimed a weapon that wasn't even that effective at subduing humans.

Mini paused, looked at the weapon in the guard's hand, and took another step forward.

He pulled the trigger. Two electrode studs launched from the gun, each connected to a wire that transmitted however many volts in an attempt to disable the mech.

Jessica13 had to resist the urge to laugh as the studs bounced off the armor and fell harmlessly.

Mini stepped forward, and she could see the grappler had disengaged from the dart it was supposed to launch as well as the cable it was supposed to tow.

It was such a simple change and yet now, she could see the compressed air cannon wind up and release to strike the guard with a blast of air strong enough to pick him up off his feet and hurl him into the table her things had been on.

Becker3 tried to back away, but Mini was already advancing on him. Before he could take three steps, her right hand caught him by the right leg and picked him up effortlessly.

The other two guards and three pilots were already rushing toward the other side of the room and away from the mech that appeared determined to attack. They seemed to have no qualms about leaving Becker3 alone and unaided.

"Holy shit," the man shouted as he was raised up to eye level—the cockpit—at an angle that allowed him to see what was inside.

Or rather, what wasn't inside.

"There's no pilot!" he shouted and struggled to twist free.

It was difficult, hung upside down as he was, but he could see that no one was there to hear his declaration—or, rather, no one who cared.

Jessica13 rushed toward the mech, yanked the chest open,

and tossed her bag inside before she scrambled in and shut the chest behind her.

"Good afternoon, Jessica13," Mini said cheerfully when she pulled the headset on. "How are you today?"

"I'll be honest, I've been better," she replied. "Do you mind if I take the controls?"

"Affirmative." The AI released control of the mech to allow her to take over.

"What do you think we should do with Becker3?" she asked.

"Make an example of him?" Mini suggested.

"There's no time. We need to get to that elevator," she replied and turned her attention to the man, who still dangled by one of his feet.

"No!" the pilot protested and shook his head wildly, but she simply dropped him despite his plea. Sure, the fall wasn't the most pleasant, but it was better than being thrown.

Jesscia13 paid no more attention to him and now focused on the elevator. The doors, thankfully, were still open but alarms would be triggered soon.

"How did you come online, anyway?" she asked as they moved as swiftly as she dared toward the doors. "I thought I needed to be around for that to happen."

"Your agreement to allow me access to the controls of the mech was not revoked," Mini informed her. "As such, the authorization of control was never relinquished and so I was allowed to access the controls of the mech at will, which included disengaging from the harness and coming to your rescue."

"And I have to say thank you for that. I was sure I was in a whole pile of shit before you came along."

"Your appreciation is noted. Although, as you have consistently helped me, you might say I owed you the help. Either that or the fact that your continued existence would allow you to consistently help me in the future. As such, we are helping each other. As I have been able to determine, that is what you humans call a friendship."

"Well...yes, I guess you're right," Jessica13 started to say but immediately increased speed when she heard the alarms activate and flashing red lights filled the hangar like they had when they were being attacked.

Most importantly, of course, the elevator doors began to close.

She pushed herself to move faster and watched nervously as the hydraulics began to protest the pace they were being used at, but she didn't dare to slow to ease the pressure put on them.

The doors were massive but slow-moving, possibly a reflection of the AI that operated them. They did inch shut, however.

"Faster, faster—must go faster!" Jessica shouted and barely registered how loudly she was speaking. She couldn't hear much of anything over the sound of rushing and thudding in her ears. Adrenaline spiked in her body, the instinctive response to her desperate need to get to that damn elevator.

The doors were almost completely closed and left barely enough space for her to squeeze through. Seconds felt like hours and each step felt like it took for fucking ever to complete before she dove forward to push through the last few feet of opening still available to her.

She made it inside and landed hard with a jarring impact on her shoulder, but the doors clanged shut an instant later.

Mechs weren't designed to dive like that, and it took her a moment to rearrange it before she was able to stand again.

"We did it?" Jessica13 asked, looked around, and pushed into the mech's natural position. "We did it!"

Mini remained silent but did show the same smiley face on her HUD when the whole elevator shuddered and began to move upward.

"Huh." She grunted and looked around in disbelief. "I would have thought they would shut the elevator down with the alarms activated."

"Normally, that would be protocol," Mini replied. "But in this case, the elevator is being sent up to the defense level because there are currently members standing guard up there who need to be retrieved before Sanctuary can be locked down."

"I...didn't know about that. Wouldn't they try to stop us before we get to the top?"

"Did you have a plan if they had shut the elevator down?" Mini queried.

"Yes—open the hatch above us, use the grappler to scale the shaft, and force the doors at the top open by disengaging the magnetic lock," Jessica13 said. It was so nice to finally have someone to discuss her plans with, even if they were ulti-mately unnecessary.

"There is a seventy-five-point-three-two percent chance that would end in success should the elevator be shut down," the AI replied after a moment of calculation. "The chances of the elevator being shut down are infinitesimal. The AI has been programmed to not allow outside tampering, and any actions would need to be taken by admin staff. It is also possible that they believe you are unable to escape as there are three Guardian mechs waiting for us at the top."

"Well, let's go prove them wrong, shall we?" She felt an almost manic kind of smile settle on her face. They had made it this far, after all. There was really no point in ever turning back.

Besides, it wasn't like those waiting for her Topside would expect her to move as fast as she could in the Minato, after all.

The elevator came to a halt and the doors began to pull open as slowly as they had closed. It appeared as though the warning had been sent to the three Guardians since they all stood in wait outside the elevator.

"Jessie, please don't do this," one of the pilots said. She recognized Lance7's voice. "Head on down with us and this will all be worked out, I promise. Armstrong7 would never let them take you away from the defense level."

"It wouldn't be his call, and you know it," Jessica13 said and shook her head decisively while she made sure to stay in motion and inched away from the Guardians. "I'm going to leave. I'm heading out! I have to see the ruins, the gold and red sunset, and the world! Lance7, what they've told us all this time is all lies!"

"No, they're not lies," he replied. "You don't know what you're talking about. You don't know what you're doing."

"Yes," she said, partly to herself as well as to the pilot who stood between her and freedom. "Yes, I do."

"As do I," Mini said. "Please place your hands up to brace your neck."

"What are you doing?" she asked.

"We're taking you back down with us," Lance7 said.

"I wasn't talking to you!" she retorted.

"I'm taking control," Mini replied. "And getting us out of here."

She did as she was told and placed her hands on her neck to brace it like she had been taught to if she expected a hard impact. The Guardians hadn't locked any weapons on her yet.

Mini took control of the mech and she could feel him going through a couple of hardware changes. These appeared to tweak the hydraulics to fit the adjustment that was required to move down on all fours on the elevator floor.

"What is this?" she asked, but Mini made no answer as the mech settled in with a shudder.

"Damn it, Jessie!" Lance7 called and moved into the elevator to restrain her.

It seemed that was what the AI had waited for.

Coils whined on what were now the hind legs and in a second, he bounded up to the wall of the elevator, used the mag clamps on the hands to provide leverage, and vaulted over the tall mech. He landed smoothly on the other side and began to run and jump in movements like a dog's, complete with a smooth loping pace.

The impact was still jarring to anything or anyone inside.

As all three Guardians attempted to converge on them, Mini navigated them around the slow-moving legs of the large mechs.

It had been a good idea to brace her neck, as each bound ended with a painful jolt across her whole body. In a few seconds, however, they were clear of their pursuers.

When the last one tried to physically block her escape, Mini ducked low and darted between its legs.

Once they were clear, the mech maintained its forward momentum and without so much as a second thought, vaulted over the edge of the cliff.

Jessica13 gasped when her whole body was caught in the vertigo of looking down to see the ground hundreds of meters below. It was an exhilarating, terrifying sight that was only made worse when vertigo vanished, gravity took hold, and they began to plummet.

"What are you doing?" she screamed.

"Trust me," Mini replied calmly.

They pivoted and the left hand aimed at the cliffside while the grappler engaged again. It fired, the retractor left as loose as it could be. The dart hammered into the wall and stuck.

They continued to fall but their momentum was arrested by the retractor, which pulled them against the cliff face. Mini immediately began to run them down the wall.

It went much faster when they were practically free-falling, but aside from a somewhat rough landing, they were none the worse for wear. The AI pushed them rapidly into motion and increased speed as he continued to move on all fours like a wild dog. They cleared the minefield quickly and smoothly, while the dart disengaged from the cliff wall and it and the cable retracted.

"You're damn amazing, Mini," Jessica13 said, unable to restrain her laughter as the whole world opened up in front of them.

"Your compliment is noted," Mini said. "And appreciated."

"What did you do to the mech?" she asked and looked at the improved movement and speed as they literally raced away. "I didn't know that it was capable of this."

"Your knowledge banks do require upgrades," he agreed. "This is the format originally designed for the Minato for all-terrain movement at high speed and also in combat situations. What it lacks in weapon capabilities, it makes up for in speed and agility. Your descendants affectionately referred to it as Bulletfoot mode."

"Bulletfoot mo— Is that why they called us bulletfoots in the bunker?" she asked and still tried to adjust herself to the changes.

Mini paused for a few seconds. "There is a ninety-three-point-seven-eight percent chance of a connection between the name for the mode and the name for mechanics. Minatos with fully-functioning AIs were a preferred support mech when I was designed."

She smiled. "I like that."

CHAPTER TEN

The afternoon light faded. Even from the ground, the sight of the sun setting and painting the whole sky with a variety of reds and oranges and even a few pinks was still a breath-taking sight.

It was difficult to see, especially since Mini had kept them in Bulletfoot mode. She had adjusted to the rhythm of the mech's movements as it ran on all fours, which provided some semblance of comfort inside the mech. Maybe comfort was too much of a stretch, though. Jessica13 knew she would be sore by the end of the day.

They were three hours into running across the landscape when what she'd done began to actually sink in. Something seemed to almost thump into her body and made her realize that she had—on some level, at least—thought about this, dreamed about it, and day-dreamed about it, but in the end, there was nothing that could really prepare her for what the Outside looked like at night.

"Mini?" Jessica13 asked. "Are you there?"

"I am always here, Jessica13," Mini replied.

She had no idea why she expected the soft voice to be out of breath and shook her head. "Do you think we can stop for a while? I think we're far enough away from Sanctuary to be safe."

"Safe from them, maybe," Mini pointed out. "We are far from being safe out here. But...my sensors do not indicate anything near us."

It took the mech a few seconds to draw to a halt as it first needed to slow after having maintained a high rate of speed for a while. Once they stopped and Mini returned them to the regular Minato mode, the silence overwhelmed her for a moment.

Beyond the almost unnatural quiet, something creaked outside and seconds later, something chirped. Night had fallen and out there and they were surrounded by life.

Life, not concrete. Sanctuary had never been quiet, not even during the evening shifts, but everything had felt so isolated. Out there, she couldn't help but feel vulnerable. The Outside was here.

"Is...is the air safe to breathe?" Jessica13 asked and peeked at the sky alive with bright, twinkling stars.

"Affirmative," Mini replied. "The air around us consists of nitrogen, oxygen, argon, and carbon dioxide, among other elements. There are no traces of chemical or biological hazards. Why do you ask?"

"I thought I could open the mech," she explained and drew a deep breath. She couldn't believe that she was doing this or saying it.

It seemed crazy that she even considered it. Her mouth was dry and her heart hammered inside her chest as she waited for the response.

"Well, you have access to the control to open the mech, if

you want," the AI said. "There's no need, of course. We have supplies in here to last you for at least a couple of weeks."

"No, I want to get this over with now. I came out here. We...came out here. We started all this and put ourselves on the line and in the end, we did it to get this moment over with. So, I say we get it over with. What...what do you think?"

"I can think of no reason why not," Mini said.

Jessica13 nodded, took another a deep breath, clenched her teeth, and steeled her nerves. "Okay...I'm opening the mech."

"You have my full support."

Jessica moved down and tugged at the levers that were all that kept everything that was Outside away from her. A horrible moment of doubt surged, swamped her mind, took control of her emotions and she began to panic.

"No. I came here for this. I'm doing it!" she shouted and yanked the lever.

The magnetic clamp released and the other locks lifted, and a quarter of a second later, the mech was open and the doors swung outward. She held her breath for a moment and covered her mouth as she was exposed to the air for the first time. Instincts kicked in and she was unable to respond otherwise. Years and years of being told how dangerous the Outside was were difficult to ignore and there was nothing that terrified her more.

And yet, as the cool, fresh air touched her skin, a small chill rushed up her spine. The gentle shiver persisted as she moved closer to the opening and inched forward until her leg protruded from the mech.

Resolute, she followed it with the other leg and soon, Jessica stepped out, although she still covered her mouth and held her breath. The surreal feeling of the earth under her feet was interesting.

Her hands lowered. She wouldn't be able to hold her breath for much longer. The seconds ticked by and the sound of her heart grew louder in her ears.

The option to get back into the mech and run the oxygen through a filter grew more and more distant. She didn't want to get back in the mech. After everything she'd been through, she wanted to be out there.

Finally, lacking any other options aside from passing out, she gave in and sucked a deep breath of air into her lungs.

It was clean, unrefined, and filled with so many different smells. Not all of them were good, but the air still tasted clean, somehow. Like it hadn't been run through fifteen different filters every hour to keep it clear of impurities. Clean and fresh were the words stuck in her mind.

And, most importantly, she wasn't doubled over while poison consumed her body.

"There…there's no poison gas!" Jessica said and released a loud laugh that echoed through the woods around her. "Only clean, fresh, beautiful air!"

"One might say the only poison gas in the air comes from the people in the cities," Mini said.

"How do you mean?" she asked and focused on the mech.

"Maybe some of the pirates," the AI continued. "They eat bad food. It makes sense that they foul the air they leave behind."

Jessica13 narrowed her eyes. "Wait, did you make a joke?"

"The possibility exists," he said.

"Okay, hold on, I simply need to…" she started to say and proceeded to climb up the side of the mech, pulled herself to the top, and balanced herself carefully on the shoulders to look upward.

"Have you never seen the stars before?" Mini asked.

"Well, I've seen pictures," Jessica13 said. "There were a couple of paintings my father made. They weren't very good, but... Well, I don't know how he would have been able to capture something like this."

There really was nothing that could have prepared her for this. While there were trees nearby, they were spread far enough apart that she was allowed a full view of the sky above. There weren't even any clouds to obscure her view and the sky opened to her in a wide expanse that took her breath away.

The sky was a deep, deep blue and acted as a dark backdrop to the pinpoints of light that filled inky canvas to cover it from edge to edge on the horizon. She had thought the most beautiful thing she would ever see was the sunset, but she had been utterly, completely wrong.

As she continued to gaze, utterly entranced, she realized there were patterns there. One in particular—a hazy band of white light that stretched across the whole of the sky—was the most beautiful.

Jessica13 lowered to sit on the shoulder of the mech. Hot tears began to run down her cheeks and she fumbled in her pocket to retrieve what was left of the picture of her parents. She couldn't stop the tears but she wiped them away quickly because she couldn't bear to not see the sky.

"Are you all right, Jessica13?" Mini asked and broke the silence that had fallen.

"I'm...yeah, I'm fine," she said and tried to laugh the tears away. It didn't work but she wasn't feeling sad.

Well, not only sad. There were too many emotions rushing through her that were difficult to describe.

"Are you sure?"

She shrugged. "I don't know. I'm a little overwhelmed, is all. I never thought it would be this...amazing. I only... I... You know, my friends at Sanctuary used to call me Jessie because the I and the E look like they might be the 13 at the end of my name."

"Are we friends?" the AI asked.

"I...think we are," Jessica13 said. "After all, we've been through more than I've been through with any of my friends."

"I've never had a human friend," Mini said and sounded pensive. "I shall endeavor to be worthy of that designation."

"You already are." She smiled and her gaze traced the different patterns in the stars. "I... Well, I don't...do your data banks have anything on what those...stars do?"

"I'm not sure I understand what stars do. A star is an astronomical object consisting of a luminous spheroid of plasma held together by its own gravity. The star nearest to the Earth is the Sun."

"Wait, the sun is a star?" That caught her attention. "But it's so big. And...well, it shines when none of the others do."

"The reason why you can't see any other stars when the sun is out is that it outshines all the others," he explained. "And it's not necessarily large, merely much closer, relatively speaking. The sun is large enough to fit one-point-three million Earths inside it and is actually not that large when compared to some of the larger stars we know of. It is almost a hundred and fifty million kilometers away and is still the closest star."

"Holy fuck, that's far away," she said. "How...how long would it take for us to get there in the Minato?"

"Well, we could start running now and not stop once and it

would still take longer than your natural life to get there. Similarly, to reach the nearest star, we could keep running for a thousand years and not get significantly closer to the second closest one. It's so far away that it takes the light from the star over four years to get to us."

"Wait, what? How… Wait, how long does it take the light from the sun to reach us, then?"

"A little over eight minutes," Mini said.

"Wow. Light must travel fast," Jessica13 shook her head to try to restore order to her suddenly rampant thoughts. "But if the light in those stars takes so long to get to us, how does it… you know, get to us? How do we see the stars?"

"The light travels and so the image travels," the AI explained. "It can be assumed that a great many of the stars have since died and all we see is the light they gave off before they died."

"How do stars die?" There seemed to be no end to the hunger for new information.

"You're full of questions, aren't you, Jessie?" Mini said although he paused before he used the nickname.

She shrugged. "I…well, yeah. Machines always made sense to me. I could look at the coding or the build and they kinda spoke to me. Even when I was a child, I could understand what they were saying. Most of the other subjects of study were difficult. But machines and computers came naturally to me. It's the Athena genes, they said, and I didn't really know what they meant. But that never kept me from being curious about it. The fact that I had a harder time understanding them meant I was much more curious about it. So…I understand if you don't like the questions. But like the machines, they come naturally to me."

The silence lingered for a moment.

"Well, stars don't die like humans do," the AI said after a few seconds had passed. "Dying is more of a human alliteration to what they do. Eventually, once the fuel that powers the stars burns out, the core shrinks and the star expands. It becomes larger and less bright until it collapses in on itself. If the mass of the star is small, it becomes a white dwarf, barely visible in the night sky as it expands and then cools off over billions of years. If its mass is large enough, it collapses in on itself and becomes what they call a black hole. It's so massive and so dense that everything that passes close enough is sucked in, even light. We don't know what one looks like since no light escapes. All we can see is a halo of light being sucked in, which we call the event horizon."

Jessica13 stared at the sky again for a moment. "That's so sad. Imagine that we see the lives of these stars and the light they give off, and for all we know, they could already be sucking some of their own light into themselves so no one else will see them."

"It is a little more complicated than that," Mini said.

"I know." She allowed herself a small smile. "But at least we get to see the light of the stars as they were shining brightly and illuminating the sky. It makes such a beautiful tapestry that we can simply stare at. I could stare at it for hours."

"We have no other engagements."

"Great!" She clambered down from the mech and moved inside to retrieve food and draw water into a bottle before she returned to her perch on the mech's shoulder. "Can I ask you more questions?"

"You are physically capable of asking them," Mini asserted. "Whether I am capable of replying remains to be seen."

"So, stars die, right?" Jessica13 stated as she prepared a quick meal for herself using the patties and the soup and mixed them for flavor. "And the sun is a star, so…will the sun ever die? And if it does, what happens to us?"

"The sun will die, yes. But it is not something you need to worry about since it will likely only happen in about two billion years. I don't think even I will survive that long."

"Huh. Still, it's sad to think about it. What happens when the sun dies? Will we simply…grow cold?"

"The standing theory is that the sun will expand into a giant and then collapse to a white dwarf and cool off," Mini explained. "Cool is relative, of course. In expanding, it will grow until it takes the Earth in as well, vaporizing the planet and turning it into dust that will float around in space."

Jessica13 tilted her head and stared at the sky. "That's sad too. But I guess all things must come to an end. It'll take longer when you're as big as a star but it has to come to an end anyway."

"I suppose that is true," Mini said. "But when you focus on what happens before the end itself, it's less sad. Like you focusing on the star's light instead of where it might come from. Celebrating life instead of mourning the inevitable death."

She smiled. "Yes, I think I like that. I like that a lot."

The food finally drew her attention and she decided she should eat while she could. It was still the same bland fare she was used to but somehow, it tasted a little better out there.

"We should push on," Mini said once she was finished. "I can keep the mech moving while you sleep inside."

"It sounds good to me." She yawned and clambered back inside.

It had been one hell of a long day.

CHAPTER ELEVEN

Once inside the mech, Jessica13 settled herself as comfortably as possible. The fresh air was liberating, but as Mini had warned her, there were still threats to be dealt with Outside, and they probably needed to keep moving. The folks in Sanctuary likely wouldn't come after her, but there was no guarantee. Besides, she had proven herself to not be the best judge of what the leaders of the bunker would or wouldn't do.

The AI returned to the Bulletfoot mode and moved rapidly across the landscape. The farther they moved from Sanctuary, the less open ground she could see in front of her. The darkness and the rhythmic movement of the mech around her were almost hypnotic, and it wasn't long before she drifted off to sleep.

It wasn't a peaceful sleep, unfortunately. She was restless, and the constant motion didn't help. But it was rest she wouldn't take for granted. It had been a long day and it was very likely that she would have many more of those in the near future.

Any sleep was welcome.

She wasn't sure when she realized the mech had come to a halt, but she could feel it starting to warm up around her. No, it wasn't the mech. Well, it was too, she supposed, but the heat came from outside.

Her eyes opened and she stretched carefully in what space was available to her inside. It was only a little less than she had learned to manage with in her tiny little room. Small spaces were not foreign to her.

As she looked up into the light that beamed down on her, she gasped, covered her mouth with her hand, and gazed at the sun that had begun to rise over the landscape below her. Mini had stopped on a small cliff, which gave her a good view of the land, most of which was covered by thick, lush green foliage.

There was life all around them. She could hear it through the speakers and see it moving and not only with her eyes. The motion sensors on the mech told her there were living creatures everywhere. They woke and went about their lives and none of them even considered the idea that they were supposed to be dead out in the open like this.

"Oh, wow," Jessica13 whispered as her gaze returned to the gorgeous sunrise. It was like the sunsets she'd seen before but much more powerful somehow. It was wondrous to realize that it was coming up, not going down.

"Good morning, Jessica13," Mini said and added a smiley face to the HUD. "I hope you rested well."

"It wasn't too bad," she said and made another attempt to stretch. "I guess I'll have to get used to resting in here for a while."

"Provided we don't find any shelter for you to use, that would likely be wise. If you would prefer, we could develop software that would allow us to continue moving in a manner that would facilitate resting for humans."

She laughed. "I'm sure we could. So, did you stop us here so I could have something beautiful to look at when I woke up?"

"The location where I stopped was for your benefit," Mini said. "It gives us a vantage point from which we can decide which direction to proceed in. The view was merely a pleasant side effect."

"I'll take it." She yawned again and settled into the controls of the mech, called up the data around her, and tried to give herself a decent view of where they were going—all while she struggled to avoid the distraction of the view. She could look at it for hours on end and accomplish nothing.

What should she do?

The question came to her and remained in her head, ticking there and begging to be answered. For the first time in her life, she faced a day with no orders and nothing she had to do. Of course, something needed to be done, but she was the one who would decide what it was.

It was an odd feeling, but one she was certain she could get used to. It wasn't like there was anything else to do but choose what she would do next. That was her life now.

Jessica13 sighed, opened the mech, and stepped outside. The air was still crisp and cool and there was noise all around her. Birds sang and trilled in the trees above, although some looked smaller and furrier than birds. No, she realized after a quick study, not a bird. It was clearly something else with a bushy tail and hands and feet and no wings, either. She wasn't sure what it was. There had been no creatures like it in the instruction videos she had seen as a child.

She took a deep breath and closed her eyes as her lungs

filled with fresh air again. It seemed unbelievable how people could ignore the fact that the air they breathed had been recycled through fifteen different filters—which left a smell. She wasn't sure what it was but it was definitely there and it did grow old and stale.

Out there, a hundred different smells vied for her attention. She couldn't identify them either but there was a cold crispness to the air that brought only the word fresh to mind.

"Are you unwell?" Mini asked from inside the mech. "Should I access my databases for some medical knowledge?"

Jessica13 laughed, shook her head, and patted the mech on the arm. "I'm fine, honestly. I only…it's weird to stand out here. I dreamed about it so many times in the past but I never thought about what I would do if I actually got this far. It was always a pipe dream—that I'd spend my whole life trying to stand out here one day. And now that I'm here, I am at a loss about what to do next."

"We could keep moving," the AI suggested. "The supplies you packed will not last for long, but I have detailed files on how to survive Outside that should prove most useful. Repairs of the mech were given the highest priority, but there is data on the collection of plants and animals that are safe to eat and how to prepare them as well as building a fire and temporary sanctuaries to protect you from the Skyfall. Those are mostly how to be safe and avoid the impact radius since it is highly unlikely that someone might actually survive being struck by debris coming down from orbit."

"But there is a chance, right?"

He paused a second. "An infinitesimal chance does exist, only slightly improved if the victim is wearing a mech. Your chances of surviving Skyfall are zero-point-zero-zero-zero-zero-zero—"

"How many zeroes are there before another number is reached?" Jessica13 asked as she climbed into the mech.

"Three hundred and forty-seven. That is based on an analysis of a direct impact by way of the calculated average size of debris falling from orbit. Of course, the smaller the piece of debris, the greater odds you have of surviving impact."

"That makes sense, I suppose." Once inside, she closed the mech behind her as she called up the data Mini used to the HUD. "I still don't know how likely it is for something falling from the sky to hit you, though."

"I do have those numbers available if you require them," Mini said. "I'm afraid they are a few decades out of date, though."

Jessica13 shrugged and studied the data displayed. "Well, I guess it's better than no data at all. And we wouldn't want anything out there to...hit us..."

She paused and stared into the distance for a moment. Something was out there but from their high vantage point, it was hard to tell exactly what it was. Not a building, certainly, but it was high in the sky.

Mini noted her interest and quickly zoomed the HUD in on it.

It wasn't a building, as she had determined already, but rather a pillar of billowing smoke that spiraled ever higher into the sky.

"What kind of smoke is that?" she asked and called up the databases. "It's not a mushroom cloud from an explosive device. I'd say it seems to be from a steady fire."

"Agreed. It would appear that something is burning."

She nodded thoughtfully. "Maybe we should see if there's anyone who needs our help. There can't be too many people

Outside and if there's a fire, it could mean there's a camp or something. It's only fifteen klicks from our position."

"A camp is unlikely," Mini pointed out as Jessica13 took control of the mech and began to maneuver them around the edge of the small decline they faced and in the direction of the smoke. "I do note, however, that there are records of one of the bunkers being built in that area, based on what used to be a iron ore mine a few hundred years ago."

"Another bunker?"

Whether there was any truth to those stories remained to be seen. She'd developed a healthy cynicism about stories and their veracity.

"It appears to be in the same rough area, although it's difficult to tell with outdated maps," Mini said.

"Well, I'm not sure we'll get a heroes' welcome," Jessica13 said as they moved across the rough landscape. "If they are anything like Sanctuary, the chances are they heard the stories of how sometimes, bunkers would send raiding parties to neighboring bunkers for supplies. Breaching the sealed environment supposedly led to mass deaths from poison and radiation, so visitors are rarely—if ever—allowed anywhere near the doors."

"How did you conduct trades if that's the case?" the AI asked.

"There are a handful of caravans that travel between the bunkers," she explained. "Some originate from the bunkers themselves and are sent out when they need some kind of resource and have another to trade for it. Others are peddlers who scavenge whatever they can find in the Cities-that-Were and come to trade. Either way, there's not too much trust so when they arrive, they're still kept under the watchful eye of the Guardian mechs and are never allowed inside. I guess that's led to the bunkers being robbed too many times before. We were allowed Topside sometimes to see what they had to offer."

"I see. How do they transport the goods?"

"Most carry what they can on the backs of their mechs—they fit them with mag clamps like the one the Minato has—but I have seen a few who use pack animals. They are big, four-legged beasts with hooves and sometimes horns that carry almost as much as a mech could," Jessica13 said. As she said that, the penny dropped. How had she missed the fact that these animals were impervious to the so-called poison in the air? The thought had never occurred to her before and seemed like another measure of her foolishness.

"What do they take for trade?"

She paused to consider this. "They're mostly in it for the resources that can be traded like copper, food, and water, but they took the canteen I offered them too."

"That is unlikely," Mini pointed out. "There appears to be no centralized currency between the bunkers and so unless they made an agreement to exchange the canteen with the bunker for resources, they would not agree to it."

She shrugged. "Whatever you say. All I know is that he didn't mind me exchanging my canteen for a couple of manus on how to fix…well, you."

"And I appreciate the effort. What are you doing down there?"

Jessica13 paused in her fiddling and watched the HUD closely. "I'm trying to see how you activated the Bulletfoot mode. It would help us get to the place faster."

"Well, the way to activate it is by giving me the controls," Mini pointed out. "Humans are not the best at running on four legs. It goes against your core programming and hardware, which makes it difficult for the human body to move the mech's controls... Well, there you go."

It was impossible not to smirk when she found the control that activated the all-terrain mode, lowered the mech onto all fours, and settled in. "No power on Earth or in the Cities-that-Were can stop me from finding out how to make a machine work. You should know that better than most, Mini. But, in the interest of helping people who might be in trouble, I'll elect not to spend the day tinkering with the mech to learn how it works. Would you mind picking up from here?"

He didn't speak for a moment but after three or four seconds, an approval message displayed on the HUD.

"Are you sulking in there?" Jessica13 asked.

"Negative. AIs are incapable of sulking."

"Well, that's good because you are the only person I can talk to out here and I would hate to lose that." She patted the inside of the mech.

"My human interaction software tells me that you are attempting what humans call emotional manipulation," Mini pointed out. "You should be aware that AIs are not susceptible to this but, as remaining where we are would put us in danger of being overtaken by possible predators, I say we should continue to move."

The approval message vanished and Mini took control of the mech to guide it between the trees and plants at an ever-increasing speed. Jessica13 wondered how long it could keep going without needing repairs and made a mental note of it by calling up the hardware diagnostics and pinning it to a corner of the screen.

They moved quickly through the forest until she could see an opening in the distance where it had been cleared. If it really was another bunker, it looked like they had a similar thought process as Sanctuary did in wanting to keep as much of the area around them as open as possible. The logic was that it would help them to see any threats that might approach in enough time to prepare for them.

Mini brought the mech to a halt at the edge of the tree line and looked out onto the clearing.

"Well, you were right," she said, softly and leaned forward until her nose pressed against the helmet. "There is a bunker here."

"The correct terminology might be 'there was a bunker here,'" the AI stated.

It was, unfortunately, true. The location looked like the scene of a battle straight out of one of the instruction programs. The minefield around the bunker appeared to have been detonated and bodies were strewn everywhere. Mechs had been damaged and left for dead—dozens of them lay in various states of disrepair and some of them still burned.

They weren't the source of the column of smoke that continued to rise into the sky, however. That issued from a heavy concrete structure which she could see was only the tip of what was likely an extensive complex that extended for kilometers underground.

"My electromagnetic sensors detect that we are about to enter a minefield," Mini warned.

"Most of the mines were detonated already," Jessica13 said. "Then again, one can never be too careful. Can your sensors give us an idea of where they are?"

"I am plotting a course now," he said after a second's pause.

The plotting took less than a minute and before too long, they moved cautiously through the open field. The safest places were, of course where the mines had already detonated to leave small, smoking craters in the soil. A couple of mechs in the area had been torn to shreds by the powerful ordinances but most appeared to have been exploded remotely. It almost looked like someone had found the mines themselves and targeted them.

This wasn't a comforting thought, but Mini navigated them through the open areas until the almost incessant beeping from the sensors told her they had found a way through.

"Nice work," Jessica13 said and realized she had held her breath almost the whole way.

As they drew closer to what appeared to be where the battle had been at its hottest, it became very evident that it wasn't only mechs that littered the area.

"Whoever did this might still be around," she warned and scanned their surroundings warily. "It's not like scavengers to leave behind this many suits without looting them first. Keep your…sensors alert. We might have more company."

"Noted," Mini said as they approached the battlefield.

The largest piece of wreckage appeared to be an observation balloon tethered to the ground to function as something of an elevated station to allow those who used it to see for miles around. Not everyone had the advantage of being protected by a whole damn mountain, after all.

It didn't look like it had done them much good, unfortunately.

"I've only ever seen one of these in books and vids," she said as they approached the wreckage. "Never in person, though, and never…shredded like this one."

"Observations indicate that the steel-reinforced balloon chamber was ruptured using high-caliber explosive shells, not rockets," the AI informed her. "That would suggest the balloon was still deployed when the fighting started. Those kinds of shells have a limited range."

"Agreed." She picked a slow path through the debris. The wreckage was the largest evidence that what had happened there had not been accidental, but there were other signs.

Barbed-wire fencing had been torn down and the electrical components ripped out before the attack. Small craters pock-marked the ground where airburst munitions had been deployed and missed their targets.

Dozens of tracks were visible in the mud as well. These were made by heavy mechs judging by the depth of the indentation and left puddles marked with streaks of oil that gleamed when struck by the rising sun like rainbows.

The smoke billowed ash into the sky and it had begun to cover the sun somewhat. Small flakes drifted down to settle on them.

Jessica13 scowled and brushed some of them off the mech's shoulder. She didn't want the fine ash to get inside the joints and turn the grease into goop, which would definitely screw everything up.

"It might not be my place to say this, but if we are to survive indefinitely Outside, we might need to collect parts and supplies from the wrecked mechs," Mini said.

"I..." Jessica13 whispered but was unable to finish. It had been different, somehow, when she had scavenged dead mechs on A7's orders. Now that she was able to choose what she did, she wasn't sure if she wanted to do that anymore.

Mini did have a point, of course. She would need parts and she couldn't really afford to turn her nose up at how she was able to get them.

She sighed. "I'll think about it. For now, though, let's focus on whether there is anyone inside who needs our help. If not…well, the supplies won't benefit the dead."

Her last statement sounded decidedly weird. Even as she said it, she realized that it sounded like something A7 would shout at her when she had cold feet. Did she miss the old man? Maybe.

Moving around the ruined mechs, she managed to find a small path that had already been beaten down by heavy tracks. The leaking oil and the irregular shapes of the tracks told her these weren't the regular mechs they would have in the bunkers. These were pirates like the ones who had attacked Sanctuary.

"Mini, I don't know if this is possible, but is there any way for you to compare the mechs on the ground, those that are wrecked out here, against the models that attacked Sanctuary?" Jessica13 asked as Mini moved them over one of the ruined ones and nudged an ill-fitting piece with a boot.

"I have some footage in my data banks," the AI said. "I'll perform the scans. You can keep moving while I do, though."

"That won't heat your core up too much?"

"Not if you take control of the mech."

She nodded and took the controls as they straightened out of Bulletfoot mode.

"Let's see if there's anyone here to save." Both inherently curious and excessively cautious, she moved toward the concrete building in front of her. The tether for the balloon came up to what looked like the second story of the bunker, one that had probably been used for observation and defense.

Maybe they had it set up in case? She couldn't tell but it was an interesting design that gave them a way to peek out instead of being buried underground and reliant solely on sensors to see around them.

Again, it hadn't done them much good. It was difficult to really determine exactly what had happened, but it was easy enough to tell from this close that the smoke issued from inside the structure. Whatever—or whoever—had attacked had gained entry.

It was a horrifying, harrowing thought. The same fear had been drilled into her since she was a child and it wasn't the kind of thing that went away, no matter how far away from Sanctuary she was.

The closer she got, the more she began to notice the smells that made it through even the filters in the mech. While she thought they were heavy chemicals, she wasn't sure which ones were present. Still, it meant the fire had burned for a few hours, at least, and had penetrated to the lower levels and seeped up slowly.

"What did they do in there?" Jessica13 asked and immediately coughed from the stench. Hell, she could even taste it on her tongue.

"My banks suggest they took what they could carry," Mini replied. "They didn't want anyone else to profit from their work, so they likely placed magnesium charges inside and set them off. It'll burn through virtually anything in the bunker and render anything that's not burned toxic. Food, supplies, and even weapons."

"That's annoyingly thorough," Jessica13 said softly. "What about the people inside?"

"There would have been evacuation plans in place like there were in Sanctuary," the AI explained. "Once the exterior was breached, alarms would have sounded and everyone taken out through other escape entrances."

"And those who didn't make it?"

A pause actually made the answer unnecessary. "They would be either killed by the pirates, fire, or smoke."

She nodded and tried to stop tears from welling up. It seemed a perfectly irrational response to cry. After all, it wasn't like she knew any of these people.

They circled the perimeter and found the entrance, from which most of the smoke escaped. As they approached the door, she could see something blocking it, at least partially.

It was large enough to cover most of the entry but there were chunks missing from it.

A few more steps revealed that it was one of the larger mechs. An Argonaut V grasped the sides of the door and shielded as much of it as possible. It had been able to slow the pirates, as evidenced by the chunks they'd needed to hack from it to get through.

They'd cut it while the pilot was still inside. Pieces of his body protruded, blackened where the blood had stopped flowing.

"A damn hero," she whispered and patted the chest plate of the mech. A7 had always said that about their fallen, and it felt fitting there too.

He had tried to slow them. The logical explanation was that he'd run out of ammo, couldn't fight much more than what his mech's fists could do, and had made sure his enemy paid dearly in time and bodies from the looks of the three pirate mechs sprawled in front of him.

Those Argonauts could do tremendous damage with their fists, she could give them that.

"Hold on, I'm picking something up," Mini said and yanked Jessica13 out of the stupor she hadn't realized she'd fallen into.

"Picking up what?"

In lieu of an answer, the AI displayed an audio file on the HUD's screen. She pressed to play it.

"Mommy!" a voice cried through static and background noise. "Mommy, where are you?"

"Where's this coming from?" she asked.

"Inside." Mini highlighted the location.

Jessica surged forward almost before she knew what she was doing, shoved past the ruined Argonaut, and slipped through the doors to stare into what looked like a massive elevator shaft like they had in Sanctuary. The cables had been cut but she could see evidence of others that had been set up to enable the pirates to descend and ascend again.

"Where?" she asked.

"At the bottom of the shaft." The AI once again highlighted the location on the HUD.

"I can't see anything."

"I pick it up based on the motion sensors and partially from the sound still coming through. It's a child. Based on voice-recognition patterns, it's a female no older than the age of ten."

"Shit." She hissed her frustration and leaned over the gaping shaft below her. "Do you have any suggestions? Could I climb down there?"

"Doing so would risk damaging your filters," Mini asserted. "Besides, a quicker rescue would be to use the grappler to let her climb up. Use the maglev to bring her up."

Jessica13 paused, considered that, and nodded. "Okay, but you'll have to fire it. I can't see down far enough and I might hit her with the dart."

"Agreed. Position the mech over the edge so I can begin the calculations for the shot."

She complied immediately and noticed the temperature in the processors spike as the AI began the necessary process.

"Firing now," Mini declared. It was followed quickly by a kick from the air cannon to fire a dart and cable down the shaft. She heard it impact and the retractor quickly reversed to leave it as taut as possible.

The maglev descended from her arm. It was meant to carry crates up and down difficult terrains using a series of magnetic coils to climb up and down the cables. It would have trouble carrying a full-grown human but a ten-year-old girl... It was possible.

"Hey!" Jessica13 called from her position at the top of the elevator shaft. "Climb onto the lev and let it bring you up."

"Are you my mommy?" said the voice from the bottom.

She grimaced and wondered what the hell she was supposed to say to that. "I...no, but I can take you to her!"

Why the hell did she say that?

"She has boarded the maglev," Mini announced.

"Oh...well, if it works, it works," she said and raised her eyebrows. "Bring her up."

"I did as soon as she boarded."

"You're so efficient."

"Your compliment is noted and appreciated."

Jessica13 couldn't help a small smile as the lev began to raise the girl. It was slow work and she needed to maintain her position. Her heart ticked a pattern to the rest of her body as she needed to keep herself absolutely still. Any movement from her could destabilize the cable and the child would fall.

"I really wish I had connected it to the ceiling first," she whispered.

"Stay still," Mini advised. "She's almost at the top."

She scrunched her face. "Oh, stay still, huh? And here I thought I could start dancing to the music in my head."

A pause followed. "Is that sarcasm?"

"Look, get her up, okay?" she muttered. There were few things in the world she hated more than standing absolutely still. It was like she was allergic to it or something.

A small head appeared through the smoke. Short red curls were clearly visible outside a filtration mask, one of those used if someone needed to dive in water tanks for repairs. It was meant to filter the oxygen out of virtually anything, including billowing clouds of smoke, but it wouldn't last in a situation like this. In diving, the water itself washed any problems away. Out in the open, the soot would build up in the filters to the point where she would have to take the mask off.

And from its already blackened condition, the kid didn't have long.

"Stay right there…." Jessica13 said calmly and softly as she stretched down, caught the girl by the collar, and yanked her out of the shaft.

The dart detached as the lev fitted into her arm and retracted as she moved through the hole in the Argonaut, stepped outside, and jogged away from the elevator door with the girl cradled in her arms.

It was a delicate balance between holding her close enough to keep her from slipping from her grasp and trying not to crush her against the chest plate of the Minato. She was relieved when they were finally clear of the smoke, for the most part, and set her on her feet.

"Where's my mommy?" the girl asked and looked around.

She pushed the door open and clambered out of the mech. She coughed reflexively as the residual smoke tickled the back of her throat.

"Let's get that off you, for now, sweetie," she said and removed the mask.

"I knew you would come for me, Mommy!" the girl squealed and wound her arms around Jessica13's neck.

She scowled. "No, no, I'm not your… Okay. Fine."

"Wait," the girl said and pulled away. The rest of her body was covered in soot but her face was surprisingly clean and revealed a mess of red hair and freckles to go with it. She had never seen hair quite so red before. "You're not… Where's my mommy?"

"See now, I needed to get you out of danger," Jessica13 said and patted the girl on the head. "Now that you're safe, we can go ahead and try to find your mommy. Did she get out of the bunker?"

"I don't know," the girl whispered. "People ran all around me, someone put the mask on me, and then I fell. When I woke up, there was smoke and I started to walk away from the fire and up to the elevator."

"Shit," Jessica13 grumbled.

"Shit?" the girl asked.

The bulletfoot's eyes widened as she turned to look at the little girl. "No…no, not that. Don't say that. It's a bad word."

"Why is shit a bad word?" the little redhead asked, her head tilted curiously.

"It's meant to represent when we're in a bad situation," she explained and shrugged a little helplessly. "It means we're in a bad situation. The word means poop and the poop is the situation that we're in."

"Oh, okay," the girl said. "Why not say poop then? And why isn't poop a bad word?"

"Because…those are actually good questions. I'll get back

to you on that," Jessica13 replied. "Do you mind if I ask you a question?" The girl nodded. "What's your name?"

"Priscilla," she replied and extended her hand. "Mommy calls me Prissy but no one else does."

She smiled, took the girl's hand, and shook it gently. "Well, it's nice to meet you, Priscilla. My name is Jessica13. And this"—she patted the mech—"is Mini. He'll talk to you too."

"It is a pleasure to meet you, Priscilla," Mini said through the external speakers. "Do not be confused by my voice. It should be noted that I was designated male upon production although they allocated me a female modulator in error. The distinction is not important, however, as I have no reproductive organs, but it is a distinction."

"What's reproductive organs?" Prissy asked and glanced at her rescuer.

Jessica13's eyes widened. "This is not the time for that question." She smiled but she didn't like where the rest of the conversation was going. That aside, she still had no idea where the mother was or if she even made it out of the bunker alive. Now, it raised the question of how to break the news to the girl. She didn't even know where to start.

"This conversation is pleasant but I regret to inform you that there is movement on the edge of my sensors," Mini said, his voice still calm—likely for Prissy's benefit.

"Okay, Prissy, you get to ride inside the mech for a while." She helped the girl inside and squeezed herself in as well.

"It's a little tight," Prissy said as Jessica13 shifted beside her.

"Well, you are a tiny little thing and so am I, come to think of it," she replied. "There might be room for both of us. Mini, are there any weapons in the mechs we can use?"

The AI conducted a quick scan of the nearby mechs. "Twelve meters to the left, there is a detachable assault rifle on the Balthazar. You won't be able to access any of the reloads so what's in the gun will be all you have. When it runs out... well, there are a couple of chain swords nearby that you could use."

"It's better than nothing," she said. "You'll need to manage the controls. It's a little tight in here for me."

"Understood. Taking control now," Mini replied and moved the Minato over to the assault rifle she mentioned.

The hand shape wasn't quite ideal, which forced Mini to keep control of it with one hand. There was the grappler on the other, however, which could also be used as a short-range weapon if they needed one.

"Okay, stay calm, Priscilla. Everything will be fine," Jessica13 whispered as Mini turned them to face the mechs that advanced on them.

"Are they pirate mechs?" she asked.

"My scans are inconclusive," the AI replied. "They're still in tree cover so all I can determine is that they are mechs—or perhaps a very large kind of lizard. The kind that aren't native to this part of the world."

"Is it weird to say I really hope they are mechs?" she asked. "Honestly, even pirates would be better."

"I don't want it to be big lizards either," Prissy shouted and made her companion duck instinctively.

"Well, it seems we have a consensus."

The movement in the trees drew closer and could now be recognized as definitely mechs, and large ones too. As they moved out of the woods, Jessica13 could identify the models. Most of them were Guardians with a couple of Argonauts among them. They were accompanied by a handful of support mechs and escorted a group of civilians not in mechs but wearing the same kind of masks they'd put on Priscilla.

"It is safe to assume these are not pirates," Mini said. "Can I lower the weapon?"

"Sure," Jessica13 said. "It's not like we would be able to stand a chance against one of those Guardians anyway."

"Put your weapon on the ground!" one of the Guardians yelled.

Mini complied and raised the mech's hands.

"What are you doing?" she asked.

"Data suggests that humans are less likely to shoot when the gesture of raised hands is offered," the AI said. "Should I put them down?"

"Well, no, obviously, keep them up. You know, just in case."

"Who are you and what are you doing here?" the Guardian's pilot said as it moved closer.

"My name is Jessica13," she replied and decided on honesty. "I'm from one of the nearby bunkers. I saw smoke rising from here and I thought someone might need help. As it turned out, I was right."

"Hey, that's my mommy!" Prissy shouted into the microphone.

One of the civilians, a woman with the same bright red hair as Prissy, stepped forward. "Is that you, Priscilla?"

"That's my mommy!" the child shouted again and in the close confines of the mech, Jessica13's ears were left ringing. She pushed the door open and let the squirming little girl out. She ran across the mud and into her mother's embrace.

"Are these all the survivors?" she asked and closed the door again.

"I'm afraid so," the Guardian pilot said and stopped a few paces away. "They attacked us from the north without much warning, heavily armed and looking to kill people. We evacuated those we could but the pirates got the rest. We came back to see if the bunker was still livable."

"I'm reasonably sure you could vent the smoke, take the oxygen out for a few hours, and let the fires die down," she said and glanced at the building. "That done, you'll have to do considerable repairs to get it working again, but… I guess it's better than no shelter."

"Not if they come back for more it's not," the Guardian responded brusquely.

"Our bunker was attacked a few days ago by pirates," she said. "We managed to fight them off but they had large numbers and serious firepower and almost got past our defenses too. Maybe they have more chavs hiding in some of the Cities-That-Were who came here for payback."

"Your bunker send a support mech to help us?" the Guardian asked and closed the distance between them to loom over her.

"Not really," she replied. Would he chew her out for running away?

The chest compartment opened and a man wearing one of the filter masks pulled clear. "Do you think they could spare any help for us here? I know it's not usual but we're desperate. Not many folks will help us."

"I'm…I don't really know but I don't think so," Jessica13 said. "Can you contact them?"

"I'm not sure," the man said. "We have a radio but we're not sure if it's working. We tried calling the Knights Mechanica for aid but had no response. "

"I've heard of them but…well, in Sanctuary, they're only a legend. So they are real people?"

"Of course. I wouldn't try to call them otherwise. In fact, they were supposed to be in one of the Cities-That-Were about fifty klicks from our location. Maybe distance is the issue for the radio."

"They're closer than my bunker if that's right," she said. "If you let me look at that radio, I think I could fix it."

"I hate to do it, but can I ask you one better?" the man asked and withdrew what was presumably the radio from inside the mech. "You might need to get closer to the City-That-Was. We're all set here but it looks like your mech could move much faster than we can. Do you think you could carry the radio out there and connect with them?"

Jessica yanked the doors open again and stepped out. The man's eyebrows raised, likely in surprise at seeing someone so young out on her own, but he didn't say anything. That made her realize that no one evidenced any concern that Prissy no longer wore a mask, so she assumed those the others wore were to protect them from the smoke. Resentment flared once again because clearly, Sanctuary must have known what these people knew. Now, however, was not the time to dwell on the lies of the past.

She took the radio from his hands. "It's a short-range comms booster and not really the best either."

"It's all we were able to salvage."

She pulled a couple of the wires out and immediately ascertained that three of the disrupter crystals were destroyed. "Nope, your message didn't get out. You're lucky it didn't blow up in your face. Old radios like this had many issues. Mini, do you think you can wire the radio up to your disrupters? I think we might get a better connection."

"It is possible," Mini replied.

"Just a sec." She climbed into the mech and removed a couple of the panels. It took her a moment to find the right wiring but once it was connected, she pinged the comms a few times to test them.

"It's working now!" the pilot outside shouted.

"Well, the good news is, I think I can get the radio to the City-That-Was to help you," she said as she exited once again. "The bad news is, I'm the only one who can do it."

"Well, we could spare a couple of—"

"No," Jessica13 said and interrupted him. "The Minato can move three times as quickly as your fastest mech and it's much smaller, so they won't be looking for me."

The man scowled but nodded. "I suppose you're right. We do need this done as quickly as possible. We're trusting you with an awful lot here, Jessica13."

"You can trust me...sorry, I didn't catch your name."

"Marcus," the pilot replied. "I appreciate your help. Do you need any supplies?"

"Some food and water would be nice."

He nodded and gestured for some of the civilians to help her. They didn't have much but she didn't need much.

"I'll be back soon," she said and mounted up.

"Be safe," Marcus replied. "And remember, when you get within transmitting distance to the City-That-Was, radio that you are looking for Hammerhand. He's the leader of the Knights and will be the one to ask for help."

"I'll remember that." She closed her mech securely.

"So," Mini said as they moved into Bulletfoot mode, "we left one bunker and now we're helping another?"

"It's not like there's anything else I can do," she grumbled. "They need my help. How could I say no?"

CHAPTER TWELVE

Most of the day was spent traveling, but there was no way to miss the City-That-Was rising into the sky above them.

It was even more difficult to miss when they entered a reasonably clear area and the absence of greenery provided them with a better view of the city in the distance. They had moved through the night hours as well, but as the sun began to rise, the massive buildings towered not five klicks from where they had stopped.

"I can't even begin to guess why all these buildings were needed," Jessica13 said in a tone of something approaching awe. "What did people actually do here?"

"My records indicate that this was once the thriving metropolis known as Séraphine," Mini said. "It was home to one of the largest open-air theaters in the world and one of the largest opera circuits in the world as well, with an influential and powerful high society. The city was known for its film production too, due to the tax benefits designed for cultural projects, but most of the GDP came from the thriving mech design work and production, thanks to the nearby iron ore mines."

"Okay," she responded with a laugh. "I think I understood about half of that. What the hell is a theater? Or an opera? Or a GDP? Film production?"

"GDP is the gross domestic product. It means what made the most money—think of it as canteen credits—for the people living in the city. As for your other questions... Well, films, theater, and opera were what people did for entertainment. When you had this many people to entertain, those who did the entertaining made considerable money too."

She shook her head and needed a while to grasp what Mini had explained. "How did they feed this many people? If there were so many of them entertaining and building mechs, who did all the farming? The..."

Jessica13 paused and tried to think of all the different kinds of jobs from the bunker that might be necessary. That led her to consider all the jobs that had been a part of the world she knew nothing about. There could be any number of things she had never heard of pursued by people who had their own lives and made their own choices.

"Mini?" she asked. "How many people lived in this city?"

"The latest census records state that fifteen million, seven hundred and eighteen thousand, four hundred and ninety-two people lived in Séraphine," the AI replied.

"Fifteen mi—holy shit." She gasped.

It was impossible for her to even comprehend how many people that was. How did you keep track of the reproductive cycles of fifteen million people? How did you feed that many? Questions flooded her mind, but she wasn't sure which one to start with.

Through all her confusion, however, one hung heavily

over her head—one she knew she wouldn't be able to avoid, even in thought, so she decided to simply ask it.

"What happened to all of them?"

Mini paused as if he sensed the weight of the answer. "The initial Skyfall came down in this area of the world. Orbital drops started about three hundred clicks from the center of the city. They sent a group of emergency relief workers thirty-eight days later, who reported a hundred percent fatality rate due to the biological weapons that had begun to spread. Then, the relief workers died too."

"That's horrible," she said softly and shook her head at the enormity of it.

"It was war," the AI pointed out. "We still don't know what the invaders hoped to gain when they attacked. It was possibly resources or maybe they merely saw humans as a threat. Either way, records indicate that they had no plans that involved humans surviving."

"I wonder if we might have simply talked to them and found a way to communicate," she said, unwilling to believe there hadn't been another solution. "Kind of like…well, like I managed to finally get the Minato working and then you. It wasn't an immediate thing. It took work and a great deal of fiddling, but it worked in the end."

"It's hard to describe the kind of fear that comes from the unknown," Mini said. "I certainly don't know how to explain it as it's a uniquely human emotion. Maybe it applies to some animals and possibly even the invaders, but it's not one I experience."

Jessica13 nodded and forced a small smile. "Well…it's ancient history now, I suppose. We should keep moving. It shouldn't be long before we're in range to transmit to the Knights Mechanica."

"It's odd but I don't have any resources regarding the name," the AI informed her. "Knights are fairly obvious and Mechanica, I suppose, indicates that they use mechs, but the combination holds no meaning."

"It's hard to say what they are exactly," she agreed. "I suppose the bunkers closer to the City-That-Was would know about them but the peddlers have talked about them. They're apparently a group of mechslingers who have worked in the Outlands. The stories mostly involve how they helped bunkers in need, peddlers who were attacked, and handed out supplies that were needed when they were needed. Which is why the bunker was trying to call them for help."

"That could be a reference to the old legends of the wandering gunslingers of times past," Mini commented. "Are you sure they even exist? As a group, I mean, because it could be that there are people who helped others and have thus been elevated to the status of a Knight Mechanica."

She thought about it for a moment and tried to recall the various snippets she'd heard during her life in Sanctuary. "I suppose it is possible but I don't think so. Outside, you wouldn't see too many people living alone and helping people like that. They might not be called the Knights Mechanica but there is a group out here that helps people. There...has to be."

Mini understood and gave her a thumbs-up on the HUD screen as they continued to move across the landscape, still in Bulletfoot mode. The trees began to thin and gave way to thick grasslands that were a little easier to traverse. It also provided a good view of the smaller buildings that indicated they were now inside the city.

"Do you think we should try to connect with the Knights?" Jessica13 asked as they moved between the walls that had crumbled for years and were already overgrown by plants and vines.

"The CO at the bunker said to be sparing with the use of the radio," Mini replied. "I don't think it was because he was afraid we would break it."

She nodded. "He was afraid someone else might listen in. Pirates are in these parts, and if they hear a random message sent out, they'll see the opportunity for an easy score. It's best to only send the message out when we're sure it'll reach someone we want it to get to."

"How will we know that?"

"Honestly? I have no idea. I guess we'll know it when we see it."

That wasn't even remotely reassuring but it was the best she could think of. The closer they got to the city, the taller the buildings became and to her, it felt like they had stepped into another forest. There weren't too many trees and the concrete structures and ground appeared to be relatively intact. Relatively was the operative word, as there were cracks from which grass and smaller trees sprouted.

Most of the foliage appeared to be from vines that climbed all the buildings as well as the steel light fixtures that looked to have been there forever.

Animals could be seen moving across the open spaces. They moved quickly in groups to keep from being targeted by the birds of prey she could see circling in the sky above them. Despite everything and all the terrifying horrors that had destroyed the human population in the area, the plants and animals had survived and, by the looks of it, thrived.

She'd never seen any of these creatures in person but some, like the deer and even a few rats and marmots here and there, she had seen before in the instructional vids that had been shown to her when she was a child.

Most of them, she hadn't seen before. Many of the birds displayed bright yellow and red plumage and chirped and chattered as if in conversation with each other up in the buildings. It created a somewhat confusing kind of harmony. The oddest creature she saw looked like a smaller-sized dog but with a finer snout, bright red fur, and a bushy tail that was tipped with white.

"Do you have anything in the databanks regarding that?" Jessica13 asked as she watched it run into the sanctuary of a building close by.

"That is a quadruped known as the red fox, or Vulpes Vulpes, common to these parts," Mini replied.

"You know that explains almost nothing, right?"

A pause followed while the AI tried to correlate it in a way that she would understand. "Think of it like a creature with dog hardware but running on cat software."

"What's a cat?"

"That is a difficult question to answer, honestly. These are the pictures in my databanks."

Jessica13 leaned forward and narrowed her eyes to study the ginger-colored creature with soft white stripes, diamond-shaped ears, a lithe frame, and a long, thin tail. It stared at the camera that took the picture with large, slitted eyes.

"Did we used to keep those creatures as pets too?" she asked.

"Well, the question remains as to whether humans kept them as pets or if they kept humans as pets, although a compromise would conclude that it was a symbiotic relation-ship where humans provided the cats with shelter and food and the cats kept smaller pests away from the humans' food."

A few more images of cats displayed, including what looked like a carving of the creature into yellowish rock. "There are also reports of humans worshiping cats as deities, although whether the worship was directed toward a deity who was a cat or if all cats were deities is hard to determine."

"Huh." She scrunched her face in distaste. "I don't think I could ever worship a creature that was an eighth of my size. I like the symbiotic relationship."

"Affirmative," Mini said. "That is the more likely scenario."

"And these foxes were like cats, then?" Jessica asked as they approached a small structure placed in a clearing in the middle of the buildings that rounded out into a circular wall about as tall as her knee, an open space, and then a taller, more elaborate structure in the center.

"They were comparable, but foxes were never domesticated by humans or, at least, not to the extent cats were," Mini continued as they came to a halt. "Although that wouldn't have explained much if you don't know how cats behaved."

"Well, they were creatures with similar characteristics," she said. "I've seen a fox and I can assume that cats would have acted in a similar fashion."

"That is an interesting assumption." Jessica13 pushed the doors of the mech open and stepped outside. "What are you doing?"

"Well, it's around the time I would normally indulge in a midday meal," she said. "As long as you keep your sensors alert to any potential threats, I would like to eat outside the mech."

"There are dangers I would not be able to see from a distance," Mini pointed out. "An attacking mech, for instance, would be able to fire rockets from a distance. Or one of those Sherlock mechs could pick us off using their long-range rifles."

"And if we were attacked by either one of those, what benefit would there be if they hit us from a distance?" she asked, chose some of the rations from the mech, and sat on the small wall.

"If they missed, we would be able to escape with more alacrity," the AI pointed out.

"Well, be that as it may, I think I need a little fresh air anyway. We've moved almost without a break for the past twenty hours and I need time to stretch my legs. I don't think I've spent that much time in a mech before."

"Given our situation, getting used to being inside the mech is likely something to consider," he said as Jessica13 began her meal.

Once again, it wasn't great but it was from a different bunker and that made it taste different. It was more savory, she realized, like someone had prepared the rations with more spices. That would have been considered an unnecessary waste of resources and time in Sanctuary.

All it really did was add a touch more flavor to the otherwise almost tasteless stew mixed with protein patty that she'd eaten her entire life.

"So," Jessica13 said, still chewing. "What is this? One of those theaters you talked about?"

Mini didn't answer for a few seconds and she wondered if he hadn't heard her. Or maybe he was sulking again.

"My records indicate that this is a popular social area, maintained outside to encourage other humans to interact with each other on a larger scale," the AI said. "The most common name for it would be a fountain. The location would have water running from the central structure to fill the outside ring, which would then force the water down into a couple of pipes and back into the spout."

"Huh." She frowned and tried to picture what it would look like. "Did they use any covering over it?"

Mini paused again. "My records indicate no."

Jessica13 scowled. "How did they keep the water from evaporating and being lost into the air?"

"It would appear that letting the water be lost to the atmosphere wasn't that great a concern back then."

That was reasonable, of course, but she couldn't help but scowl at the small bottle of water she had for herself. It was a wonder that people could be so wasteful, even people who lived over a hundred years before. Folks living in a time of plenty never quite imagined that their situation could change so drastically.

"I wonder what it must have been like," she said softly, finished her food, and packed everything into the mech before she climbed in.

"Being that wasteful?" Mini asked.

"I wonder what it must have been like to be around so many people simply...well, enjoying themselves. Not having to worry about things like wasting evaporating water. Is that crazy?"

"I can assure you that your wondering does not classify as a mental illness," he replied as they began to move again.

"That's not quite what I meant, but I guess it still answers the question." Jessica13 turned and retrieved the radio. "Do you think you could get us to a higher point? I think I'll be able to manage a focused comm burst to reach the second bunker to tell them I'm here in the city."

"Hold on." The AI reverted the mech to Bulletfoot mode, settled onto the ground, and ran quickly to one of the smaller buildings that looked more or less intact. A few calculations crossed the HUD before the grappler fired to enable them to climb to the top. A host of birds flew up from inside the building, startled by the sound, but settled slowly when the mech began to clamber up the side of the building.

"Sorry," she said softly, not wanting to disrupt their lives any more than was necessary.

Once they reached the roof, Mini maintained the connection with the cable. The building didn't appear to be that stable, to begin with, and adding the full weight of the mech in the wrong place could bring the structure crumbling down.

"I'm calling up a location for the second bunker now and giving you the most direct connection," the AI said and brought more computations up on the screen to run them through a variety of different algorithms. Jessica13 could comprehend most of them and thought she could probably make them herself but nowhere near as quickly as Mini performed them. In under a minute, a comm line was opened.

"This is Jessica13," she said into the mic. "Can anyone hear me on this frequency, over?"

A moment passed before a soft crackle and hiss was heard over the line and finally, a voice. "We read you, Jessica13. How goes the search for Hammerhand, over?"

"I've just reached the city," she said. "It's mostly deserted, over."

"You might...find the industrial complex on the western end of the city," the voice said but crackled severely with the interference and distance. "Knights Mechanica...defenses up in the area. Advice...short-range bursts over general comm channels...should respond, over."

She nodded and thought she'd at least understood the general idea behind what was said. "Roger that. How are you guys doing there, over?"

More crackling. "...better if we...the Knights are coming.

Still rebuilding otherwise, over. You should send the communication…head on back, over."

"Well, I'll get back to you once I know more. Out," Jessica13 said and cut the communication.

"Connections over that kind of distance are probably what burnt the disruptors in the radio the first time," Mini said. "Ours are currently well above recommended heat settings."

"We probably shouldn't contact them again until we have good news to share." She studied the wiring behind her. "Anyway, can you put out a short-range, general burst?"

"I'm connecting with as many channels as possible," the AI said and activated the radio transmitter. "You're connected."

"Connecting to Hammerhand of the Knights Mechanica," Jessica13 said. "Repeat, connecting to Hammerhand of the Knights Mechanica. Your help is desperately requested."

She cut the connection quickly.

"Is that all?" Mini asked.

"If you can send that message on a loop with five-minute intervals as we move through the city, they will be able to receive it once we come inside their connection range," she replied. "That way, the word that we're looking for Hammerhand will reach them while we still continue to move so no one can triangulate our position."

"Preparing the connection."

"Great, and I'll get us down from here," she said and quickly let them down from their position at the top of the building which, while good for sending messages, also made it very obvious where they were.

"Loop and intervals set," Mini said after a minute or so.

"Then we should push on to the industrial complex on the western side of the city." She smiled. "I'm not sure what an industrial complex is supposed to be, but I have the feeling we'll know it when we see it."

Moving through the ruined streets of the city revealed exactly how much life had spread into what had been a mostly human domain. She remembered thinking about how the cities must have been a wasteland, barely habitable by the humans who had once lived there and who now scavenged for parts and riches left by those who had come before.

From what she could see, animals and plants were what had benefitted from the absence of the people who had built all this.

Mini took control of the mech to move them more quickly and glided smoothly over the ruins using Bulletfoot mode. She sent out the message every five minutes as they progressed. It was quicker to move in the city than it had been in the forest, and with the roads cutting clearly through the land, they were able to reach the industrial complex the CO at the bunker had mentioned.

And, as Jessica13 had predicted, she knew it when she saw it. Massive steel crates made up what looked like a small city inside the city and took up as much land as Sanctuary did fifteen times over, at least. The crates were the largest pieces of the landscape, stacked on top of each other and sometimes taller than the buildings in the city itself, but the ground was littered with piles and piles of mechanical junk.

Her heart almost skipped a beat as they headed between the heaps of scrap and pieces and parts of thousands, if not tens of thousands of mechs scattered across the kilometers and kilometers of space.

"I have the feeling this isn't what the industrial complex looked like when there were humans aplenty," Jessica13 said and studied a few of the mechs that were the most interesting.

"It would have been a little more organized," Mini said. "This was where most of the mechs that were made in the factories a little farther inside the city were brought for testing, organizing, and shipping. Back when they built hundreds of thousands of mechs every year and sent them out to prepare for the Invasion, this was a hub of activity."

"I can't imagine what it must have been like to work with everything all new and shiny and still in perfect condition. I suppose it has appeal but...well, they didn't know what they were missing." She brought them to a halt in front of a larger pile of mechs that had been discarded, likely by scavengers who had no idea what they were looking at and had tossed them aside, thinking they had taken all that was worth anything.

"Back then, people had no reason to do what you do. They had everything of the best and besides that, they didn't even think to pick up the pieces others had discarded. They would simply make replacements."

Jessica13 shrugged, pushed the mech open, and stepped out. "Again, they didn't know what they were missing. There aren't many better feelings in the world than being able to pick things apart, find out how they work, and put them together to make something others would simply throw away work again."

"It sounds like a kind of revenge against the people who threw it away in the first place."

"Possibly, but in the end, all that matters is making something work." She shook her head and gestured at the closest mech. "For instance, whoever scavenged from this took most of the chest plate armor and probably thought that since it was thicker, it was better, but ignored the shoulder pads made from steel titanium-alloy. They are cut and bunched together to not only be effective armor against even the highest-caliber rounds but also good at absorbing explosives. Basically, it's about knowing what are the best while not being the obvious pieces. Hold on."

She climbed into the Minato, retrieved her tools, and chose those she needed before she scrambled out and set to work on the shoulder pads. She wasn't sure when she would have the opportunity to install them, but they would still work as functional armor until then.

"While you're looking around there, I don't suppose you would be able to find proper power cells to work with?" Mini asked.

"Oh." Jessica13 grunted in surprise and turned to look at the mech. "What's the matter with the ones you have now?"

"Well, cycling the power from only a couple of cells would be enough for short supply runs. For longer stays Outside and with the added drain of not only my AI core but a dozen other functions that were upgrades from the original design, you run the risk of draining the cells and having them short."

She scowled. Adding to the weight with more armor would create similar problems with the power cycling.

"Shit, I should have thought about that." She rubbed her temples, irritated at her short-sightedness. "Sorry, Mini. I'll try to find something that'll work."

"There is no need for apologies," he responded as Jessica13 continued to dig through the pile of scrapped mechs. "You've already put enough work into keeping me functional."

"Well, the idea is for you to stay functional for as long as possible. In case you haven't noticed, I need you out here."

"Well, yes, that is fairly clear, but suffice it to say that I need you too," the AI pointed out.

Jessica13 nodded. Sure, Mini could probably operate the

mech on his own without her, but maybe he liked having a human around.

It didn't seem like something an AI would care about, but that didn't matter. The idea made her feel good.

She continued to rummage through the mechs until she found something they could use. "The Watson is a comparable size to the Minato, right?"

"The Nordicgear WTS-N?" Mini asked. "Accessing data banks..."

The Watson was the support mech most of the other bulletfoots used in Sanctuary. It was simple to maintain and easy to learn how to use and was also capable of carrying considerable weight on its squat frame. It was still a little larger than the Minato at a little over nine feet tall, which meant it would take a little adjustment of the power cells.

Which really wasn't a problem as she thought she could do it.

"The power cells from the Watson should be compatible," Mini said. "But you weren't waiting for my assertion, were you?"

Jessica13 shrugged, pulled the cells clear, and gently severed their connection to their mech of origin. "I thought you liked the fact that I'm impulsive and adventurous."

"Agreed. That is why I stole you away from Sanctuary," the AI said as she put the cells on her back and climbed onto the Minato's back.

"Excuse you, I'm the one who stole you," she pointed out, pulled the power cell isolation plates up, and opened the back to give her access to the functions there. "You were the mech that moved the fastest and had an AI I liked."

"Why do you think it moved the fastest and had an AI you

liked?" Mini asked. "Do you think that was merely a coincidence?"

"What are you saying—you chose me when you weren't even functional?" she asked, spliced a couple of the power wirings from their original couplers, and guided them out. "Let me know if the energy spikes start to reach a dangerous level, would you?"

"Of course. And note that is an answer to both questions. I guess you could compare my state before I was functional to the human subconscious."

"Huh." She grunted and mulled that statement over while she connected the wiring and slipped the new nuclear power cells into the appropriate compartment. They were slightly too big but there was a little space to work with. It would feel tighter inside the pilot's area, but that was actually not a terrible thing.

"What's the matter?" Mini asked when she noticed her sudden silence while she installed the shoulder plates.

"Nothing," Jessica13 lied and shook her head quickly. What was the point of lying to the only companion she had? "It's only...well, I'm here having fun, inspecting mechs and upgrading you, while people at the bunker are waiting for me to bring them help. I can't help but feel a little selfish, is all."

"Your mech requires care as well," the AI pointed. "As do you. Your own care should not be neglected in order to provide care for others."

"I guess you're right." It was quick work to install the shoulder pads, and while they were better than having none at all, she would feel more comfortable when she found the time and materials to weld them in place. For now, bolting them in would work. "Still, the sun is starting to set and we haven't heard anything from the Knights so we should probably find someplace to spend the night that isn't out in the open."

"True, although the fact that we have remained in the same place over the past three transmissions of your message might indicate that we have remained too long," Mini pointed out. "We might want to move away from these coordinates as others could have listened in on your transmissions."

"That sounds like a plan," Jessica13 said. "You might want to stop transmitting at those intervals while we're still here. I wouldn't want those pirates to find their way to us before the Knights do."

"It might be too late already," Mini said.

"What?"

Jessica13 climbed down as she'd finished installing the upgrades and moved inside to look through the HUD at what Mini saw.

A group of Mechs moved through the junkyard, climbed over the piles and piles of metal carcasses, and appeared to be searching for something specific.

"Shit," she snapped. "Do they have our location?"

"That is unlikely, or they would have already attacked us," Mini replied. "Unless those mechs are the Knights Mechanica?"

She shook her head. "To quote you, that is unlikely. Look at the way they've built those Lancers—like they don't even care about repairing them. They'll simply discard them when they break and pick up the ones they killed others to find. That's not like the Knights."

"You don't know what the Knights are like," the AI reminded her.

"I still know it's not what the Knights are like," she retorted tartly. "Hold on, I think I saw a couple of things we could use for weapons—"

"Weapons were likely the first things to be stripped from these mechs," Mini pointed out.

Jessica13 grinned manically and scrambled out. "Only to those who don't know what they're looking for."

She moved through the pieces and tried to make as little noise as possible as she worked. It wasn't long until she tugged something up from the pile and struggled somewhat with the piece.

"What is that?" Mini asked.

As the AI undoubtedly already knew what it was, she assumed he had asked what she planned to use it for.

"An old battery pack used to store energy from the nuclear reactors from one of the older Cable mechs," she said as she worked. "It was one of the last models to use acid-based batteries to store power instead of cycling it like the Minato does. They were replaced mostly because the batteries had a tendency to short when they were overloaded. Sometimes, when the container was compromised, the short caused them to explode and coated virtually everything in the vicinity with acid powerful enough to eat even through steel plating."

"A battery bomb," Mini said when he realized what she was working on and watched her wire the battery up to a handful of power cells nearby.

"Yes," Jessica13 said with a small grin. "It's why they never let us have these in Sanctuary. We didn't even collect those from the mechs that were destroyed. Not only is the explosion powerful enough to be dangerous in and of itself, when the acid eats through basically anything, it could fill a room with toxic gas in seconds. We…uh, probably don't want to be around this when it goes off."

"Remote detonation does seem to be the best idea. Which begs the question of how we'll use it."

"Probably more like a booby trap in case the pirates try to follow us," she replied, picked up the cells and the battery they were connected to, and loaded them on the mag clamp on Mini's back. "We could probably find a couple of cables…here!"

She moved over another mech that had a grappler and, with some effort, carried it quickly to the Minato as well.

"And now we have two grapplers," he said. "How are we supposed to run if we carry all of this weight? I still need to manage the weight distribution with the new power cells to work the Bulletfoot mode."

"Don't worry. We'll drop all of this when we need to run," Jessica13 said. "With that said, we should probably move away now."

She froze when the radio behind her crackled to life. "Connecting to Hammerhand of the Knights Mechanica. Repeat, connecting to Hammerhand of the Knights Mechanica. Your help is desperately requested."

Never before had the sound of her own voice been so horrifying as it was in that moment. She spun to see the pirate mechs turn to face them.

"Run now?" Mini suggested.

"Yes please," Jessica13 said, her mouth suddenly dry. "And maybe next time I tell you to stop the loop, you do it!"

"Registered, now climb aboard!" The AI sounded annoyed for the first time since she'd known him.

CHAPTER THIRTEEN

The pirates had their location and were almost able to visually confirm where they were so they could attack. The sick feeling seemed to spread from Jessica13's stomach to her legs and arms and made her feel like she had no possible avenue of escape.

There were a dozen of them by her count from this distance. At least she knew for a fact why no one else had taken the time to scavenge in this junkyard. It also explained where the pirates who had attacked the bunkers had taken their firepower from. She only wished she hadn't found out while they were this close.

"We need to move now!" Mini stated.

She nodded, scrambled into the mech, and yanked the doors shut behind her.

The AI turned and they began to move away from the pirates who had advance slowly toward them.

As they moved, however, the added weight settled on the mag clamp with a loud clatter. It wouldn't dislodge, of course, but the noise it made could be heard for kilometers. If any other hostiles were in the vicinity, it would very clearly betray their position and they might find even more pirates hot for blood.

"You know, Mini, if we ever get out of this," Jessica13 said," I think we need to work on being a little more discreet. Not only you, of course, but me as well. We should both learn from this."

"Lessons are already being pasted to my core programming and should be useful in the future," Mini asserted.

"Assuming we have a future," she muttered despairingly.

The AI didn't pause to wallow and merely continued to move them out of the bottleneck they'd found themselves in. Jessica13 could see the numbers more clearly now. There were actually thirteen of them. Twelve were the regular Lancer designs full of the implanted modifications made by people who didn't know what they were doing. The rough and ready patchwork gave the mechs a decidedly scavenged look with pieces that protruded untidily.

One of them stood out from the others, an Ominium B4 in almost perfect condition. The model was nicknamed Balthazar, although she had no idea why. It had been designed to integrate bits and pieces from practically any other mech and was highly sought-after for that reason. Some of the older ones could be described as having almost no original parts and were called walking corpses.

This one looked like it had escaped that fate thus far. A couple of jet-engines were mounted on the back but aside from that, it looked fairly intact, something unique among those models.

"Shit, shit, shit," Jessica13 said and shook her head as the pirates accelerated their advance, obviously determined to pursue their prey.

Something weighed her arms down. She wasn't sure why but she suddenly couldn't move. All she felt able to do was stare as the pirates advanced on them with every intention of killing her and stripping Mini for parts to fit onto their own mechs.

The AI realized what was happening and immediately took control of the mech away from her. He moved them into what could pass for an attack position, retrieved the battery bomb she had built for them, and attached it to the air gun usually used to launch the grappler dart.

In this case, it was powerful enough to launch the bomb well above their heads. It hurtled toward the mechs, who either didn't realize they were under attack or didn't care.

Her eyes widened as she watched the lethal arc of her improvised weapon before Mini delivered a targeted burst from the radio to activate the power cells.

She wasn't at all sure that it would work and could only hope fervently that the reality would match her intention. It landed heavily in the middle of the enemy group and it seemed her fears rather than her hopes were realized.

A moment of breathless silence passed during which she attempted to refocus her brain on finding an alternative. A loud pop curtailed her efforts and a couple of the Lancers toppled clumsily and immediately writhed and flailed as clouds of green smoke rose dramatically when the acid began to eat through their armor and into the men inside.

Or women. She really had no idea.

"Let's move!" she said. The knowledge that at least two of them had been eliminated was gratifying and gave her a little hope.

Mini responded to her prompting and set them in motion without hesitation, but a loud crack drew her attention. She twisted and gaped as the Balthazar glided smoothly in flight. The jets on its back propelled it easily to an elevation of almost twenty meters and drove it forward much faster than the Minato could ever hope to move.

As it advanced, the pilot drew the two assault rifles it carried and opened fire.

Mini jumped back and evaded the gunfire smoothly but a few pings here and there indicated that a couple of rounds had impacted the armor.

The Balthazar cut off their escape and the gunfire drove them toward the Lancers that continued to advance on them.

It wouldn't be quite as simple as that, of course, although they were in a real predicament. Mini now moved diagonally. The airborne mech continued to hover above and maintained a steady barrage of bullets while the Lancers moved quickly to cut them off again.

"Hold on," the AI warned her, and Jessica13 braced her neck hastily with her hands again. Calculations scrolled across the HUD and indicated that Mini attempted to recalibrate the weight. After a few seconds of running, the joints jerked downward and the mech settled on all fours.

The Lancers hesitated and even the Balthazar paused its assault. Maybe they were surprised to see a support mech that could do something they had never seen before.

Or maybe they merely needed time to readjust to catch up with them again.

Mini turned the Minato with surprising speed, skidded across the scattered junk in their path, and tried to gain purchase to leap toward one of the crates nearby. The mech used it for leverage and launched them over one of the lower stacks nearby.

The lancers hadn't been fooled and moved immediately to

intercept. The Balthazar certainly wasn't deterred and merely jetted on a new trajectory to enable it to fire at them again.

"We need that monster to run out of fuel sooner rather than later," Jessica13 snapped and scowled at it. "Or...overheat or something."

"The chances are increasing of a shot that will break through the armor," Mini alerted her. Not that either of them really needed to be reminded of the fact. The Lancers now circled rapidly and would soon be in a position to attack again. They clearly realized this too, as indicated by the distinctive sound of their chain-swords activating.

"I have an idea but I'll need to be able to operate the grappler we picked up," she said. "Do you think you can keep the Minato running while I'm out there?"

Mini paused, but the calculations she ran didn't show on the HUD's screen. "I believe so. But your chances of surviving out there are remote at best."

"What are my chances while I'm in here?"

Another pause followed. "Point taken. I urge you to be careful, though."

That particular request was essentially pointless given what she would try to do. "I'll try."

It was something she had always imagined herself doing but she'd never actually considered doing it. Exigent circumstances were a bitch, however, and Jessica13 pushed herself farther into the pilot's compartment and pulled the containment padding away until she was able to reach past it into the back compartments and finally, to the trapdoor.

This was usually only accessed when she needed to do repairs, and she was used to being outside when she needed to open it, but she would have to work around the challenges.

Dealing with the Minato moving in Bulletfoot mode was

difficult enough when she was inside the compartment and could hold on for dear life. It was so much more difficult to move now that the entire mech contorted and moved. The g-forces dragged her back and forward as Mini navigated them around dangers and obstacles.

The hatch pushed open and the stench of gunfire and smoke immediately swamped her. It was all she could do not to pull it shut again and trust Mini to get them out of this.

"Come on, you can do this," Jessica13 whispered fiercely, pushed out of the hatch, and tried to establish some idea of where they were.

Mini had navigated the two of them out of the trap the pirates had tried to close around them, but they remained in close pursuit. The Lancers were slower than her mech, but the Balthazar in the sky still prevented a final break for freedom.

It took barely a second to scan and assess the situation. Her heart beat hard enough that she could feel it tick in her fingertips and it seemed like the world had slowed to enable her to take everything in. She wouldn't be able to shoot the Balthazar down. While she was a fairly good shot, even with a grappler, she wasn't that good.

And she would have only one attempt.

"Well, I'd better make it count," she grumbled and stretched her hand to the mag clamp on the back of the Minato. It was a struggle to avoid being bucked off her position still halfway inside the mech while she pulled the scavenged grappler up to where she could operate it.

Maybe it was because everything around her was in chaos or her body somehow knew they were dead if she didn't get this right, but a calm filled her. Even though she was jostled with every move Mini made, Jessica13 found her focus was suddenly razor-sharp and she could easily splice a couple of wires and connect them to the spare grappler.

The mechanism whirred to life and she found the external controls, guided it into position, and nodded with satisfaction when it responded to her control.

The Balthazar immediately realized the danger he was in, pulled back, and descended hastily to avoid being caught in the open.

Its evasive tactic worked out for the best, really. She didn't plan to shoot it directly anyway.

She turned to look where they were going. It wasn't the smartest move and a cloud of dust whipped into her eyes, but she saw all she needed to see. Her focus settled on the side of the group of steel crates around them and she swung the grappler to aim it toward them and counted the seconds down in her head.

It wasn't often that she wished for the calculating powers of an AI but in this situation, she really wished she could run the calculations Mini could.

She would have to call it by sight.

"I hope I'm right," Jessica13 whispered as the countdown ended and she fired.

The dart rocketed forward, powered by the air cannon, and spun to drive into one of the crates above them. When it connected, their speed decreased and she disengaged the magnetic clamp that held the grappler in place.

Once it came free, Mini surged forward and increased speed when the crates began to slide and topple on the Lancers that were closing in pursuit.

The Balthazar saw the danger and pulled back sharply to avoid the steel avalanche, but two of the Lancers weren't so lucky. These were caught entirely unawares and only looked up when the sun was suddenly shadowed around them.

No screams were uttered and no sound could be heard but the roar and clatter of tons and tons of steel. Even inside Mini, Jessica13 felt the ground shudder beneath the force of impact.

Mechs tended to be tough to eliminate, but she doubted anyone would walk away from that.

Well, aside from those that hadn't been struck, but it had at least given them some space and time.

Mini took advantage of it and raced forward at a speed that seemed even faster than they'd achieved when they evaded capture at Sanctuary. She closed the hatch again and wiped the dust from her face as she returned to the pilot compartment.

"Nice work out there," he said as she settled in. "I think I could have performed it if you had told me what you had in mind, though. It was illogical to risk your life."

"You didn't have access to the spare grappler and it would have taken too long to set it up for you," she pointed out and closed everything down behind her. "And it wouldn't have worked if you needed to stop to use the grappler attached to the mech. It needed to be done and it needed to be me."

Mini didn't respond, although Jessica13 had a feeling he knew he was wrong, somehow, and didn't want to discuss it further since it had worked out for the best in the end. She had disabled a couple of the mechs and given them breathing space that would hopefully get them out of the junkyard.

It wasn't over, however, as the remaining Lancers clambered over the fallen crates. The Balthazar elevated once more, still reluctant to risk itself in case she had any more tricks up her sleeve.

She didn't but hopefully, that wouldn't matter.

Mini still increased speed and it seemed that the added power cells gave them more power to work with. There would be downsides. Adding more stress to the mech would make mechanical stress skyrocket in turn, but those were problems for later.

It seemed as though the AI had adapted well to the added weight and the Minato raced out of the junkyard and reached what appeared to be a road before their pursuers could stop them. The Balthazar accelerated dramatically and would overtake them soon, but that was a risk they would have to face.

Jessica13 turned, retrieved the radio again, and keyed the next broadcast. She needed to find the Knights now more than ever, not only for the sake of the folks in the bunker but for her own as well.

A second later, a sharp crackle issued from the radio and a connection was established.

"This is Hammerhand of the Knights Mechanica," said a thick, gravelly voice from the other side of the connection. "Get the hell off the radio before you give your position away to pirates. Are you trying to get yourself killed, over?"

Her eyebrows raised in surprise. She hadn't actually expected anyone to answer, but if they did, it meant they were inside the three to four klick range of the transmission.

"Roger that, Hammerhand," she said as she pressed the control on the radio. "Unfortunately, it's too late for that. If you're able and willing to help, it would really be appreciated, over!"

Mini halted abruptly and the Balthazar and Lancers gained quickly and opened fire on them. They were attacking with more ferocity than before, likely pissed about their comrades being killed and determined to exact revenge. The sight was enough to spur them into motion again.

No answer issued from the radio. She could only hope they wouldn't ignore her cries for help. It was time the Knights Mechanica proved the truth of their legends or she wouldn't last much longer.

CHAPTER FOURTEEN

The world flashed past as Mini found them open space and Jessica13 almost couldn't believe how quickly they moved. The additional cells she had fitted were being used to their full potential and pushed power into the mech to give Mini everything he needed to sustain the Minato at a speed she would never have believed was possible.

It was terrifying, breathtaking, and almost beautiful to see the mech brought to its full potential, or as close to that as she had ever seen in a mech before. Support mechs weren't given much attention based on the assumption that the combat mechs needed most of the upgrades.

Adrenaline surged within and brought an entirely new thrill. Her whole body seemed to vibrate with energy as Mini pushed on at a reckless pace. Bullets kicked up the concrete of the road around them but the rounds that did actually impact the mech merely bounced off of the armor.

It wouldn't last, unfortunately, especially since even at breakneck speed, the Balthazar gained on them slowly and maintained a steady and relentless barrage of fire at them.

They would need help but until then, Jessica13 couldn't help but admire the kind of effort Mini coaxed out the mech.

"Alert, there are mechs ahead of us." The AI sounded calm despite their predicament. "According to your parameters, they are not friendly and are likely to be pirate reinforcements."

"Noted," Jessica13 said. "Is there any way that we can fight back?"

"Not without compromising our escape," Mini replied.

She made a face. "Evasive maneuvers, please."

"Evasive maneuvers starting."

The mech changed direction abruptly while she held on and braced her neck for each impact. She twisted when two rockets were fired at them from the buildings nearby.

The mech's stride didn't falter and it surged smoothly into a jump, bounded over to the buildings, and ran a couple of steps along the walls. The buildings themselves looked gutted, with scorch marks that had only begun to be covered by the vines that slowly invaded the rest of the city. Mechs were scattered haphazardly over the destroyed lots and the road, all of them destroyed like they had been at the bunker.

The devastation explained why no one else had settled in the city. This area was a damn war zone and these pirates refused to allow any semblance of life. Even animals avoided this part of the city and any involvement with the monsters who held sway there.

The air around them exploded with bullets and rockets when the pirates sprung their trap. They had obviously hoped to catch Mini and Jessica13 off guard with their attack but had mistimed it and were left to try to keep up with the smaller, faster mech as it raced past them. The Minato repeatedly ran up the walls around them to stay out of the way of the majority of the assaults directed at them.

"Woooo!" Jessica13 couldn't restrain a yell but still braced herself and held on desperately as Mini thrust into a smooth momentum again and raced forward, still ahead of the enemy that continued their pursuit.

To her surprise, Mini trilled with excitement as well like he had when the AI was still dormant. The core itself revealed the kind of activity she had never seen in any of the mechs she'd worked on. It suggested an AI that was fully released and now performed under the harshest of circumstances and reveled in it.

It was something intriguingly new, and despite the horde of dangers they faced, something within her simply wouldn't let go. She wanted—no, needed—to keep going.

This was what she was born to do, she realized suddenly. It was like this was what she had always wanted to be and yet had always found herself held back somehow. This was where she was meant to be and what she was meant to do. Strike and run, using her brains while the skills of her AI thrived under the pressure as all the dangers of her world threatened her from every side.

This was her world and her destiny. Her future was not to be huddled in a bunker, afraid of the slightest movement or what happened beyond the protective confines that held her in check. She wasn't made to live in fear of anything that might attack. Maybe this wasn't true for everyone, but it defi-nitely was for her.

It reminded her of the piece of junk armor she'd peeled off one of the pirate mechs that had attacked Sanctuary. At the time, the lettering on it had caught her eye and her imagina-tion. She frowned as she tried to recall the words.

"Live free or die hard, bitches!" she yelled almost before she knew what she wanted to say. The outburst was followed by another excited call from Mini. The road made a sharp curve to the left, which would give them temporary cover from the bullets that continued in an unrelenting fusillade that showed no signs of slowing. A few warning messages displayed when the armor was pierced in a few of the non-essential areas of the mech.

She would take the time to repair it when they got through this.

Not if. When.

Mini approached the curve at high speed and rather than slowing, engaged the legs more forcefully to give them extra traction as he tried to take the curve as sharply as possible. The mech twisted them to the left in response and Jessica13 was shoved into the side of the compartment.

When she straightened, she froze instinctively. The Balthazar had launched a volley of flechettes and a handful were on target with no way to avoid them. They seared through the armor like it was made of soup. The alarms blared inside her compartment to warn her the hydraulics in the left arm were destroyed.

A quarter of a second was all it took to reduce her elation to panic as the Minato lost control of its turn, skidded across the pavement, and tumbled awkwardly. Inertia carried them across the street and into the building that blocked their path.

Jessica13 felt the impact of the mech with the structure and it drove through it almost completely. She looked up as the wall collapsed on top of them and turned the world around her pitch-black.

CHAPTER FIFTEEN

It was difficult to immediately recall what had happened. The blackness faded but it was replaced by flashing red lights and the ringing in her ears was swamped by the blaring of at least three different alarms.

She wasn't sure what was going on around her and as she tried to move, every inch of her screamed in pain.

"Fuck," she whispered and sagged with a soft whimper.

"Are you all right?" Mini asked, his voice still as calm and composed as ever.

"I'm alive," Jessica13 groaned. "Very short of all right, though. Ouch...what happened?"

"A building fell on top of us," the AI said. "The Minato appears to be in need of repairs before it can climb out from under the rubble."

"How are we still alive?" she asked.

A short pause followed. "It was a small building."

"Small comfort too," she muttered. "I think I passed out for a while there. How long was I out?"

"Only for seven-point-three-four-seconds," Mini replied.

"Which is fortunate. Any longer and you would have required medical attention."

She tried to move again and groaned when her own body fought the effort. "I'd say I need some anyway. Although if what I think is happening around us is correct, medical attention for me might be the very essence of a futile endeavor."

"Why do you say that?"

"Because the pirates are still out there and they likely aren't too happy with us," she pointed out. "I doubt they'll simply leave us down here."

More processing time passed. "Agreed. Although the hope is still that we survive long enough for someone with the kind of expertise necessary to help you heal arrives."

"I know," Jessica13 replied softly. "I wish I had the time to restore you and the mech to fighting form. You really were magnificent out there."

"Your compliment is appreciated, although tempered by the fact that a stray round managed to sever the hydraulics in my left arm, thus landing us under a falling building instead of making our escape," Mini pointed out.

She shook her head and took a deep breath of the air that was somehow still clear. At least the filters were still functional. "Even with all the processing power of all the most powerful computers in the world, you won't be able to account for a variable known as blind, dumb luck."

A few calculations scrolled across the HUD when he began to run diagnostics on the mech.

"What are you doing?" she asked.

"If luck or chance cannot be accounted for as a variable, it stands to reason that a chance still exists of our exiting this situation still functional," the AI pointed out. "In which case, some of my processing power can and should be devoted to helping to fix the Minato. If chance does not favor us, it won't matter."

Jessica13 couldn't really argue with that. A few seconds ticked by as Mini pulled up all the mechanical issues the collision had caused in the Minato. The rubble shifted above them and caught her attention. She wasn't doing that, of course, which could only mean there was someone who wanted to reach them—probably with vengeance on their mind.

She blinked instinctively when sunlight streamed between the chunks of the broken building that were removed one by one. Jessica13 tasted blood in her mouth and now that she had the light, she looked hastily at her body to see what was wrong with it.

Thankfully, nothing appeared to be broken. The pain that came from moving could be the result of a few jolted joints and bruised muscles. Hopefully, that was the extent of her injuries, not that it would matter anyway.

No, Mini was right. As long as they were alive, there was the chance they could remain that way. Despair would do no one any good and she wasn't about to give up yet.

Her eyes adjusted to the light but she couldn't make out who worked to clear the rubble from around them. When she was finally able to squint and focus, however, she looked into the sky and her breath caught reflexively.

The Balthazar hovered, framed in the sunlight, and descended slowly. It seemed to take up the whole of the sky. This close, she could see the details like the ugly yet effective welding job that had attached the jets to the mech's back. As it moved inexorably toward them, one hand grasped one of the assault rifles it had fired at her and held something else in the other.

It looked like one of the chain swords the Lancers had

carried. The weapon whirred and spun and she couldn't help but gulp nervously.

The ground vibrated ominously when the jets roared in such close proximity and set the Balthazar onto its two feet before they shut off. Their noise was replaced by a low, annoying whine as the mech climbed on top of the fallen Minato.

The cockpit was framed by reflective glass, which made it impossible to see what or who was inside, but her imagination could fill in the gaps. No doubt, there were teeth missing and the pilot would stink and be absolutely filthy, having been inside the mech for longer than was recommended. Worse, they'd likely had problems with the filter systems in the mech due to gunk buildup.

She stared as it raised the chain sword and aimed it at the Minato, then flinched when a shower of sparks erupted from where it was cutting. It didn't last very long. These pirates had likely taken apart enough mechs to know where to cut when they wanted to reach a particular part of the mech.

A few seconds passed and it reached down into the hole it had cut, grasped and yanked the cockpit cover free, and tossed it aside.

"No...no," Jessica13 protested and tried to fight but there was nothing she could do. The powerful mechanical hand took hold of her and hauled her out of the Minato, then dragged her down the mountain of rubble she had been buried under for the other pirates to see. She noticed immediately that their numbers had swelled somewhat and assumed he'd gathered additional forces while in pursuit.

The man inside the Balthazar was perfectly audible. The outer speakers were on, and it laughed scornfully, obviously at her.

"Poor little bunker rat!" he declared to the vocal amusement of his comrades. "Caught out in the open with only a tiny little mech to help you. A quick mech, but nothing's too quick that it can't be caught. Ask any other rat you find."

It released her abruptly and she sprawled in the dust while he continued to laugh at her with his pirate cronies.

Jessica13 glared at him, wiped the dirt from her mouth, and attempted to push herself to her feet. Her body rebelled and shrieked in pain at the attempt. Hot tears rushed down her cheeks as she looked at the other mechs.

She wasn't afraid of them, she told herself. They were nothing more than worthless pirates who didn't even know how to put a proper mech together. She refused to be cowed by them.

The Balthazar pilot seemed determined to gloat over her and acted like he thought disabling the Minato was some kind of feat. "Did you think this would be a walk in the park, little rat? You pathetic little piece of shit. Do you think you can take four of us down and live?"

Her scowl turned into a sneer and she gave up the attempt to stand that her body resisted so painfully. Instead, she began to drag herself across the ground toward the Minato. "If I'm such a pathetic little piece of shit and I'm such a bunker rat, what does that make the four I killed, huh? What does that make all of you that you needed luck and so many of you to defeat a fucking support mech?"

She punctuated her angry retort by spitting the blood in her mouth at the Balthazar. Her spittle landed a few meters shy of its feet.

There was a moment of stunned silence among the pirates, but it was ended by another fit of laughter from the apparent leader.

"I have to say, you have more fight in you than most bunker rats," he said and laughed derisively. "That's not saying much, mind. Most of you pathetic excuses for breathers tend to lay down and die. It doesn't really matter since it'll end the same way for you. It'll only last a little longer."

Jessica13 paid no attention and continued to drag herself up to the Minato.

"Feel like dying in your mech?" the leader asked. He walked over to her and made the ground shake with every step of the heavy mech. "I can respect that, I suppose. We can take it apart with you still alive inside. It doesn't really matter. I think my boys actually prefer to have a squishy inside the mechs they pull apart."

She still made no reply. There was no way she would give the asshole the satisfaction of thinking he had rattled her. The horrible truth was indisputable. She had lost and there was no way to get around that. But they wouldn't break her spirit. She would believe they could get out of this until her very last breath.

Something caught her eye in the distance, and she narrowed her eyes to focus on it. A gleam of green light moved and definitely look like a mech, but it was too far away for her to be sure. It made little difference if it signaled the approach of reinforcements, so she ignored it in the same way she ignored the jeers and laughter from those assembled.

Fuck them. Fuck the pirates.

She stretched up, caught the jagged edges of the Minato, and winced when the steel cut into her fingers. Blood seeped from beneath her fingers but she ignored the pain, hauled herself into the cockpit, and settled in with a soft sob.

"I'm so sorry," Mini said and the speakers crackled with

interference as more alarms now blared inside despite the fact that there was no HUD to tell her what the problems were. "I failed you. I was supposed to get you clear of the danger and help you in your quest to save the people in the bunker and contact the Knights Mechanica, and…I failed you. I'm so sorry."

"You don't owe me any apologies," Jessica13 said. She tried to fight back a cough that constricted her lungs and moved the radio to where she could fiddle with it and maybe send one last emergency message. "You did everything you could and more. You got me farther than any other AI could have done. For that, I can only thank you. It was my recklessness that got us in this mess in the first place. I thought I could help on my own like I was some kind of hero. There's not much else to say."

She continued to fiddle with the radio while Mini processed her words. There was still the chance she could get the message out. The Knights were out there somewhere, and even if they couldn't save her, they could still save the people in the bunker.

"Your compliment is appreciated," he replied after the pause. "Your appreciation for a compliment from me is an unknown factor but know that I consider you a hero. You saved me. And tried to save others, to whom you owed nothing."

That teased a small smile from her and she patted the side of the mech. "Your compliment is appreciated."

Jessica13 activated the radio again, coughed, and cleared her throat before she focused on the Balthazar that now moved in to finish her off once and for all.

Fuck them. She stared at the barrel of the assault rifle that was aimed at her and keyed the broadcast button as her mind went back to the five words that had stuck with her for some reason.

"Live free or die hard, motherfuckers!" she shouted as loudly as her lungs could make it, closed her eyes, and waited for the inevitable end. She wouldn't die cowering but she didn't need to watch.

CHAPTER SIXTEEN

Her mind had already accepted the finality of it. She hadn't really expected to go out like this. It wasn't like she intended to end up there, waiting for death from the barrel of a powerful assault rifle aimed at her head, but in all honesty, there were worse ways to die. At least this way, it would be quick. Almost instantaneous, she reassured herself.

Jessica13 took a deep breath and waited, and her body flinched instinctively.

The earth shuddered violently and a thunderous boom assaulted her ears. She was knocked deeper into the mech and sucked in a deep breath she immediately regretted. A mouthful of dust triggered a fit of violent coughing.

Which beat being dead, she supposed.

One eye opened and then the other when she realized she wasn't quite dead and from the looks of it, something had happened to stay her execution for the moment. The barrel of the assault rifle was still visible but it now pointed away from her and aimed upward, which made it look like the arm that held it was pressed into the ground.

The dust began to clear, and after a few more coughs, she tried to wave some of the dust away from her face to see more clearly.

A mech stood at the base of the pile of rubble and she gaped at the sight of it. Painted bright green, it was the same one she'd seen earlier and thought it had been one of the pirate reinforcements. It seemed impossible that it had reached her so quickly.

There were scores of carvings cut directly into the green paint. She was too far away to see what they actually were but the silver beneath was clearly visible. Vents hissed steam from both the rocket behind the hammer as well as the hips of the massive mech as it straightened to compensate for the impossible weight of something that large. Even more improbable were a couple of banners hung from the shoulder pauldrons in the same green as the mech but a little brighter somehow. These displayed a group of lettering she couldn't understand painted in red and silver.

Flames still surrounded the rocket pack it carried on its back, powerful enough to launch it into space if what she'd seen about mechs that size was true. They framed it in what looked like wings of flame and smoke as it adjusted its position.

The dust continued to clear and the pirate Lancers came into focus. They still stood nearby and had apparently been joined by a considerable number of others, and she realized that the newcomer must have jumped from one of the nearby buildings. It had no doubt used the power of its landing as well as the rocket behind the massive hammer it held to completely flatten the Balthazar and the man inside it. Only most of the arm and the assault rifle next to it seemed unscathed.

"Impossible," she whispered and pushed herself out of the mech to confirm what she was looking at.

Jessica13 had read about Excalibur-class mechs before but only a handful had ever made it out of the manu plants before the war began and destroyed the factories. At least, that was what she had read.

But, large as fucking life, one now stood in front of her and damned if she didn't believe it was the most powerful mech ever built. The pirate Lancers that had dwarfed her Minato were in turn dwarfed by the massive form that towered over them and lifted its heavy hammer from where it had flattened the Balthazar like a fucking pancake.

The weapon all but confirmed to her mind who piloted the mech. It could only be Hammerhand of the Knights Mechanica.

The mech took a step that made the ground shudder and looked at her.

"Good thinking!" The thick voice boomed through the massive outside speakers loudly enough to burst her eardrums. Dust was shaken from the buildings surrounding them and a group of birds took flight, probably thinking their homes were about to collapse.

Her ears were still ringing but she raised her thumb at the gigantor.

"Thank you!" she shouted in response, unsure if the pilot had heard her.

Still, it wasn't like he really needed any input from her. He had his own problems to deal with as the Lancers came out of the stupor they had been thrust into when a mech the size of smaller buildings descended from the sky and crushed their leader into paste. It was the kind of thing that required a moment to think about.

They now fired their weapons at the cockpit and tried to find a weak place but nothing penetrated, and the Excalibur swung the hammer once again. A jet fired from the back to power it earthward almost impossibly fast with a thunderous crash. The blow flattened one of the Lancers in much the same way the leader had met his end.

Hammerhand wasn't alone, Jessica13 suddenly realized. Another group of mechs had arrived—members of the Knights Mechanica, she assumed. Their mechs appeared to be in good shape—fighting shape, as A7 had been fond of saying—although a couple of them had a few bits and pieces that didn't fit their model types.

Two Nordicgear mechs—one a tall, fast Sherlock and the other a squat Watson to back it up—both wore the same green banners on their shoulders. They lurched in front of Hammerhand to take advantage of the opening the falling hammer had given them and advanced on the pirates. The Sherlock picked up the fallen Lancer's chain sword and leapt smoothly over the Lancers around it.

It was almost possible to forget that it was a ten-ton mech that stood a good five feet taller than the Minato when it moved like that.

The chain sword flashed and a shower of sparks erupted in all directions as it attacked. The weapon slashed smoothly at anything close enough while the rifle the mech carried selected its shots to fire into the openings the sword created. The deliberate, coordinated assault felled the mechs quickly and efficiently.

Those that weren't eliminated suddenly experienced issues and seemed to have difficulty staying upright. The Watson moved through the distracted pirates and consistently fired the filaments from the needler it carried. Each one delivered the kind of electrical charge that could kill a human on direct impact.

For the mechs, though, their electronics would experience fifteen different kinds of problems, as enough of the filaments could fry a mech's electronics for good.

The Watson had no real interest in permanently disabling anything and seemed content to distract as many of the pirates as possible to support the Sherlock that did most of the real damage.

The hammer swept into another powerful blow that pounded another couple of mechs under the weight of the strike while the ground shuddered from the force of it.

Jessica13 had difficulty taking it all in. The Knights Mechanica surged onto the offensive as a group and seemed to deliver their deadly attacks almost without effort. While she'd been otherwise occupied, enemy reinforcements had, in fact, arrived and the pirates outnumbered her rescuers, but it didn't seem to matter. They were apparently too afraid to take advantage of their number superiority and chose not to put themselves in the path of the hammer that swung relentlessly whenever an opportunity presented itself.

She climbed out of the cockpit, stood on top of the Minato, and watched the fight as she and her mech were forgotten by both the pirates and Knights alike. The combatants appeared to be thoroughly engaged in wreaking destruction on one another.

"Mini, do you see this?" she asked, almost breathless, and ducked when a few stray rounds ricocheted near her.

"Most of my sensors have been damaged and those that are functional appear to be malfunctioning," he replied but still sounded as calm and collected as ever. "Are we experiencing an earthquake? Maybe Skyfall near our location?"

"Not really," Jessica13 said and slid into the cockpit with a groan. She attempted to fix some of the broken electrical equipment inside the Minato that might allow it to move again. "It's the Knights. They're fighting the pirates and one of them is piloting an Excalibur-class mech. With a fucking rocket-powered hammer."

The ground shuddered again as if to emphasize what she had said.

"That is odd," Mini said. "My data banks might be malfunctioning from the damage, but the data I have would indicate that only a handful ever made it off of the production line."

"That was what I heard too," she said with a weak laugh. "As it turns out, there's one Hammerhand got his hands on, no pun intended, and he's earned the nickname too. That hammer of his turned the Balthazar into fucking paste."

"Another malfunction, possibly, but I think I would have liked to see that," Mini said as she brought a few of the electronics back to life.

Jessica13 laughed again. She simply felt the need to laugh now, for some reason. Like the bright and beautiful world around her had somehow become brighter and more beautiful. "I think I would have liked to see that too. Unfortunately, I thought I was about to have my head shot off so I closed my eyes and missed the whole thing. But seeing the result was gratifying enough."

There was no HUD but there was still life to be had in the Minato. She would need to clear the rubble that still held its limbs trapped but there was no real way she could help the Knights in the fighting without a mech of her own.

"Oh, and for the record, Mini, wanting to see a pirate asshole eat shit will never be considered a malfunction to my eyes," she said before she hauled herself from inside the cockpit.

"Noted," Mini said. "I will add that to my databanks as well. Assuming they haven't been corrupted in the damage."

She stayed as low as she could and grimaced at the reality that her body still ached from the damage it had taken. The fighting had moved away from her for now, but stray bullets and pieces of shrapnel from explosives as well as the massive hammer were a reason for caution. It meant that if she stood, she was likely to be caught and killed accidentally by a stray projectile. She began to remove the rubble from Mini's arms.

While it was slow work, it was better than waiting for something bad to come their way.

Jessica13 looked up when more explosives detonated around them and made it difficult to focus on her work. A handful of the pirate Lancers remained and attempted to slow the Knights, while the remainder looked like they were beating a hasty retreat. They'd obviously had way more reinforcements than she had first noticed, and she assumed they had been lurking in the nearby buildings or had been close by.

With a mech that stood thirty feet tall and swung a hammer that could flatten them with one stroke, she really couldn't blame them for choosing flight over fight.

But they'd return when the coast was clear, and she wouldn't leave Mini behind to be scavenged.

"They retreat but do not surrender!" Hammerhand boomed to the Knights who fought beside him. "Like roaches, they pull back to strengthen themselves and then try to rise again. It is our duty, my Knights, to crush each and every one of them until they realize there is still honor to be found in these wild lands!"

The other Knights raised their weapons and cheered. Jessica13 couldn't help but feel inspired herself by the words. While his terminology did feel a little antiquated, the spirit behind it was something that couldn't be ignored. It was as if he was a physical embodiment of what it was to be a member of the Knights Mechanica.

And there was also the fact that the man piloted a mech that could literally crush the pirates like the roaches and pests they were. He didn't even need the hammer for that, although it did help a great deal. She thought he could probably lift a boot and stamp them to death if he didn't feel like swinging the weapon.

The other Knights gathered again and the pirates huddled nearby, mostly piloting Lancers that were barely held together and in a condition much worse than those she had seen before.

Maybe the few that had followed the Balthazar were an elite unit and those who remained were only the grunts who had managed to piece something together that could only barely be classified as mechs.

Stupidly, they seemed to believe they had an advantage since they had the greater numbers and charged forward, shooting and spinning their chain swords as they advanced.

Hammerhand was, predictably, at the front of his troop. He raised his hammer in the air like some kind of symbol to the rest of his fighters to stand by him, come hell or high water. Suddenly, the rocket on the other end of the weapon activated and launched it into an arc that made landfall hard enough to shake the ground to the point that Jessica13 wasn't sure how the buildings didn't collapse.

She covered her head when a few pieces of debris plummeted but thankfully, that was all. The blow had struck close to the pirates, though, and made a couple of them stumble and fall.

"It's probably only bad hydraulics," she said, more to herself than her AI.

"It is interesting to note that the impact of the hammer with the ground causes a seismic event that registers at 2.3 on the Richter scale," Mini told her as she continued her work to clear the rubble.

She had no idea what a Richter scale was but she assumed it was impressive. "All I know is that I wouldn't trade places with those pirates for all the best mechs in all the world."

CHAPTER SEVENTEEN

As much as Jessica13 wanted to continue to free the Minato from under the rubble, it was almost impossible not to watch the battle as it unfolded. Despite the fact that she knew flesh and blood piloted the mechs, something like awe came over her.

She'd heard of the Knights before, of course. Peddlers had told tales of watching them fight and said it was reminiscent of watching the battles when the planet was how it used to be.

Damned if they weren't right, although she wasn't sure how they would know about how battles were conducted in the past.

The earth shuddered every time the Excalibur touched down and it advanced on the pirates who were, for some reason, pushing into the attack rather than running the hell away.

Jessica13 looked at the top of one of the buildings when she caught the movement of three individual mechs that seemed to be attempting to find a position from which to strike from the flank—or maybe an angle that would allow them to fire at the massive mech on the ground without being hit themselves. The chances were that one blow would be all Hammerhand needed anyway.

A Cinder and a couple of Lancers jumped from their position on the building and abandoned the high ground in favor of a surprise attack.

Hammerhand looked up, saw them approach, and raised his left hand. He held something large and square-shaped in the massive fingers.

A loud crack preceded the sudden smell of ozone as a blue layer, almost a film, emerged from the square contraption and expanded into the area around it to form a rectangle that almost matched the size of the mech that held it.

The device looked like a shield, and when the two lancers bounced off it like they had been electrically repelled, she realized that it was exactly that. Maybe he activated it now because it was necessary but otherwise, it took too much power to maintain it constantly.

The Cinder was quicker than the other two but could not alter its trajectory to avoid the barrier that prevented it from delivering anything even remotely like an effective attack. The mech tried to move away while it was still in the air but there was nothing it could do other than brace for impact and use it to slow its descent.

It landed clumsily but still on its two feet and mostly intact, although the experience was likely uncomfortable for the man inside. A couple of joints had loosened when it jarred against the ground and it would need more than a few repairs.

The Lancers were not so lucky and fell heavily on their backs.

They probably didn't have any inertia dampeners installed,

and from the way they remained where they had fallen, the pilots were either dead or severely injured.

Jessica13 tried to think of some form of commiseration, but all she could think was good riddance. Shitty pirates weren't good for much else—not for building mechs and definitely not for helping people.

The Cinder activated both its main weapons and aimed the shotgun at the Excalibur first. It fired a sheet of flechettes that either pinged off the thick armor or simply embedded themselves into it with no damage. It was a distraction, meant to hide the use of the flame-thrower that snuck in beneath in the hopes that it would find something that wouldn't be resistant to a tongue of plasma.

It didn't work out quite the way the pirate had hoped as the shield thumped down quickly, caught the pirate's flame-throwing arm, and pinned it roughly to the ground.

The head of the Cinder pivoted to look up and a hand raised to try to block the deadly hammer.

Jessica13 doubted that he would have survived even if the rocket in the back of the hammer hadn't suddenly activated. This provided all the speed it needed to pound the Cinder flat with a loud yet somehow anti-climactic boom.

Hammerhand lifted his hammer and flicked it to the side to remove any bits and pieces from the mech it had crushed that might have adhered to the surface of the weapon before he turned to face the remaining pirates.

It was difficult to tell if there was any reaction from those involved in the attack at seeing their comrade turned into paste, but they didn't falter in their attack. Maybe they hoped they could use the distraction to their benefit, or something equally stupid. She wasn't sure how they could think that as none of the others appeared to have any luck.

It only took one, though.

A couple of Lancers managed to skirt the shield before it swung toward them and attempted to flank the larger mech, only to be reminded that Hammerhand was not alone. The Watson and Sherlock team were quick to intervene. The pilot of the Sherlock attacked with his chain sword and a shower of sparks followed the weapon.

The cockpits of both Lancers were hacked open, which left the pilots exposed and the Watson moved in and quickly fired a few of the filaments with an electrical charge. While the armor would have normally absorbed that kind of attack, without anything between them and the projectiles, the pilots writhed and screamed while the electricity coursed through their bodies.

It would most likely kill them since it was intended as the kind of charge that would disable the isolated electronics in the mechs they attacked.

The pirates continued the assault, however, and a horde of them charged forward once they realized that ranged attacks wouldn't do much against the shield Hammerhand had activated. They had apparently decided to close the distance and overwhelm their adversaries.

The shield suddenly deactivated. Jessica13 wasn't sure why she'd thought the rounds fired by the Knights would go through the shield when those from the pirates wouldn't, but the thought was quickly banished. The line of pirates was thrust back by a flurry of rounds from the Sherlock. There weren't too many bullets but their effectiveness in piercing the half-assed armor the pirates used was telling.

Each round was targeted into cockpits of the Lancers, and the armor-cutters sliced through them easily. Jessica13 had seen the effects of the ordnance. Not in person, but the informative vids they'd been given explained that the cutters would create considerable shrapnel once they were inside the cockpit.

Five Lancers collapsed as their pilots were shredded and they were suddenly left without input. If they couldn't get functional armor, they wouldn't have AIs that operated the suits if the pilots were rendered unable to do so.

Jessica13 was suddenly incredibly thankful to have Mini on her side. The AI had certainly been what kept her alive through her time Outside. The thought reminded her that she had left her still buried under rubble while she watched the battle.

"Sorry, Mini," she said and once again turned her efforts to the chunks of building materials that pinned Mini's right arm down. "How's the suit working? Can you operate any repairs from in there?"

"The electronics are still in diagnostics," the AI replied. "A few functions are still intact."

"How about your right arm?" Jessica13 asked as she dragged the last few pieces of debris from the arm in question. If she could get some of the mechanics working again, maybe the mech would help to clear the rubble.

"Nothing."

She leaned in a little closer and pulled away a little more rubble to reveal a few dented armor plates. Deftly, she peeled the plates up slightly to reveal the issue. Mini would be able to send the electrical impulses to the hydraulics but most of the signal was blocked as the dented armor had cut through the isolation and pressed directly on the wire.

Jessica13 cut off the power to that section of the suit and after she'd applied isolation tape and hammered out the dent in the armor, she reassembled it again.

"How about now?" she asked and patted her work.

With a soft whir, the fingers of the Minato wiggled before it bent slowly at the elbow, which forced her back a step.

"You're a genius," Mini said. "Warning: I cannot see what I'm doing and therefore would not be able to move without help from you."

"Don't worry about that. I can be your eyes," she said and patted the chest plate reassuringly.

Out of the corner of her eye, she caught sight of a couple more mechs that approached from behind the Knights. A moment of panic surged and she jerked up. How had the pirates managed to circle the Knights? Had they called someone else in to help them in their attack?

It took a moment before she realized these Lancers were in significantly better shape than those the pirates had manned. Even those that had accompanied the Balthazar had been assembled with lesser-quality pieces, likely those that had looked the flashiest and would have appealed to the eye of someone who didn't know what they were doing.

In fact, the pirates both she and the Knights had faced had nothing near the quality she had seen in the mechs that had attacked Sanctuary, she recalled, and were much, much worse than those that now marched up behind the Knights. These appeared to almost be in perfect factory condition, although the mismatched colors and shapes told her they were created from three or four different Lancer models.

The other distinguishing feature was the fact that they were all painted the same brilliant green Hammerhand's was and a couple of the banners hung from their pauldrons.

It took a moment before Jessica13 realized that the new arrivals weren't there to reinforce the attack on the pirates. The assault proceeded as a spearhead pushed forward by

Hammerhand's Excalibur, which was supported by the Sherlock and Watson. These three held the line in an orchestrated and measured maneuver. The Excalibur alternated between a thrust of its shield before it deactivated it, followed by a swing of the hammer to demolish any that were still in range. At the same time, the Sherlock picked off those that tried to out-flank him with precise shots and a little support from the Watson.

The new Lancers weren't there to support them, although they did fire intermittently whenever the Excalibur's shield was down. It seemed, however, that they were in place to protect and support another almost impossibly large mech.

It was still smaller than the one that maintained the front of the line, and it appeared to be far less mobile as well.

The Raptor/Sargossa was hunched over, mostly top-heavy. It stood at eighteen feet tall and looked like what she had seen labeled as an ostrich in the instructional vids. It settled in place and braced itself as the two rocket launchers on its back came up into firing position.

"I can't explain why it intrigues me, but I want to have a look at that," Jessica13 said aloud. "To see how it works."

"What are you referring to?" Mini asked and still moved his free arm around blindly.

"Oh, right, sorry," she replied and scrambled to the other side of the mech to help get the camera feeds back online while she attempted to also keep an eye on what was happening on the battlefield. The Excalibur had settled into something of a rhythm, one the pirates hadn't been able to circle effectively for a flank attack. Now, however, they pressed in and seemed to have something planned. The way they positioned themselves suggested they were getting ready to try something.

Pirate mechs had somehow appeared to supplement the numbers and almost three dozen were now gathered there, she realized. Again, she could only assume that they had made their way to the battlefield under the cover provided by the derelict buildings. From what she could judge with her limited experience, they seemed geared to make a push and would probably time it for the moment when the shield was dropped and before the hammer completed its swing.

The Knights were communicating, however. That much was obvious as the Raptor settled into its firing position and waited for its opportunity to strike. She had no idea what they planned but the unfolding drama was engaging enough to keep her riveted lest she miss any of the action.

Hammerhand coordinated the attack, that much was clear, and Jessica13 couldn't help but want to be in on that conversation.

The signal was given, apparently, as the flaps that covered the rocket launchers were yanked up and the Raptor pivoted to face where the fighting was at its hottest. As she had expected, the pirates waited for the opening between the shield deactivating and the hammer blow and the anticipated moment came in a few seconds. Ten of the enemy Lancers activated what looked like rockets on their backs to thrust them forward.

The rockets fired from the Raptor and pale white smoke trailed behind them, but they hadn't targeted the enemy directly. Instead, they arced upward into the shell of a building above them. The explosives detonated and destroyed the supports, and a large section of the building broke free and plunged earthward.

The shield dropped and Hammerhand was open to the Lancers that immediately attacked. Only those who brought up the rear looked up in time to see the chunk of masonry that plummeted toward them.

One darted through safely but fell quickly when the Sherlock fired a single precise round. Three more were caught under the falling rubble although they raised their hands and stumbled frantically in an effort to avoid the inevitable.

Those that remained, perhaps eight or nine, were able to deactivate their rockets and come to a halt before the building collapsed on them.

Their heads jerked as they looked around them and it was evident that panic had begun to gain the upper hand once more as they tried to pull back again. In their haste and confusion, they milled frantically and tried to avoid one another but remained closely bunched as a perfect target. The rocket behind the hammer lit up while some were quickly eliminated by the Sherlock's pinpoint shots.

More rockets were fired into the pirate group by the Knight's lancers to drive them back farther while their ranks were decimated by the ongoing assault. The Excalibur no longer actively fought but Hammerhand gestured for them to maintain the barrage. The idea seemed to be to continue the relentless attack until there were none left to retreat.

This was a battle waged by a team that had fought together for a long time, and while Jessica13 had seen some spoken coordination, they appeared to already know what Hammerhand would order. It was as if they were prepared in advance to initiate whatever tactic or maneuver he had in mind before he even called it.

For her, it was breathtaking, the kind of thing she had always wanted to see in her team in Sanctuary although she was unaware of what her dissatisfaction had really meant until this moment.

Hammerhand deactivated his hammer and placed it on the rubble in front of him. The servos whined and the vents opened to release steam into the air. She wondered if that was a cooling mechanism for the mech. Something that big had to generate considerable heat.

As the steam hissed out, it almost made it look like the mech had huge, fluffy white wings.

"And so, the chaff was broken from the wheat," Hammerhand intoned through the powerful external speakers on the Excalibur. "Lifted, crushed, and removed by the fist of God."

She had no idea what he made reference to, but it was impossible not to feel awe when she heard it. Maybe it was an effect of the speakers or merely because what he said made no sense, but she simply wasn't able to understand it. It reminded her of most of what she had been told about the Great Prophet Sagan.

Jessica13 then realized that another mech now moved toward her. She hadn't seen anything quite like it before. A few parts of a Watson protruded from what had originally been a General Robotics Mark II chassis and it even had an older version of the grappler she had on her Minato.

It was hard to not like the way the mech walked, though. The smooth motions showed that while it had been put together with various pieces, it had been done with the kind of thought and presence of mind to make sure the modifications improved the mech.

There was no green paint and no banners on the pauldrons, unlike the others, but it didn't look like a pirate mech.

Sure enough, as it approached, the headpiece on the cockpit—which made the mech look like it had a small head—popped up and an actual head emerged from the top.

She wasn't sure what she'd expected, but a thick bushy

beard was not what she'd had in mind. Most people who spent time in mechs didn't have beards because of filtering problems.

They certainly didn't live long enough for their beards to turn grey as this man's had. He was otherwise bald except for a pair of bushy eyebrows that framed what looked like a smaller and kinder face than she was used to seeing Outside.

"Hello there, small one," the man said in a rough accent that she found hard to understand. "In something of a bind there, are we? Well, I'll tell you something, I learned that there lesson the hard way too. I was strolling about during the battle, trying to collect some pieces I needed for me baby here, and ended up on the ground when they dropped a building on me. It took them two days to dig me out, and you'd better believe I cussed at them over the radio the whole fucking time, too. They don't leave the Tinker behind, buried under rubble."

"The tinker?" she asked.

"Oh, yes, that's my name, see?" the man replied with a small grin. "Well, not really my name, but I done forgot my real one, so everyone calls me Tinker. Even me, sometimes."

"I can see that," she replied.

"What's your name, little one?" he asked and took a tentative step closer as if he didn't want to scare her but also wanted her to feel welcome.

"Jessica," she said, a little out of her depth but determined not to let it show. "Jessica13."

"Jessica13. That's an odd name," he commented, his tone curious rather than insulting.

"So is Tinker, but you didn't hear me complain," she snapped in response but good-naturedly. She could see he saw it that way as well and he laughed at her words.

"Well, you have some spark in you, make no mistake." He rumbled another laugh. "And sure I am that's required for surviving out here in the wild, so it's always nice to hear and watch. But in all seriousness, only one group of folks are the kind who put numbers at the end of names. The kind of folks who like to keep track of how many people have the same name."

She nodded and stepped forward. "I'm from one of the bunkers. One out to the east of here, about a hundred klicks, called Sanctuary. I had to leave and go out on my own."

"Well, don't think we judge the folk who come from the bunkers," Tinker assured her and raised the hands of his mech defensively. "Or the ones who chose to stay. The folks around here, pirates and the like, tend to call you bunker rats or something of the sort. Very derogatory is what I say."

She nodded. "The pirates called me something like that. Well, the one who rode the Balthazar you're currently standing on."

"I don't much like them that hate on folks who know how to survive, no matter the manner, especially when it comes with a society," he said. He took a moment to realize that he was, in fact, standing on the mech that had been flattened by the Excalibur's hammer. "Well, I'll be fucked. Hammerhand does like to make him an entrance, but don't think there'll be much to salvage from a mess like this. It's best when they're shot up or blown up. Well, no, best is shot like Carson does in there. Punches one right into the cockpit, kills the pilot, and leaves the mech intact and wide open for scrapping."

"Carson," she said and looked around. "Is that the one in the Sherlock?"

"You've a good eye for the models, little one." He glanced to where the other Knights had begun to take the fallen mechs apart. "Yeah, Carson's riding that Sherlock. He's a shit pilot, between you and me, but he has one hell of a shooting eye and knows how to choose the target to shoot, so I'll never tell him that to his face. It's good for him to have Taylor riding next to him in the Watson—keeps them all alive. They've fought together since before they joined the Knights Mechanica so they know what they're doing. Again, I won't ever say that to their faces."

"Are you a member of the Knights Mechanica?" Jessica13 asked and returned to her efforts to remove the rubble from Mini. "I mean no disrespect, of course—keep working on what's around the legs, Mini, and I'll get the other arm free— but you don't look quite like the rest of them."

"You mean I don't coat my baby in cheap green paint and put little flags on her?" Tinker asked and raised an eyebrow. "Well, if you knew what they used to make that paint, you wouldn't want it on your…I'm thinking a Minato? They hard to find these days, honestly."

"You have a good eye too," she noted.

"Well, yes, but that's because I play the most important role in the Knight's Mechanica." Tinker moved closer and dragged a couple of the larger pieces of rubble away. "It's right there in the name. I'm the Mechanic-a. I work all these mechs to their full potential, get them all roaring and humming and ready for a fight when they need to be. D'ya think these assholes could keep their own pieces running without me?"

"Fuck you, Tinker!" the pilot of the Raptor shouted, having listened to what they had discussed.

"Yeah, I'll remember that when it's the next time to oil your joints there, Bessie," the man yelled in response. Jessica13 couldn't tell if Bessie could hear him but the lack of any kind of response suggested that either she hadn't or she knew she needed him to keep doing good work on her mech.

"If you get you a big fucker that needs to bend over to fire off, you need a better grease feed into the joints or they gonna burn right the hell off," he said and shook his head. "I like the thought behind the design but that's lazy finishing."

"It seems like something that top-heavy wouldn't have a good way to get the oil all the way down to the legs," she said as she freed the Minato's left hand and checked the electronics. "You'd need to put something near the ankles. It helps to give it some ballast against falling over on its side, and with the grease box on the bottom, it'll be simpler to pump it up to the rest of the mechanism. You'd need to refill it twice as much, of course, but it's better than doing it manually."

Tinker eyed her for a few seconds as she adjusted the electronics that allowed Mini access to the limb again before she shifted her position to work on the legs.

"You really have a mind for this," Tinker said. "Of course, it's not that easy to find the right kind of grease boxes. I would have to build it almost from scratch and maybe integrate it into the foot."

Jessica13 looked up from her work and wiped the sweat from her forehead. "Sure, but you need to give it some kind of mechanism to pump the stuff into the joints above."

It was an odd thing, she suddenly realized. She was talking about mechs and how to improve them to an almost complete stranger. It should have felt weird but it didn't. Having someone of like mind to share the conversation was interestingly relaxing. She could feel the terrifying sensation of almost being killed slipping away.

The feeling was still there and would likely be a part of her life, but it was a lesson learned. The negatives of it had begun to fade.

With Tinker's help, she soon finished clearing the rubble from around Mini. The AI still couldn't see anything but the stabilizers were working again, which enabled him to stand the Mech on its feet and she climbed inside and took control.

"There we go, good as new," Tinker said with a chuckle. "Well, we have to think about getting you a new plate for the front of the cockpit, anyway, and then you should be good as new."

"I don't suppose we'll find anything good on the mechs around here," Jessica13 complained as she moved clear of the demolished building and out to the road again. "There aren't many Minatos up and running around here, so I'll need to figure something out to fix it."

"Don't worry about it none, Jessica13," he replied and walked beside her. "The chances are there are more than enough Minato pieces in the scrap yards and if not, we'll find something that was an upgrade on what you had before. For the moment, though, I think the big fella wants to have a word with ya."

There was no point in asking why he thought that as she could see Hammerhand striding to where the two of them now stood. Even in the Minato, she could feel the impact of the steps on the ground like it was a minor earthquake each time. It was irritating to the point where she began to struggle to remain on her feet before he came to a halt in front of them.

He remained in place for a few seconds and looked at her. The size of the mech was impossible and she knew for a fact that something so big would never fit inside the elevator at Sanctuary.

"Your bravery will not be forgotten," Hammerhand said, his voice a little quieter and less booming than before. "Standing your ground before insurmountable odds is not something to be discarded from the mind."

She inclined her head and tried to analyze his speech. His accent was a little easier to understand than Tinker's but there were a few odd word placements and inflections that ticked her off for some reason.

Not that she would mention it to the pilot of a mech that could stamp her to paste with one foot.

"Honestly, I didn't so much stand my ground as run away," Jessica13 admitted. "You arrived a little late, but by the time I stood my ground, I really didn't have anywhere else to go."

"I saw everything, child," Hammerhand replied. "How you stood your ground when you could, fought back when you could, and remained brave in the face of what must have appeared to be the very end. To my mind, that is bravery."

"Oh…well, thanks," she said and her face heated in response to the praise.

He'd seen everything? She hoped not. He would have seen how she careened into the building that had buried her under it. Or worse, he would have seen how they drew the pirates on them when they were trying to be stealthy.

Either way, if his conclusion was that she was brave and not stupid, she would leave it at that.

"You spoke of others who might need our help," he continued.

"Oh, right," Jessica13 said. "I almost—well, there's a bunker to the east, a little closer than the one I'm originally from, but…anyway, they were hit hard by a group of pirates that attacked my bunker first. They're well-armed, well-led, and have considerable firepower behind them. We barely survived the attack, but the other bunker wasn't so lucky. There were survivors and they are starting to rebuild, but they need protection while they set their defenses up again. I was asked to come and see if…well, the Knights Mechanica could help."

She had worded it as officially and eloquently as possible but by the end, she began to feel she had rambled on. Hammerhand looked at her after a moment of silence.

Had she worded it wrong? Had he expected her request for help with some kind of pomp and ceremony? In neglecting that, had she somehow offended him?

The questions buzzed around her brain like insects, unwilling to be controlled as the seconds ticked by.

Finally, the enormous mech turned to face the other Knights.

"Then we shall go!" Hammerhand roared and his speakers boomed again to the point that she could almost feel his voice in her bones. "Our hands to those who need them! Our weapons to defend those who cannot defend themselves!"

The other knights raised their weapons and cheered.

Tinker nudged Mini in the side with his hand and almost knocked him over. Alarms blared over the stabilizers, but his intention was clear enough.

"Mr. Hammerhand," Jessica13 called and the Excalibur stopped and turned to face her again. "Hammerhand? Hammer?"

"Hammerhand is fine," he replied in a quieter tone.

"Hammerhand it is," she said with a nervous chuckle. "As you can see, my mech is in need of repairs, and—well, it seems a little wasteful to see all these mechs around here and simply leave them to whatever vultures might come to collect them. I thought we could probably…uh, maybe…scavenge them ourselves before we go to the bunker?"

There was no response for a moment but then the large shoulders began to rock alarmingly. When he shook his head, she realized he was laughing.

"Welcome to the Knights Mechanica, my girl," Hammerhand said finally and chuckled. "I think you'll fit right in."

The massive mech moved away, and Jessica13 wasn't sure what to make of his statement until Tinker nudged her in the shoulder again.

"I think the big man likes you," he said and laughed.

"Is that what that was supposed to be?" she asked. "I thought he made fun of me."

"We don't leave anything for the pirates to take again," Tinker said. He glanced at the crushed Balthazar and nudged it with his boot. "Nothing they can use, anyway. Anything useful is collected and carried to where I can put it to good use in one of the other mechs. It was my and Hammerhand's idea to set things up that way, and you have the same spirit of a scavenger in you. Like the big man said, you'll fit in right with the Knights Mechanica."

It was quick work to scavenge most of the mechs. A good portion of them had been reduced to little more than scrap metal after Hammerhand had destroyed them with his hammer, but those that had been eliminated by the other mechs were still in good enough shape.

Once she had the parts she needed, Jessica13 retrieved her tools from the Minato and laid it on the ground since she didn't have the harness to hang it while she worked. She used a pair of cutters to peel away the sections of metal she wouldn't be able to use in that position anymore.

Even so, she hated to waste anything. The chunks were shoved in a bag she could fit on the back of the Minato and kept going without so much as a pause.

Tinker watched her work as she began to install the new front panel in place of the one that had been torn off. As she continued to fit the new piece, a few of the other Knights moved in closer as well and tried to get a good grasp of what she was up to.

Most talked on the private comms she wasn't privy to, but as they leaned in closer, she wondered if they hadn't seen Tinker work this way before.

The panel fit rather well and only required a few minor cuts and adjustments to settle into the place she had created for it. While it wasn't a pretty fit, she had already decided she would have to get used to something like that since she was Outside now. It seemed logical that she would have to accept that her mech wasn't as nice and clean as she was accustomed to.

"Nice work on that panel," Tinker said once she had finished fixing it in place. "How do you think you'll see through it, though?"

"There isn't a problem with that," Jessica13 said and patted her finished work before she pulled a few of the armor sections up from the panel itself. "I only need to fit it with the sensors in the Minato. That, plus the ones I need to fix on the head section, means I'll be able to settle in there with a full view. They didn't design these with see-through panels. They were always meant to work with full armor and visuals provided through sensors on the outside."

The wiring was jumbled near the head of the mech and she began to sort through the issues manually.

"Why would they make a mech you couldn't see out of?" the Knight riding the Watson—Taylor was his name if she remembered correctly—asked. "What if the sensors go down and you can't see anything at all?"

"Minatos were fitted with AIs originally to resolve that," Jessica13 said. "They were finicky bastards, every one, but you can work the sensors without the AI. If you do have one in, though, you get to see why they didn't want panels with a weaker structure on the front."

"It's when you go down on all fours, yeah?" Carson, the pilot of the Sherlock, said, likely having watched her run from the pirates like Hammerhand had.

"That's right," she replied, finished her work with the sensors, and set them to a timed restart to bring all the systems up again. "When you run on all fours, you don't want to have the underside of the mech weaker in case something catches the bottom and breaks it. It's best to have the whole thing as structurally sound as possible."

"Agreed," Tinker said. "Though I'd still rather have a way to see something with my eyes out there than have to rely on machines."

"We already rely on machines," Jessica13 pointed out and patted Mini's hull. "Do you think you can get up now?"

"What's that?" he asked.

"I wasn't talking to you," she responded and after a few seconds, her mech began to move on its own and managed to climb slowly onto his feet and settle without issue.

"Repairs are…adequate," Mini said through the external speakers. "Running diagnostics now in case you missed something."

"It's odd to let your AI talk back at you like that," Tinker told her as she pulled the door open and climbed into the cockpit. "I'm lucky if I can get me three or four words out of the one running mine. Not that it runs much."

"Like I said, the Shimura-Sendai manufacturers designed their AIs to be finicky and, I think, as close to human brain processing as possible," Jessica13 explained and studied all the diagnostics Mini ran through her HUD. "It's absolutely worth the effort, though, once you do get them functional."

"Your compliment is noted and appreciated," Mini replied.

"Enough dallying!" Hammerhand roared at them. "Those who need our help will not wait, nor will those who wish them harm!"

"Ready to move, Jessica13?" Tinker asked.

"Affirmative." Mini answered the question and completed the diagnostics.

"Let's move," she agreed.

CHAPTER EIGHTEEN

The day had begun to wind down by the time the mechs were ready to move. None were quite as fleet of foot as Jessica13's Minato but she lacked the kind of firepower they had.

Whether they had killed most of the pirates in the battle or whether those who survived knew better didn't matter. The fact remained that as the group moved through the city, they were left unhindered.

"Do you think the pirates will try to attack us again?" Jessica13 asked Tinker, who had opened a comm line with her.

"Well, you can't ever account for stupid," he replied with a chuckle. "But many of them only survived this long because they know who they can attack and who is best left alone. When an Excalibur wanders around the city with a mech-flattening hammer and flanked by a group like ours, those who know their way around the world stay away. Those who don't won't last very long anyway. The fun thing about natural selection is how brutal it can be in weeding out the weak."

"Natural selection?" she wondered.

"The evolution of animals," Mini interjected and displayed a couple of diagrams on the HUD. "Animals tend to evolve according to a fundamental premise that those with the best traits for survival in their current environment tend to pass those genes on to their progeny, whereas those that don't die or are killed off. Tinker's reference implies that those intelligent enough to stay clear of the Knights Mechanica are those who will survive long enough to pass that intelligence to their progeny."

"Oh." She frowned as she considered this. "How come this wasn't taught to us in the instructional vids?"

"It is possible that those in charge of running Sanctuary did not think of it as relevant to your education," the AI pointed out.

"You know, I can tell when you're still talking to your mech," the man interjected. "Even if you don't have your speakers on. Most folks don't really take small things into account like body language. If you shrug, tilt your head, and do anything, the mech moves too so it's like I can see a quarter of the conversation."

"Oh, I didn't mean to be rude," she said, still not sure what the etiquette between these knights was supposed to be. "It was only...it's a little embarrassing. The AI was explaining a part of what you said to me to give me context."

"Don't you worry about anything. We all have gaps in our knowledge," he reassured her. "Was it about the accounting for stupid?"

"No, I understood that part," Jessica13 said. "I've actually heard it before from my CO at the bunker. He liked to say it almost every time the pirates attacked us."

"You don't say?" The man grunted as if surprised. "Ah, well, it's good sense, I suppose. What was the part you needed help with?"

"It was mostly the 'natural selection,'" she explained. "But Mini already explained what he thought was the context you used it in."

"He?"

"Yes. They originally fitted him with a female voice modulator, and because the AI wasn't functional when they brought the mech to operation, they didn't think to fix it."

"I...huh." A pause followed, and she waited for his response. "Have you thought about whether you wanted to fix that?"

"What do you think, Mini?" Jessica13 asked. "Should we start looking through the scrap yard for a modulator that best fits your personality?"

"My personality is perfectly adapted to my current module," Mini replied. "I am finicky, as you said."

"No, I said that AIs can be finicky to get to working," she clarified. "And I'd say you're less finicky and more...sassy, I think the word is."

"Sassy. I like that," he said. "I suppose I will continue to be sassy with a new modulator. Therefore, if it makes you feel more comfortable, we can search for one."

"You're doing it again." Tinker laughed.

"Sorry," Jessica13 said. "We're discussing getting him a male modulator instead of the one he has now. He's a little iffy about it but doesn't mind if it would make me happy."

"Oh, well, it wasn't a complaint on my part. I only assumed the AI was...well, based on the voice..."

Tinker didn't appear to know where to go from there and she wondered if he was not used to having someone to talk to.

She could understand the sentiment. Machines and mechanical things talked to her in a way she couldn't get from other humans. She even got along better with an AI than she had with any other human she'd met. Maybe the man was the same way and that was why everyone called him Tinker instead of his real name.

"Well, it's not something we're really thinking about," she continued in an attempt to break the awkward silence with the older man. "It's something to talk about as we make our way to the bunker to see if we can help the people there."

"I can understand that." Tinker sounded a little relieved. "Priorities are important and all that. Hammerhand will likely keep us moving through the night to make sure we reach the bunker in time to help them. Although I guess you can move faster in that Minato. Tell me, does it operate with the Bulletfoot mode? Is that what the others were talking about when they said you moved on all fours?"

Jessica13 hadn't expected someone to know about the Bulletfoot mode. She hadn't found any reference to it in the manus she'd been able to get her hands on so it had surprised her when it happened the first time.

Then again, none of them had been about the Minato itself, so it made sense that she had missed much of the specific information. There was also the issue of her experience with mechs as a whole being limited to what was available to her in Sanctuary.

Still, it seemed odd that he would know something about her Minato that she hadn't known until recently.

"Yes," she answered finally. "There's an actual name for it, but the AI told me that people back in the day called it Bulletfoot mode. It seems like an odd name, but I get the feeling behind it. A support mech supposed to deliver bullets by foot is suddenly able to move quicker like it was shot out of a gun."

"It seems to work on two levels, that name," Tinker chuckled.

"It's odd, though, since our mechanics at the bunker were called bulletfoots too." She once again considered this, still no closer to a real explanation. "I haven't been able to find out if the mode came before the nickname or the nickname is what caused the mode."

"It will be one of those mysteries," Tinker replied as they pressed on. "Something to keep your mind busy on the boring nights. You'd be surprised how many of those there are out here."

He wasn't wrong. The team of mechs marched through the night and pushed through the same forests she had come through, but at a much slower pace. The Excalibur and the Raptor were the slowest of the group, of course, and both needed time to cool off every hour or so. Tinker had to exit his mech to put grease into the lower joints of the Raptor as well.

While having those mechs with them meant there wasn't much in the world that would fuck with them, it also meant they would travel for the whole night. They couldn't cut across the forest either as they had to stay on the paths where the less agile and mobile of the mechs were still able to move.

The Excalibur would probably be able to push through the forest, Jessica13 thought, but it would mean pushing trees and even felling them, and that would do all kinds of damage to the mech itself. It was far more sensible to simply stay on the road.

It had been a long day, and Jessica13 eventually curled in her cockpit, found a reasonably comfortable position, and turned control of the mech over to Mini so she could sleep for some of the night. There wasn't much movement, which meant it was far more restful than her previous night's sleep when Mini had moved them at high speed.

She had wanted to spend time looking at the stars for a few more hours first, but the deliberate movements of the mech quickly lulled her into a deep sleep.

It had actually been a long couple of days, and she couldn't ever remember sleeping quite so well.

Despite that, she still felt like she could use a couple more hours when she was dragged slowly from her dreams of fighting alongside the Knights Mechanica by a light flashing in her eyes.

She rubbed her eyes and took a deep breath. The memory of the dreams began to slip away as she stretched as well as she could inside the cockpit. There was a trace of pain in the back of her neck that would prove to be annoying later in the day, but all she could think was she was being alerted that they were under attack.

"What's the matter, Mini?" she asked around a massive yawn.

"There is nothing to be alarmed over," he said in his calm, feminine voice. "I didn't want to interrupt your sleep but I thought you would want to know that we will arrive at the bunker in a short while. Being awake for that is advisable, according to communication from Hammerhand."

"Wait, Hammerhand is communicating with you?" Jessica13 asked and looked around hastily to confirm there was actually an external comm link open.

"We were included in the Knights' group comm link during the evening, courtesy of Mr. Tinker," Mini replied.

She grunted. "That was nice of him. How far are we from the bunker?"

"About a klick and a half," Mini replied quickly, then paused. "How did you sleep?"

Jessica13 smiled. "It was the best sleep I've had in a long time, I won't lie. I'm a little stiff and sore in places, though."

"You might want to think about installing some kind of modification that would make sleeping in the mech a little more comfortable."

She nodded agreement and focused on the fact that the group hadn't slowed their pace. The sun had begun to rise in the distance and painted everything in a wide array of golden rays. If there was one thing she was sure of in her ever-changing circumstances, it was that she would never get tired of the many gorgeous sights that filled a world that was supposed to be desolate of all kinds of life and beauty.

Or, at least, that was the impression she had been left with before her first time Topside with Armstrong7.

She settled into the controls but let Mini retain them for a few seconds while she adjusted to her surroundings before she took over. The structure of the Bunker was now visible ahead in the road, almost impossible to miss as they approached the wide area that had been cleared around it.

Since she'd left, the road had been opened and it appeared that most of the mines had been removed to be repositioned when their defenses were set up again. There was no point in leaving them out for someone to step on accidentally when they worked to restore their security measures.

As they approached, Jessica13 realized that a handful of temporary living quarters had been erected outside the bunker, watched over by a group of mechs that assumed the responsibility of temporary security. They made use of what had once been their balloon tether station as a location to start rebuilding from.

The smoke no longer seeped from the bunker behind them, but the ground was still covered by a light dusting of ash that had settled from the pillar of smoke that remained a vivid memory in her mind. Hundreds of tracks crossed the ash, and most of them weren't large enough to be made by the mechs.

It meant the air was clean enough to breathe out there again, at least. They had likely run the venting mechanisms inside the bunker, but it would be a while before it was fully clear of the toxic fumes that had flowed through it.

Jessica13 wasn't sure what to expect when the mechs activated at the sign of intruders. They obviously expected an attack by the pirates and assumed they had returned for what couldn't be carried away the previous time.

She increased the speed of her gait to make sure she was at the front of the line when they approached the group of people who waited silently for them.

While they would probably note that these mechs were different from those that had attacked them, there was no guarantee that they were there to help. Caution was the sensible response.

As they moved closer, she realized that a large group of civilians stood outside the small buildings they had erected. It was larger than the group that she had seen before. Whether they had been trapped inside the bunker and rescued or if there had simply been other survivors who managed to escape during the attack, it didn't really matter to her.

She was happy to see that so many had survived the attack and had worried that most of them had been killed.

Hundreds of people began to emerge from the shelters.

The men, women, and children all looked a little tired and smeared with soot but were alive and well.

One of them raced away from the group and past the mechs that stood guard but were still a little unsure as to who these newcomers were. The child looked a little dirtier than the rest of them.

"That's Mini!" she shouted in an impressively loud voice. "That's Mini and Jessica13! They came back!"

It was Prissy, she realized suddenly, and warmth rushed through her along with gratitude that she'd managed to pull the girl up the elevator shaft while the bunker had still been filled with the noxious smoke. Thankfully, she remembered them, and the little girl's words immediately eased the tension in the faces around them. They smiled and laughed when the mother hurried to retrieve her daughter before she got hurt.

The little girl evaded her and rushed closer as the line of Knights came to a halt. None of them wanted to somehow injure the child who raced toward them.

Prissy all but bulldozed into her and wrapped her arms around Mini's right leg.

"I knew you'd come back, Mini," she said with a grin. "The others thought you wouldn't, but I knew."

"And we are happy to return, Priscilla," Mini replied. Jessica13 almost thought she could detect a hint of genuine warmth in the AI's voice. Of course, with the outside speakers still not working, the girl wasn't able to hear the response.

"I can't say we thought you were coming back," said a voice through the radio she'd installed.

"So I heard," she replied.

"We're glad you did, anyhow," the man said. Marcus, she thought his name was. "And glad to see you brought friends with you. Are these them? The Knights Mechanica, I mean?"

She was about to answer when the now-familiar shaking underfoot silenced her. Hammerhand stepped to the front of the group and approached the Guardian Marcus piloted.

"My name is Hammerhand and these are the Knights Mechanica," he bellowed over the external speakers. He spoke directly to the leader but it was meant for all of the survivors of the bunker to hear. "News of the attack on your bunker saddened us deeply, and we are here to make sure you are allowed to rebuild and restructure your home so you can live in peace as all are meant to do."

A low cheer issued from the people gathered around them, and Jessica13 couldn't help a small smile.

Marcus took a step forward. It was surreal how the Guardian—which she had for so long seen as the largest mech ever—compared against the sheer size and power that radiated from the Excalibur as it vented steam once more.

Tinker moved in beside her. It appeared as though Marcus and Hammerhand were speaking or exchanging greetings.

"I've been wondering," she said as he came closer and she connected with him on their private commlink. "How is it that he's able to cool something that large? He can't carry very much water and certainly not enough to keep the mech cool for longer periods of time."

"Actually, that's an interesting question I don't quite have all the answers to," the man replied and sounded excited to be able to discuss it. "I've looked into how it works, and from the way I've managed to piece it together, the Excalibur has about twenty different fusion reactors running each element of the mech individually. These are different reactors than what's in your mech or mine. A new kind of tech from the Cities-That-Were had those reactors made to produce supercooled carbon dioxide—or what was called dry ice back in the day. It warms and turns into the steam, you see, and that steam is cold enough to cool the mech off without causing any kind of corrosion. There might have been pressure issues early on, but that was solved with the vents."

Jessica13 listened to the man and a small smile played across her lips. He couldn't see it, of course, but she did appreciate that he had a great deal of passion for his work. It also seemed like he was glad to have someone he could share his knowledge with.

She knew the feeling, having watched as even fellow bulletfoots dreaded her verbal involvement. More than once, their eyes had glazed over when she began to talk on a topic she really, really cared about.

"So, how is the supercooled carbon dioxide produced by the reactors again?" she asked.

"I'm not sure, but it's made as a byproduct of the reactors, so while the mech is heating up, it cools itself off too," Tinker continued. "It's really an ingenious piece of technology. People kind of focus on the sheer size of it—and I can understand how that would happen because it is a monster—but that usually makes folks ignore the small things that make it much more special. Even Hammerhand sometimes. He gets tired of me talking about the fucking thing, and it's his mech."

"I know the feeling," she said with a laugh. "I would like to take a look at it. That one and the Raptor."

"Tinker?" a voice intruded on their conversation. It took Jessica13 a few moments to realize it was Hammerhand but without the booming voice.

"Right here, sir," her companion replied quickly.

"I need you to bring the Beast to see if we can't find a way to help them get the Bunker working once more," their leader said, his voice a sudden and uncharacteristic divergence from his usual cadence.

"Right away, boss," Tinker replied and spun away from her to hurry back the way they'd come. For the kind of mech it was, it moved surprisingly quickly.

"Is there anything I can do?" she asked Hammerhand.

"For now, we need to help these people get back into their bunker where they can set up their defenses," he replied. "Your technical skills would absolutely be appreciated."

"I'll get right on it." She joined the other Knights as they moved toward the civilians. Prissy had been dragged away from Mini's feet by the girl's mother, which enabled them to move again.

She realized the civilians had gathered along the road that had been cleared of ash and soot. They held armfuls of wildflowers collected from the forest and as the mechs marched past them, they cheered and threw the flowers at their feet.

It was a heart-warming sight and she couldn't help but smile as they passed. The group moved in closer to the bunker itself, where they immediately set up to help them not only to repair the bunker itself but modify their temporary living structures to be more effective.

The Watson was otherwise occupied, having settled on the ground. Taylor, the pilot, began to draw parts of the mech out in sections in an area that had been cleared of ash. It was immediately apparent that these compartments contained everything needed for a temporary medical location, and the wounded bunker folks or those who needed other medical help began to draw near for the assistance they needed.

She liked how the Knights seemed to be prepared for almost anything and ready to help in a variety of different ways. Plus, more was on its way from the sound of it, as Tinker had been sent off to find the Beast, whatever that was.

She scrambled out of her mech and strode to where some of the Knights worked to improve the temporary living areas. They appeared to be somewhat confused about the water filters. This had been one of her first jobs in mechanics and she knew it like the back of her hand.

It was quick and easy work and they would definitely need a few upgrades. She saw that condensers had been set up outside to collect water from the air, although they were what was usually used to collect water from the air inside the bunkers to avoid waste.

The system they'd created wasn't all that efficient but out in the open, there was likely enough water in the air to make up for it.

One of the women whom Jessica13 recognized as Prissy's mother came over to where she worked.

"Thank you so much," she said and sat beside her. She smiled at her little one who ran around Mini's legs. "The Knights Mechanica have really been a blessing in our time of need. A godsend, I think they usually called it in the Cities-That-Were."

"I'm not one of the Knights," she said. "I'm only a messenger."

"The Knights Mechanica need messengers too," the woman said with a small, tired smile. "And you're helping like one of them. That makes you one of them."

She opened her mouth to counter the statement but she wasn't sure why she would do so when she wanted to be a part of the Knights. It had been a decision she made almost without realizing it the night before. Why would she want to dispute it?

Her thoughts were interrupted when the Excalibur approached the entrance to the bunker where the Argonaut that had been there when she had arrived still remained to partially block the entrance. She once against felt a thrill of awe at its final act of courage and defiance to attempt to defend the people inside from the pirate attackers.

The trapdoor at the bottom of the body of the Excalibur opened and a man climbed out. It was Hammerhand, obviously, although he didn't quite align with how she had pictured him. A part of her had vaguely assumed he might have a thick bushy beard, but this wasn't the case. Like almost everyone who spent most of their time inside mechs, he was bald and clean-shaven and yet still a tall, powerful man with broad shoulders that bulged through his flight suit.

He held something in his hand and knelt in front of the Argonaut, lowered his head, and said a prayer for the man who had died within. After a few moments, he placed what looked like a gear from his own mech at the Argonaut's feet before he took a piece from the thigh's armor and tucked it into a pocket.

Jessica13 wandered over to where Taylor operated their improvised Med center while a handful of the other Knights moved to the Argonaut as well and followed Hammerhand's lead to kneel in front of it and place pieces near the mech before they took a piece from it.

"What are they doing?" she asked the man.

"Paying their respects to the fallen," Taylor explained. "A prayer, of course, and then a memory. It gives them something to take with them. You leave a part of yourself behind and take something with you. The last exchange of humanity, Hammerhand calls it."

"Do you think I should?" she asked.

"If you like," he replied as he applied bandages over a woman's burns. "No one will force you to but it's a good way to remember them and carry them with us."

She nodded and decided she would engage in the last exchange of humanity. It felt like the right thing to do, but only once she finished fixing the water filters.

CHAPTER NINETEEN

It felt impossible that she was back where she had started.

Returning to the mountain had been something she had dreaded during the past few days, but as they worked on restoring the bunker to full operation, it became more and more clear that they didn't have all the parts necessary to do it. Tinker returned with his Beast—which was called a Beast of Burden and was an improvised bandwagon that he used to carry all the parts he wanted. It was massive, almost the size of the Excalibur, and piled high with parts. Even so, they had nowhere near enough to accomplish what was necessary.

Given how she felt about the bunker she'd once called home, it was odder still that returning to Sanctuary had been her suggestion. They would have the parts that were required and from her recollection, they had many to spare too. Besides, from the kinds of parts that had been piled on the Beast, there was bound to be enough for them to trade for what they needed.

It was a good idea. Tinker and Hammerhand had both agreed and so had most of the Knights.

Then why did she feel so shitty about it?

The answer was simple and possibly entirely selfish. She didn't want to go back. Not after everything that happened.

"Do you think they got the message, boss?" Tinker asked.

"They heard us," Hammerhand replied across the comm-link. "They are trying to decide whether or not to let us in."

Jessica13 scanned their surroundings. They had found a way around the minefield and tried to hail the AI that would allow communication with those inside. If they were willing to trade with the Knights, someone would be sent up on the elevator and cables would be let down the cliffside that would allow them to climb up.

Either that or they would open the entrance on the lowest level on the other side of the mountain, but she hadn't ever seen them open that one in all the time she'd lived there. She had dreaded the dire circumstances that would make that necessary when she was inside but now, she couldn't help but feel a little foolish about her fears.

She took a deep breath and looked around again.

"You nervous?" Tinker asked and shuffled a little closer to her. "There's no need to be, you know. If they don't want to trade, we can head over to one of the other bunkers nearby."

"I don't think I'll be welcome there," she admitted. "I didn't part on the best of terms."

"I don't think they much like anyone leaving Sanctuary," he replied with a shrug that triggered a comically exaggerated reaction from his mech. "They tried to stop me from leaving when I did, but as long as you did it without killing anyone, they're not too sour about it. Of course, they're not happy about losing one of their own but they don't want someone who drags morale down to stick around. That's simply bad manners."

"Wait—you came from Sanctuary too?" Jessica13 asked. "How come you didn't say that before?"

He turned to look at her. "I must have. I feel like I talk so much, it's bound to come out eventually."

"When did you leave?"

"I can't rightly remember but it can't have been more than twenty, thirty years, though," he said. "Odd how time doesn't pass the same out here as it did in there. I'm not sure which one I prefer. Not too many people want to get out so they probably scrubbed my existence out of the books and started the replacement process."

She nodded and wondered if the same had been done for her position. Someone would have been brought up to replace her from one of the other levels, likely with mechanical knowledge. The exchanges between levels would have continued until it reached one of the less-vital stations. Finally, the process of replacing her would culminate when they found one of the waiting mothers with the right genetic conditions who were ready to reproduce.

It was a process that usually only occurred when someone inside died but maybe to the people inside, she had died.

"There's our answer," Hammerhand said and raised his hammer to guide their gazes to the top of the cliff where a handful of Guardian mechs lowered the cables to allow access to the Knights.

Only five lines descended, and it was quickly decided that Tinker, Hammerhand, Taylor, Carson, and Jessica13 would go up first. The leader's massive mech required the combined strength of the cables to hoist him upward, and the other four waited until the lines were free once again before they followed. The other Knights would either hold their positions or join them later. She could understand why they would want to allow as few of the newcomers up the cliff as possible.

Her chest pounded with every step she took closer to the home she had rejected. Mini was suspiciously silent on their return and she wasn't sure if it was because he had almost been "killed" when the Librarian tried to wipe his databanks or if he merely had nothing to say.

They reached the top, where a group of mechs waited for them, but none had assumed any kind of attack position. She recognized Armstrong7's Argonaut standing tall in front as well as a couple of Guardians, one piloted by Lance7. It was a greeting party, and from the look of the open elevator door behind them, it seemed more welcoming than intimidating.

"Hammerhand," Armstrong7 said an took a step forward. "It's been a while since I've seen that big ugly mount of yours, old man."

"I'll bet you were counting the days, my friend," the Knight leader replied and extended his right hand forward, closed in a fist. The Sanctuary OC tapped it with his own before they turned toward the elevator.

Jessica13 couldn't tell if they didn't recognize her or if they simply didn't care. Either way, it didn't really matter. She was far more intrigued by the fact that Hammerhand seemed to be on friendly terms with her erstwhile boss. Although she wracked her brain and sifted quickly through her memories, she couldn't recall a single moment where the CO had mentioned personally knowing the Knights Mechanica or their leader. For the life of her, she couldn't understand why the truth of the matter had been clouded and perhaps even deliberately obscured by the myths and legends that filtered through to the rank and file.

Not only that but for the first time as far as she could

recall, traders were actually invited into Sanctuary. This seemed entirely contradictory, and she could only assume that the CO was, in fact, well aware of who and what they were—to the point where they were given an open invitation. She wondered how in hell they would explain that to all the folks who suddenly saw one of the most basic rules being broken. It honestly made no sense at all.

Once they were inside, Tinker moved to where Armstrong7 stood and nudged him in the shoulder the same way that he had with her, although the Argonaut was nowhere near as affected as her mech had been.

"Xander, you son of a bitch, is that you?" the CO asked and turned his mech to face the man.

"Hah, I thought you wouldn't recognize me in this little fucker." Tinker laughed. "How the hell have you been, Armstrong7? Do people still call you Xander?"

"From time to time, yes," he said with a chuckle. "Not nearly as much as you did, though. How did you end up with Jessie over here?"

Her ears perked up when she heard her nickname mentioned. There had been no indication that they recognized her, but who else would wander Outside in a Minato?

Tinker leaned over and nudged her shoulder. "She came into the City-That-Was trying to help the bunker we mentioned in the message. And, mind you, tangled with a few bad eggs while there and killed a handful of them too before we had to step in and teach them a lesson."

"How did you—" Armstrong7 turned to her. "How did you get that right? Installed new weapons on the Minato, did we?"

She was almost stunned that they acted like she hadn't even left. While she appreciated the fact that she hadn't been tossed out, she hadn't expected them to react like nothing had happened.

"I...well..." she started, stopped, and tried again. "We were in a scrapyard. There were weapons that could be used around us so I improvised. It didn't work out great since I still needed to be rescued."

"Well, that's why you don't fight combat mechs with a support mech but hey, that's still better than what most would have been able to do," he replied.

"It was mostly the work of the AI but I guess I did contribute a little."

Tinker laughed again as they continued to descend until they reached the hangar. Reeling from the apparent contradictions and feeling way out of her depth, she simply remained silent and hoped something would be said to clear up her confusion.

It was all so familiar and yet, as she stepped inside, it seemed that what had once been home was now utterly strange. She looked at the lines and lines of mechs set up on their harnesses while the bulletfoots she had worked with for years labored studiously on those they were supposed to fix, upgrade or clean. The scene was vividly familiar but it was still somehow foreign.

She acknowledged with both a sense of relief and a slight pang of regret that she wasn't a part of this world anymore.

When they saw the foreign mechs approach across the causeway, the workers began to pull away, a little nervous of the newcomers. More than one astonished glance flashed over the visitors and it was obvious that they had no idea what to make of this unprecedented bending of the rules. They didn't run, though, as the Sanctuary mechs remained close and escorted them through until they could find harnesses for the new mechs.

They didn't bother trying to find one for Hammerhand, though, and he simply deactivated his Excalibur and climbed out.

The bulletfoots and other mech pilots still regarded the newcomers with suspicion but seemed to have adopted the stay away approach. She understood the feeling and knew it wouldn't pass. There was a mistrust of anything from the Outside embedded in them, and from what she remembered of her own education, she couldn't blame them.

No explanation was given as to who the newcomers were, which certainly didn't help. It seemed that even now, with an obvious opportunity to present the truth, the status quo would be perpetuated and the Knights Mechanica would remain mere legend. She'd been present on a few occasions when a caravan had been allowed access to the plateau but they didn't arrive often and it was usually peddlers. While she'd heard that other bunkers had sent a trade deputation, she'd never seen it herself.

Little wonder then that her erstwhile colleagues felt uneasy and discomforted by the arrival of these unusual visitors. She could already imagine the CO's brusque explanation —probably that they came from another bunker and he knew them personally, which was little more than a partial truth— in the tone that precluded argument. Perhaps that was why he hadn't introduced them or mentioned the Knights Mechanica. He could simply pretend they were someone else.

The Knights dismounted and moved to Armstrong7, who had exited his mech as well and now headed toward his office.

"I can't guarantee that the admins will be willing to trade the parts," the man said and shook his head. "But we do need those you mentioned. The reactors especially—we're running low on those for the filtering systems. I'll put in a good word for you and maybe, just maybe, we'll be able to arrange a trade. You can wait here while I work on that."

Hammerhand nodded. "Your assistance in this matter is appreciated."

"There's not much I wouldn't do for you, old friend." The CO patted the taller, leaner man on the shoulder. "In the meantime, I think you could all use work on your mechs. Let our bulletfoots know if you need anything. I'm sure they'll be glad to help."

"They won't," Jessica13 said under her breath.

She wasn't sure if he heard her but returned to the Minato without waiting to find out.

The negotiations, as it turned out, dragged on almost interminably, which allowed her the time she needed to work on Mini. There were a few improvements she had planned and with help from Tinker, she was able to retrieve a few legs the man had recommended from his hoard.

"Why are you giving the girl chicken legs, Tinker?" Carson asked, who approached while they worked to replace the limbs. "No need to waste the good parts on the new girl."

"It's better than wasting them on you, you old mange-covered mutt," her companion retorted and continued to remove the old limbs from the Minato.

"Why are you putting new legs on me?" Mini sounded a little anxious about the changes.

"I have footage of you running from the pirates," Tinker explained without pausing in his work. "Impressive running, of course, but I noted that you had far more traction on the back feet than the power that was transferred there. The balance was a little off too, so that would have been helped with these limbs. I'll keep the old ones in case you don't approve or have stability issues."

Mini remained silent and Jessica13 could tell that he calculated how the change would affect his Bulletfoot mode. They would continue to make him more and more efficient as they initiated improvements.

No mech was ever finished according to the Shimura/Sendai motto, which they printed on the front of the manus she'd gotten her hands on.

"Hey, you!" Tinker called, and a head turned toward him. Jessica13 recognized the bulletfoot who worked on one of the other mechs but couldn't recall his name. "This one here needs a new paint job. Do you know how to make up green paint?"

The kid tried not to look hostile in any way as he approached them and shook his head.

"You take a load of grease out from the joints of…let's say that baby over there." Tinker pointed at the Excalibur. "You mix it with a little engine oil until you get the right shade. When you're finished, come over because this Minato needs a new paint job to make him fit right in."

Jessica13 couldn't help a small smile when the bulletfoot rushed away to collect the ingredients. "I thought you said you didn't like the green."

"Well, I won't be out there representing the Knights Mechanica," Tinker said. "You will, so you need to look the part. We'll fit Mini with one of those banners once you've been in a tussle or two."

"But I'm not a Knight yet," she pointed out.

"Well, you can be if you want to," Tinker replied and looked at her while he wiped the sweat from his bushy eyebrow. "Or you can tell him to go back to whatever he was doing before."

"No, no, that's fine," she said and turned to help him. She liked the idea of looking the part of one of the Knights.

It was quick work to replace the legs, made easier by the harness that held Mini up when he didn't have any other support and gave them time to fit the new parts without difficulty.

Once they released him from the harness, Jessica13 held her breath as Mini settled into them. She wished she could have been inside but since he was the one who would operate the mech at the high speeds that would make it matter, it was better for her to simply let him move the mech alone and run his calculations.

Once he was finished with those, he would be able to factor her added weight in.

"Well, you are right," the AI said finally and moved experimentally on the causeway. "I do have better balance numbers with these legs than the others. I'll have to give it a proper test once we're outside."

Tinker nodded. "Of course, and I'll keep the legs from the Minato original on the Beast if you want them back. It won't be as easy to get them on when we're out of here, but we can do it. I think I have a couple of harnesses on the Beast if you need them."

Jessica13 frowned when Mini moved the mech in an odd up and down motion like he tried to do something with it and it wasn't working. She tilted her head and studied his efforts for a few moments.

"What are you doing?" she asked finally.

"I'm trying to crouch," Mini explained.

She shook her head. "No, no, you can't do it that way. It's

against the joint lines. Your legs now bend backward, like a... What was the animal we saw in the city?"

"A fox?"

"Yes, a fox. The legs bend backward, which gives you better mobility when you're on all fours. I think it might slow us when we're on two legs, but it should give us better stability."

The AI paused for a moment to adjust the coding that controlled the movement, then crouched, settled on the new legs, and moved tentatively in the fairly limited space. Jessica13 watched intently as the mech gradually adjusted to the new legs until they visibly worked better.

She knew for a fact that she wouldn't have been able to get them working so quickly. Those with the legs that bent backward would always be more difficult.

"Where's that kid with the fucking paint?" Tinker asked, looked around, and waved the young man toward them. He carried a can of the paint he'd whipped up and held it out for approval. It did have the greasy, green look the other Knights had, she had to admit.

"Watch it with the joints," Mini warned him. "I don't want to have to clean them out before I can move properly again."

Jessica13 could hear the Knights laugh at a bulletfoot being bossed around by an AI, but she didn't laugh. Not too long before, she had been the one doing that kind of job.

While that was a recent enough memory to still be valid, it also felt like an age had passed since them.

Armstrong7 stepped through the door of his office. He seemed tired and carried a jug she had seen in his office before. He put considerable work into it and because having alcoholic drinks in Sanctuary was frowned upon, he usually kept it secret.

She often wondered how much of a secret it actually was since she knew about it, but it wasn't like the admins would punish their head of security for making alcohol in his spare time.

"They're discussing it, but I feel hopeful," the CO declared. "And it might be a little premature but I thought we could share a drink. A toast for the exchange, sure, but also to drink in the presence of old comrades."

"Are you still making that shit from the barley cakes?" Tinker asked. He withdrew a handful of aluminum cups from his coat and handed them to the Knights and any other takers. None of the bulletfoots or mech pilots from Sanctuary responded. They still looked less than trusting of the Outsiders.

"It's the best in the world and you know it," Armstrong7 replied and poured from the jug into the cups. Jessica13 took one for herself, held it while the milky-white liquid was poured, and frowned at it a little dubiously before she took a sip.

It burned like battery acid and the moment it was clear of her mouth, she coughed and wheezed from the heat of it.

"You know it's working when it makes you cough like that, little one." Tinker laughed, as did the other Knights as they drank.

"You know she needs a drink when she's been working with you, Tink," Taylor said, still laughing and now a little red in the face. "But her work on the mechs is better than yours, so maybe you need some too."

"Bah," Tinker spluttered and shook his head. "I'm a fucking genius and you damn better know it. You can always tell who's the genius because they're the ones getting laughed at. Remember that, Jessie."

"But the fact that some geniuses were laughed at does not imply that all who are laughed at are geniuses. They laughed at Columbus, they laughed at Fulton, and they laughed at the Wright brothers," Armstrong7 interjected and sounded more serious than before. "But they also laughed at Bozo the Clown. A Prophet Sagan classic, and definitely one of my favorites."

"The hell with your Sagan quotes," Tinker grumbled and swirled the drink in his hand. "No one knows who the fuck Bozo the Clown is anymore, so how do we know he wasn't a genius too? But I guess she might be a genius in the making, no mistake."

"The clown part in it does give it away," the CO pointed out. "And yes, she is. Even if she did decide to take off on her own."

And there it was—the hard edge to his tone that betrayed his real feelings about her escape. She knew beyond a shadow of a doubt that if she'd arrived without the protection of the Knights, the reception would have been exactly what she'd dreaded.

"Don't you punish her too harshly for that, Armstrong7," Tinker replied in a warning tone. "You remember how her father was, which means it's in her blood to be curious and adventurous."

The man nodded. "Indeed. But he at least had the benefit of being able to run away with you."

"Wait—what?" Jessica13 asked and fixed her attention on the two men. "Did both of you know my father?"

Tinker took a long sip and swallowed before he replied. "Aye, little one. The man was a nutter to start with, but he had a mind for metal, exactly like you, and when they threatened to take that away from him, he ran. I never knew he had left a child behind until after, though, and never understood why he would leave a tiny one like that. It broke his heart every time he thought of it and you."

"Conflict of duty, perhaps, to a higher cause over his duty to the bunker and his daughter," Armstrong7 said and shook his head regretfully. "He grew disillusioned with the bunker but maybe he sacrificed his relationship with you because he knew that Outside is no place for a tiny child. Hell, I could tell you that. Where is he, anyway?"

She pushed back the protest that clamored to be heard, driven by indignation and anger. For her entire life, she'd been told her father had perished in a pirate attack. This seemed the greatest affront of all. It was one thing to lie in a misguided attempt to protect the structure they rigorously enforced in the belief that it was for Sanctuary's protection. But to lie to a child and have her believe her father was dead when he might well be alive and out there somewhere?

Caution forced her to remain silent, however. She knew that if she so much as voiced a single word, she'd be unable to stop the inevitable tirade. It served her purpose to not confront Amstrong7. She needed to remain calm until they had what they needed and could leave. Common sense told her Tinker would be more understanding and willing to fill in the missing details. She had left Sanctuary because of the lies. That meant she was free and could now choose whether to let them continue to affect her or not.

"I'm not rightly sure where he is," Tinker said. "He spent time with the Knights for a while but one day, he picked his mech up and was gone, out into the Wastelands. He's likely dead since I haven't heard nor seen sign of him for the last ten years, give or take."

"I'll drink to the crazy bastard," Armstrong7 said, raised his cup, and downed what was left in it. She took another sip and focused on the burn to quell her emotions.

A short silence followed and desperate to fill it and distract herself from the rampant thoughts that bubbled below the surface, Jessica13 looked at the corner of the hangar where Hammerhand sat on the boot of his mech and toyed with something in his hands.

"Think we should get him a drink too?" she asked, her voice a little rough but easy enough to blame on the alcohol.

"Leave him be, little one," Tinker replied and placed a hand on her shoulder. "He needs him some time to think before we head out."

She nodded and glanced at the other side of the hangar, where a group of security guards entered, escorting what looked like the parts they needed.

"I guess that's our answer," Armstrong7 said with a chuckle. "You can take those to the other bunker and help them get started again in exchange for the pieces you offered."

Hammerhand stood quickly and strode to where they finished the last of their drinks. He took Armstrong7's hand and shook his firmly. They cut a fine figure, the two of them, and she wondered what things would be like if they ever fought side by side.

"Your help in this will not be forgotten, my friend," the Knights' leader said softly.

The CO nodded firmly. "You know, the parts you're selling to us are worth a little more than what you're getting in return. I won't tell the admins, but if you need anything from us, you only need to say so."

"We have what we need as provided by God and Outside, friend," Hammerhand replied with a smile.

Jessica13 raised a hand and stepped forward. "Ah…excuse me?"

The two men turned to her.

"Was there something you wanted?" Hammerhand asked. He seemed a little confused but not disapproving.

"If you would like to stay with us, you'll always have a place here at Sanctuary, Jessie," Armstrong7 said, which she hadn't expected at all. "I spoke to the admins about you, and they said that you would be welcomed with open arms. We would need you here, though. No more foolish runs Outside."

"You'll also have a place with the Knights," Hammerhand countered. "Tinker might not be the mechanic he once was, although he is still the best. You could do worse than learn the craft at his hand. You won't be as safe as you are here, of course."

"Your choice," Armstrong7 said and gave the other man a glance tinged with annoyance.

The thought of staying did appeal to a small part of her, but after what she'd heard and seen in this visit, she knew that was impossible. Her old CO seemed to want her back, but her suspicions wouldn't subside. What was to stop him placing her under arrest when the Knights left? Maybe he did want her to stay and work with them, but it was unlikely that those in control would be willing to forgive and forget. He might not have the power to override their decisions.

Aside from that, she couldn't help but wonder what life had waiting for her out there. It was in her blood, as they had said, and as she looked at Mini who attempted to assist the bulletfoot to apply the paint, she couldn't help a small smile.

"I'm sorry, Armstrong7," she said. "But I need to go with the Knights. I can't explain it but I feel like I need to be Outside now."

The man chuckled and nodded. "I can't say I'm not disappointed, but I'm not surprised either. You could do worse than a group like the Knights Mechanica."

"I know," Jessica13 replied. "But, if I could, there is one thing I'd like to take as a memory of Sanctuary."

"Anything," he replied, then paused. "You know, within reason."

She looked around to the pile that had once been hers and located a sheet of light metal scrawled with faint red lettering. *Live Free or Die Hard.*

"I think I need a little more armor on the chest plate," she said and picked the sheet up.

"It's yours," Armstrong7 replied, although he looked a little confused as she headed to where Mini was still engaged with the frustrated bulletfoot. The CO glanced at Hammerhand. "She always was an odd one."

"Agreed," Hammerhand replied. "She has her father's spirit, though. And that'll take her anywhere she wants to go in the world."

The story continues with The Auburn Rebellion, available now at Amazon and Kindle Unlimited.

From all of us behind Bulletfoot, we'd like to first express our gratitude to you for reading book one in this trilogy. We hope you enjoyed it.

We get it. Times are hard, friends. But we believe people are tough. So we wanted to write a story about people who get over adversity with their friends - as we all do when things get rough. A tale that covers the hope and grit of people in tough situations that will fight for revival and recovery in a world that is well past that. We wanted to share with you our own hope in and for a better world, that people, no matter how much things go badly around them, are good-- can be good.

That we believe all of us have the potential to overcome even the apocalypse.

So thank you for joining us on this journey. Stay tuned, and let's get through the harsh world of Bulletfoot - together.

- Rust, out.

ABOUT THE AUTHOR

Marshal Rust was born in Boulder, Colorado, where he still resides to this day. His parents - both hard-working blue-collar folk - made sure he got a good education and ensured that included reading as many books as he possibly could. And it's no surprise he came to absolutely love science fiction and fantasy. He cut his teeth on the works of Heinlein, Asimov, Tolkien, and more. He later progressed to the works of Robert Jordan, Terry Brooks, David Brin and Cormac McArthy, and many of their contemporaries through and over the years. He's worked in his father's trade as a welder, moonlighted as a delivery man, sold computer hardware, and done a brutal stint as an animal massage therapist (yes, it's a real job), and has even had to chase a goat that made off with his paper bagged lunch, but nothing makes him happier than clear skies and a blank sheet of paper to write on.

OTHER LMBPN PUBLISHING BOOKS

To be notified of new releases and special promotions from LMBPN publishing, please join our email list:

http://lmbpn.com/email/

For a complete list of books published by LMBPN Publishing please visit:

https://lmbpn.com/books-by-lmbpn-publishing/

ALSO BY MARSHAL RUST

Bulletfoot Series

Origins (Book 1)

The Auburn Rebellion (Book 2 coming soon)

At Athena's Gates (Book 3 coming soon)